# The Road to Mercy

# THE ROAD TO MERCY

Kathy Harris

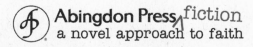
Abingdon Press fiction
a novel approach to faith

Nashville, Tennessee

*The Road to Mercy*

Copyright © 2012 by Kathy Harris

ISBN-13: 978-1-4267-4193-7

Published by Abingdon Press, P.O. Box 801, Nashville, TN 37202

www.abingdonpress.com

The persons and events portrayed in this work of fiction
are the creations of the author, and any resemblance
to persons living or dead is purely coincidental.

Library of Congress Cataloging-in-Publication Data

Harris, Kathy, 1951–
   The road to mercy / Kathy Harris.
      p. cm.
   ISBN 978-1-4267-4193-7 (pbk. : alk. paper)
   I. Title.
   PS3608.A783134R63    2012
   813'.6—dc23

                                                    2012012565

Scripture quotation is from the *Holy Bible*, New Living Translation,
copyright © 1996, 2004, 2007. Used by permission of Tyndale
House Publishers, Inc., Carol Stream, Illinois 60188.
All rights reserved.

Printed in the United States of America

1 2 3 4 5 6 7 8 9 10 / 16 15 14 13 12

To Mom and Dad

God blessed me with you

## Acknowledgments

A heart full of love and gratitude to my husband, Larry, who never let me quit, even when it meant takeout instead of home-cooked.

Linda Cox, my sister since second grade, you made the story better. Thank you for countless hours of dedication to this book.

I can't imagine life without "girlfriends" to share the journey. Hugs to all of you, especially Chaz, D. J., Linda K., and 'Nita.

A shout out to eight special encouragers from American Christian Fiction Writers who are known collectively as the Naners: Alice, Amy, Carol, Kassy, Pat, Peg, Rita, and Tiff.

I owe an incredible debt to everyone at Middle Tennessee Christian Writers, especially my critique partner, Rebecca Deel, an amazing writer and cheerleader; Kaye Dacus, a mentor to many minions who walked this road with me from beginning to end; and Tamara Leigh, who believed in the story before it was written.

Kyle Olund, thanks for taking a chance. Working with you is a blessing.

Ramona Richards, I'm grateful to you and the entire Abingdon team. May the music play on!

I also want to express my appreciation to those who assisted with research. Steve Rowitt, you helped breathe life into Isaac Ruben. Sabrina Carver, your faith has always been an inspiration to me. And I lift my thanks heavenward to the late Shirley Harkins, a special writer whose path crossed mine when we met at the ACFW conference in Nashville in 2005.

My hope is that this story will reflect the Word, Jesus Christ, who was, is, and will be forever. I write to the rhythm of his song.

*Sing a new song to the L*ORD*! Let the whole earth sing to the L*ORD*!*
Psalm 96:1

# PROLOGUE

*God blesses those who are merciful, for they will be
shown mercy. Matthew 5:7*

## October 10, 1959

Jack Randall jerked his foot from the accelerator and instinctively applied the brakes. His mind raced as his Plymouth Belvedere slowed to a stop. Police cars with lights blazing blocked the intersection that led to his home. The reflection off the wet pavement created an eerie blur, and shadowy figures danced across the sides of the squad cars.

.*Must be a bad accident.* The storm that passed earlier in the night had soaked the black asphalt.

As he watched the policeman walk toward his car, Jack cranked down the driver's side window. The uniformed officer flashed a bright light in his direction, not quite in his eyes.

"Sorry, sir, no through traffic this morning. A small plane crashed on the Neimann farm."

Jack's heart pounded. "Anyone hurt? I need to see if my family is—"

"No one on the ground was hurt, sir. Everyone in the plane was killed. May I see your driver's license?"

Jack reached into a back pocket for his well-worn wallet. From it he pulled a small piece of paper, which he placed into the gloved hand of the Illinois state trooper.

"Did the storm bring it down?"

The officer nodded while studying the license. "Lightning took out the engine. It was en route to St. Louis." His brusque demeanor softened and he returned the paper to Jack. "A family of four. Two kids onboard."

"Terrible." Jack tucked the license back inside his wallet.

"You can go home now, Mr. Randall. Hug your kids. Life is short." The trooper tipped his hat and stepped away from the blue sedan.

---

Jack punched his pillow down. Sleep would not come. Thoughts of the plane crash crowded his consciousness. His wife lay beside him. His children were safe in their beds. Why did he have such an uneasy feeling? Why did he feel compelled to go to the crash site?

He prayed softly and sat up on the side of the bed. "Lord, what should I do?"

Running his hands through his hair, he stared at the fluorescent green numbers on the clock face. *Five thirty.*

"Jack?" His wife roused beside him.

"I'm sorry." He turned to her. "I didn't mean to wake you, honey."

"What's wrong?"

"When I came home this morning, the state police had the intersection blocked. A plane crashed on the Neimann farm. I'm thinking about driving over there."

"What can you do?" She propped herself on an elbow.

He kissed her on the forehead. "I don't know. I just have to see if I can help."

A few minutes later, Jack turned left out of his gravel driveway, his headlights illuminating the heart-shaped leaves of the tall catalpa trees growing in the vacant lot across the street. Pods dangled from the branches like bony fingers, sending a chilling reminder of death through him.

The Neimann farm lay to the southwest, about a mile as the crow flies, toward the small town of Mercy. He had been there last year for an estate sale after old man Neimann passed away. The Neimann children had auctioned off the farm equipment and livestock. Mrs. Neimann continued to live in the house, while the land had been rented to other farmers in the community.

Sunrise streaked the twilight sky by the time Jack approached the turn onto Mercy Road. This narrow strip of asphalt led all the way into town, no more than ten miles past the farm, which was less than a thousand yards beyond the intersection.

He pulled his sedan into the gravel driveway and recognized the face of a friend, Canaan County Deputy Sheriff Harold Chester.

"Hey, buddy. How are you?" Chester said, walking toward him.

"Good, but I heard about the plane crash. Anything I can do?"

Deputy Chester shook his head. "A real shame. Two beautiful kids, maybe five to seven years old." A tear welled in the deputy's eye. "Not much older than my kids or yours."

"Need any help documenting the scene, measurements, anything?"

Chester smiled, brushing moisture from his cheek. "You're still a law enforcement man at heart, Jack. Gets in your blood, don't it?" He nodded toward the barn. "We've got it done. I'm just waiting for the Feds to come in and do their assessments before we cart off the wreckage. There's metal all over this farm."

"Not surprising," Jack said.

"I'm not sure how the bodies were so intact. Not much trauma, except for the pilot. He had a gash on his head. We're pretty sure he was the father. He was still inside the plane. The mother and two kids were thrown out."

"Would you mind if I look around?"

"Not at all. You know not to move anything."

"Sure. No problem."

The deputy pointed toward the orange streaks in the awakening horizon. "The main wreckage is about five hundred feet beyond the barn."

Jack pulled his flannel shirt collar up around his neck and set out toward the deteriorating structure that stood between him and the crash site. The chilly wind chastened him for not wearing a jacket. Thankfully, he had worn his boots. Weeds had taken over the lot. The rain still clung to them, and his pants legs were quickly soaked to the knees. He scowled. If old man Neimann could see the shape this place was in, he would turn in his grave.

Jack noticed the faint odor of decaying cow manure as he walked through the open livestock gate. The old hayfield beyond had grown past the time to harvest, and ragweed stood half a foot higher than the tops of the fescue, alfalfa, and red clover.

He saw the plane wreckage straight ahead. From this distance it mimicked a kind of abstract sculpture someone had dropped onto the field. The wet surface glistened in the early morning light, creating an unnerving glow. As he approached, Jack noticed beads of moisture covering the white, twisted metal.

*Four people died in this wreckage.*

The distinct odor of burnt wiring filled his nostrils. No doubt lightning had struck the plane. Fortunately, the whole thing hadn't gone up in flames. Not that the outcome would have been any different.

There was an unpleasantness in thinking about the bodies now lying in the county morgue. It was a far cry from the destination they must have had planned in St. Louis. Lord willing, those four souls had reached an even better place, the throne of their Creator.

Had it not been for such a terrible accident, the beauty of this quiet morning would have been refreshing. He loved the open land. Especially when it stretched farther than the eyes could see, as it did on this estate. Old man Neimann had certainly enjoyed a gorgeous piece of nature. Perhaps he was part of the welcoming committee for the . . . the . . . Jack realized he didn't even know the names of those who had died here.

He reached out to touch the squared-off tail section of the plane. Teardrops of moisture clung to his fingers. He wiped his hands on his trousers. There was nothing he could do. He might as well go home to his family.

Turning toward the barn, a piece of trash from the plane caught his attention. A familiar shape out of context. It took a moment for him to process what he was seeing. Something was missing. What was it? Lack of sleep had slowed his cognitive processes, and he strained to put the pieces together.

*A bottle.* It was a rubber nipple from a baby bottle.

He thought back to what Chet had said. Two children, five and seven years old, had been found. They wouldn't need a baby bottle. So what was . . . ?

The realization hit him hard. An infant had been onboard. There was another body. *Oh, God. Help me find that child. He needs to be with his family, not alone in this field.*

Jack scratched his head. Where should he start looking? If only he knew where the other bodies had been located. The mother had likely been holding the child in her arms during the flight. Chet had said she was expelled from the plane, but where had she been found?

He scanned the weeds for a sign. A red kerchief lay east of the wreckage. Perhaps the mother had worn it over her shoulder when burping the baby?

*Come on, Jack, you're grasping at straws. Just walk around the site in a grid. You know the rules,* he reminded himself. Search and Rescue 101.

He set out to walk every inch of soil in the field. It took more than thirty ever-widening circles before he reached the fence line. When he approached the final turn, he debated what he should do. No doubt he had scoured the entire field. Perhaps it was time to call in assistance.

Then he heard a sound.

He stopped to listen.

Nothing.

Only the low chirping of birds filled his ears. Must have been a barn cat.

Wait! He heard it again. It was coming from that haystack, and it sounded like . . . a baby.

Jack sprinted toward the loose mound of hay. How could a child have survived such a horrendous crash? What would he find? Walking closer, he saw what appeared to be a newborn. The baby was dressed in bright blue and lay motionless in a crater of gray-green straw.

Energy drained from Jack's body. Had he arrived too late? When he touched the infant, he knew he hadn't. The child's soft, pale skin felt moist and warm. Jack gently picked up the sole survivor of the crash and held him to his chest, shielding him from the cold wind.

Panic replaced relief. The baby needed immediate medical attention. He could have internal injuries, complications from exposure, or even shock.

Lack of sleep had begun to take its toll, and Jack operated on remote power. He traversed the uneven terrain back to his car as fast as he could without jostling the fragile life cradled in his arms. If Chet was still there, he could drive them to the hospital in the squad car. If not, he would find a way to secure the baby in the front seat of his Belvedere.

When Jack passed through the gate, he saw the deputy's green Bel Air, but no sign of Harold Chester. "Chet! Chet! I need help!"

A few minutes later, Jack watched Harold Chester's right foot hover close to the floorboard of the police cruiser. His other leg jiggled nervously, as if peeved that it had no particular task in this special mission. They had decided to take the baby to Mercy Hospital. Although a small facility, it was the closest to the farm.

Despite the upset and commotion that had come into his world today, the infant lay quietly in Jack's lap, swaddled in Chet's olive-green jacket. The siren screamed, making conversation impossible. Jack cupped the baby's ears between his hands and tried to focus on the narrow road ahead.

A patchwork of color blurred in his peripheral vision as they sped past white clapboard farmhouses and red barns with silver silos. He imagined farmers interrupting their chores and wives peering from porches to investigate the early morning disturbance. They would soon be the talk of the neighborhood. In fact, the party lines were probably already buzzing.

When Chet pulled into the hospital parking lot and stopped, Jack jumped out of the car and ran to the hospital entrance. Because the deputy had radioed ahead, a group of doctors and nurses met him at the door. As he transferred the baby into the arms of a nurse, the infant opened his blue eyes and held Jack's gaze—for what seemed like a lifetime.

Three days later, Pastor Sam Lewis caught Jack's shoulder and spun him around. "I heard about the rescue. Good work, brother." He reached to shake Jack's hand.

Jack smiled and thanked the reverend. People had made over him like he was some kind of hero. But he had done what any other man would do. "Right place at the right time," he said. "That child is fortunate to be alive."

"Blessed, I would say." The reverend nodded. "In fact, I believe God has plans for that young man."

# 1

**Present Day**

Josh Harrison looked into the eyes of five thousand people, but he felt only the presence of one—the spirit of the Almighty God.

"Thank you, Lord," Josh whispered as he lifted his hands toward the multicolored light truss above him. He stood motionless, soaking in the warmth. "Praise Yeshua," he said.

"Praise Yeshua," voices in the auditorium echoed.

From the stage, Josh could hear them. First one thousand, then two thousand—and finally all five thousand—praising God. Spotlights flashed across the crowd. The blue-white glow illuminated ten thousand hands in the air, an almost unearthly vision. Some swayed back and forth. Others held up lighted cell phones.

He signaled Ryan Majors, his lead guitar player. Ryan struck a low, reverberating E chord, which grew in intensity. At its high point the tone seemed to ricochet off the civic center walls. The crowd fell silent, still on their feet, when the hall went black.

Exactly three seconds later a laser light split the stage in two. The drum thundered and the cymbal crashed.

"He is the Light in the darkness," Josh shouted. "He has come."

The audience cheered and the band commenced a familiar melody. Josh began to sing the tender lyrics of "He Has Come," his biggest single yet. He loved to sing it. The song was the main reason he had been invited to join the Triumphant Tour, the most successful U.S. concert series in Christian music—ever.

God had blessed him with the privilege of doing what he loved. He often wondered why people thanked him for his music. His reward came from doing the will of the Lord, whose presence especially filled him when he was onstage. It was a complete and awesome substantiation of his chosen career. A confirmation he was doing what he had been born to do, praising Jesus in song.

A few hours later, Josh sank into the comfortable leather seat next to the front door of his bus. More than a day stood between Rapid City, South Dakota, and his wife, Bethany. He longed to see her. To be home. He could be there sooner, but he hated to fly. It would be a long ride to Nashville.

"Do we have any jelly beans, Danny?" Josh asked, settling into the seat just as the bus rolled forward.

"You betcha, boss." The driver glanced at his side mirror, assessing the lane to his left. "Look in the drawer under your seat."

Josh leaned forward and pulled the drawer open. He found five or six bags of the colorful candies. "You're too good to me, man." He grabbed a bag and tore it open.

"Just trying to get on your good side." The stocky driver laughed while merging the bus into the late-night traffic to head east on Interstate 90. "Actually, I need a favor. My mom's surgery has been scheduled for next week, and I'd like to be with her if you don't mind hiring a substitute driver."

"How's she doing?"

"As well as can be expected when you're facing major heart surgery. I know I need to trust the Lord to get her through this, but I've only got one mom. It's hard to imagine. . . ." The driver choked up.

"Let's pray for her right now." Josh stood and laid his hand on Danny's shoulder. "Father, I know how much you love Danny's mother. I ask that you wrap your arms around her and her family. Give them peace—and bring something positive from this trial. I ask for complete healing, Lord, and pray for your will in Jesus' powerful name. Amen."

"Amen . . . and thanks." Danny took a hand off the steering wheel to swipe his face.

"Can Mitch do the Tulsa trip on his own?" Josh asked, returning to the jump seat.

"He could if Ryan will lend a hand. He's had an attitude lately when I ask him for help."

Josh threw too many jellybeans into his mouth and contemplated what Danny had said. "What's the problem?" He chewed through the words.

"I . . . I'm sorry. I shouldn't have said anything. I didn't mean to be disrespectful. Ryan has a lot on him with playing guitar and road managing."

"Don't worry about it. I'll talk to him. You just take care of your mother." Josh stood, stretched, and stifled a yawn.

"You need to get some sleep instead of feeding that sugar addiction."

"You're right. I think I will. Let me know when we stop for fuel. I want to pick up a paper at the truck stop. Alabama played Tennessee tonight."

"Will do, boss. See you in the morning."

"Get us there safe, man." Josh pulled back the thick black curtain that separated the driver's compartment from the front sitting area of the bus.

He walked across the dimly lit lounge, between empty sofas and captain's chairs, and pushed the white button on the far wall of the kitchen galley. The bunkroom door opened with a whoosh. The sliding air lock door always reminded him of a device from *Star Trek*. If only he could be beamed home instead of having to endure an eighteen-hour bus ride. Yet, at this point, he was thankful a comfortable bunk awaited him.

In a few seconds his eyes adjusted to the low light in the windowless hallway, which was little more than a twenty-foot compartment that had been divided into stacked bunks and skinny closets.

The band and crew had turned in for the night, which was evidenced by six drawn curtains. Sleep would pass the time and help heal the stress of the last few weeks. So could a phone call to his wife, but it was after two in the morning and Beth would be in bed. He would call her tomorrow.

Josh reached to switch on the overhead light inside his bunk. Because he was the lead performer and business owner, he could have commandeered the back lounge for a star bedroom, but he enjoyed being with the others. Most buses had bunks stacked three high. His 2003 Prevost had two stacks of two on each side of the aisle. Eight bunks. Enough for him, his band, and Mitch, his merchandise manager, plus one for Danny when he napped between shifts. They stowed miscellaneous gear and bags, or an occasional guest, in the extra bed.

Josh's bunk was in the first stack on the left. Climbing in, he decided not to turn on the small television bolted to the wall. He pulled the covers up, tucked himself in, and prayed silently for a safe trip home. He knew it wouldn't take long for the purring of the diesel engine and the gentle motion of the big bus to rock him to sleep.

# 2

**Present Day**

Bethany Harrison measured a cup of chocolate chips and poured them into the soft cookie dough. Ordinarily she would have popped a few of the delectable morsels into her mouth, but not before breakfast. She glanced at the clock. *Eight a.m.* She hadn't even dressed for church.

The smile on Josh's face would be worth her rushing around this morning. It had been a month and a half since she'd seen him. She hated the separation.

Thinking about him temporarily stilled the nagging headache that had awakened her. No doubt the Nashville weather had taken a toll on her sinuses again. Allergies were part of the Middle Tennessee Welcome Wagon. One negative in her otherwise blessed life.

*Help me, Lord, not to complain. But, please, relieve me of this headache.* And soon?

After rolling dollops of the cookie dough into balls, she placed them onto prepared baking sheets and reached for her secret ingredient—raw sugar to sprinkle on top. The caramel colored crystals added sparkle and sweetness to what Josh called her Chocolate Chip Pizzazz Cookies.

She popped the two pans into the oven, fed Buster, their one-year-old Boston terrier, and then sat at the kitchen table to sift through her Bible study materials and nibble on a breakfast bar. Alexandra Hayes would arrive soon to pick her up for church. Maybe she would pack a few cookies for Alex to take home.

The sweet aroma of sugar and butter prompted Beth to check the oven just as the timer chimed. Perfect. She grabbed a potholder and moved both trays to the nearby stovetop. With a metal spatula, she transferred the warm cookies onto a cooling rack.

She had just enough time to change into church clothes. When she turned toward the hall door, the pain hit her. The most devastating pain she had ever experienced, like a bolt of lightning had struck her left temple.

Clutching her head, she fell to the floor.

⋯⋯

The siren shrieked as the ambulance made its way through the East Nashville streets. Beth tugged at the oxygen mask covering her mouth and nose. If she could only ask the driver to turn off that intolerable noise, her head might not hurt.

She couldn't remember: had the discomfort come first—or the noise? Pain blurred her normally focused vision. She no longer had her bearings. The throbbing in her head drew a line between reality and illusion, trapping her on its jagged edge. She could only pray that, if she fell, she would fall the right way.

Blackness began to overtake her. And silence chased away the noise. Only the feeling of motion remained, as the ambulance rolled through time and space.

Suddenly, a herd of horses thundered through her head and arcs of white light shot across the horizon of her semi-consciousness. Her dreamlike existence unlocked an aural display of colors, sounds, and memories. She could almost reach out and touch the special moments from her life.

Delicate pink roses adorned her wedding bouquet. Josh stuttered as he proposed. Bright yellow galoshes splashed through buckets of rain on her first day of school. Growing up in Kentucky . . . her first pony . . . sleeping in the backseat of the car on the way to her grandparents' house in Illinois. The memories came faster and faster, reminding her that she had enjoyed a lifetime of love.

Loving and being loved had taught her the greater love of God. She knew she could rest assured that the Giver of all good things had plans for her, whether in this life or beyond. She ached to know him better. *Now I know in part; then I shall know fully.*

Perhaps this was her time to know fully.

Warmth and peace enveloped her, and when the ambulance pulled into Davidson County Medical Center, Beth felt closer to heaven than to earth.

# 3

**Present Day**

A vibrating phone jarred Josh from deep sleep. He fumbled with it in the darkness.

"Hello."

"Josh, it's Alex Hayes. Beth is on her way to the hospital."

"What's wrong?" He wiped the sleep from his eyes.

"She's complaining of a headache, and she's disoriented. I found her passed out on the kitchen floor and called an ambulance."

"An ambulance?" Josh threw back the curtain that separated him from the bunkroom hallway. In the soft glow of the hall light he could read the numbers on his watch. 9:36. "Is she o . . . okay?" The words caught in his throat as he dangled his legs over the side of his bed and then jumped to the floor.

"What's going on?" Ryan interrupted, poking his head outside his curtain.

"She's in a lot of pain, but she's responsive," Alex said. "I'll know more when I get to the hospital. They took her to Davidson County Medical Center. I'll call you after I talk to a doctor."

By the time Josh ended the conversation he was standing in the front lounge of the bus with several members of his band gathered around him. After a brief explanation, and each person's assurance of prayer on Beth's behalf, Josh set the wheels in motion for the quickest route home.

He consulted with Ryan and then Danny.

"How far are we from St. Louis? Can I catch a plane and make it home faster than we can drive?"

"We're about a hundred miles from St. Louis," Danny estimated. "Maybe more."

"I'll check flights." Ryan pulled a phone from his pocket and punched in numbers.

Josh settled onto the jump seat and stared at what seemed to be a never-ending white line in the center of the highway. For the first time in his life he regretted his career. He should have been home with his wife when she needed him.

Danny interrupted his thoughts. "Boss, I just saw a mileage sign. I can make it to the St. Louis airport in about ninety minutes."

Josh turned to Ryan, who stood with a phone cradled between his ear and shoulder. "Will that work?"

"I'm talking to the travel agent now," Ryan mouthed before he paced toward the back of the bus.

Josh gulped air. Why was it so hard to breathe?

*Lord, I know you love Beth; please protect her until I get there.* He had prayed the same prayer a thousand times in the past half hour.

Ryan stepped back to the driver's compartment. "That's the earliest flight? What time does it arrive in Nashville?" He directed his attention to Josh. "I can get you there at ten o'clock."

"Tonight?" Emptiness hit Josh in the gut. "I can't wait that long." He turned to Danny. "How soon can you get us to Nashville?"

"Maybe six hours."

"Then do it. Get me to my wife."

Josh's cell phone rang as he retreated to the back lounge of the bus. It was Alex's number on the caller ID.

"How is she?" he asked, forgoing the pleasantries.

"She was disoriented and vomiting when she got to the hospital. That has been over an hour ago. They won't let me see her, but the nurse says she's stable." Alex hesitated. "Josh, the doctors believe she's had a cerebral aneurysm."

"What?"

"A tear in an artery in her brain."

"Is she conscious?"

"Yes. They're doing a CT scan now."

Josh heard himself breathing into the phone. He latched onto the side of his bunk and held on.

"Josh, keep the faith. God will see her through this."

"I want to talk to a doctor."

"I'll do my best. How soon before you're here?"

"Five o'clock—or before."

He put the phone down and stared out the window of the back lounge. From a cloudless sky, the autumn sun highlighted the rich colors of the Midwestern farmland. A few red leaves still clung to the woody skeletons of nearby trees, and the green fields wore a partial camouflage of yellow and brown in preparation for the coming battle with winter.

Josh felt his life changing just as the seasons.

A panorama of Americana sped past. Modest white houses snuggled near gray and red barns. Livestock grazed peacefully. Cars meandered a country road that paralleled the superhighway on which his bus traveled. Although within plain sight of each other, the two roads ended in different places.

Had he taken the right one?

The technician stroked Beth's forearm. His eyes offered reassurance. "Can you hang in there for a little while longer?"

Beth nodded and pulled the white sheet closer to her body. Her teeth chattered, making it difficult to speak. The temperature in the exam room had to be freezing.

"You look cold. I'll bring you a blanket."

"Th-thank y-you." She tried to form the words.

He returned with two warm blankets and a clipboard. "I need to ask you a few questions. Do you remember what you were doing when your headache started this morning?"

"Yes. I-I was in my kitchen baking cookies."

"So you had no intense physical activity? Just a normal morning?"

"Yes." She watched as he jotted down notes.

"Is there any possibility you could be pregnant?"

"I don't think so."

"Are you allergic to any medicines?"

"No."

He finished his note taking, then laid the clipboard on a nearby table and picked up a needle. "Have you had a CT scan before?"

"No." She shook her head, rousing the pain.

He thumped her left forearm. "Okay, you're going to feel a little stick."

She closed her eyes when he inserted the tip of the hypodermic needle into a vein. Seconds later the sensation of heat scurried up her arm. It dissipated when it reached her shoulder.

"You should be feeling a little warmth. It's a benign dye we need to view the arteries in your neck and head." He laid a heavy quilt across her midsection. "As a precaution against the radiation, I'm covering you with a lead blanket."

The weight of the blanket heightened Beth's awareness of breathing. Or trying to breathe. Everything she had once taken for granted seemed now to be in question. Would she live or die? And would she ever see Josh's face again?

*Dear God, please bring my husband home to me.*

Within seconds the platform underneath her began to move.

"Try to relax," the technician spoke from behind a glass booth. "After we're finished, the doctor can give you something for pain relief. Now I need you to lie very still. On the count of three, breathe, exhale, and hold. One . . . two . . . three."

The giant metal ring encircling her head began to rotate.

"Good. Now breathe and relax. Let's try it again."

The whir of the machine reminded Beth of airplane landing gear being lowered, the memory taking her mind momentarily off the pain. Her thoughts took her back a year and a half. She and Josh were on their honeymoon, flying toward Jamaica and . . .

"Mrs. Harrison, are you awake?"

"Yes-s-s." Beth bit her lip.

"I'm Dr. Abrams. I've given you something for pain. You may drift in and out for a while."

She stared at the stranger dressed in white, not quite comprehending his words.

"We've completed your CT scan and located the source of your problem. I believe you have suffered a spontaneous dissection in the left carotid artery."

Beth searched his face for better understanding.

"This is a serious condition. I want to schedule another test to confirm it."

She tried to sit up. "M-my husband is coming home today. Is he here?"

The doctor gently pushed her back down. "I'm sure you'll see him soon. First, I need you to tell me about your headache. Do you still have pain?"

"Yes." She raised her left hand to her head.

"On a scale of one to ten, how bad would you say it is?"

"It's the worst headache I've ever had in my life. A ten."

"We're doing our best to make you comfortable. Relax as much as you can. That will help."

<hr />

"Josh? Where are you?" Alex asked.

"We're pulling up to the hospital now. Where can I meet you?"

"I'm on the sixth floor. Beth is in a room."

"I'll meet you at the sixth-floor elevators." He snapped his phone shut and hit the button on the outside air lock doors. The bus was still rolling as he leaped to the parking lot. His knees buckled when his Nikes hit the pavement, but he managed to stay upright.

*When had he eaten last?*

He sprinted into the lobby and pushed the elevator button twice. Seconds later, the doors opened to an empty lift. He stepped inside, jabbed at the faded number 6, and waited for the metal room to ascend. His heart poked at the wall of his chest, and his pulse quickened.

When the doors opened to the sixth floor, Josh breathed a sigh of relief to see Alex waiting for him. She was still wearing her church clothes. Her red hair fell in tired ringlets around her face. But just seeing her encouraged him.

His relief dissolved quickly when he realized they were standing in the lobby of the critical care unit.

"How's she doing? Can I see her?"

"I don't know. They won't let me go in, but maybe you can." She pointed toward the waiting area. "There's an attendant over there. Let's ask."

They hurried to the desk and explained the situation.

Josh paced the floor while the woman made a phone call.

"Mr. Harrison, you can see your wife now. Her room is down the hall, past the elevators. Take a right, and then a left."

Josh waved a thank-you to the receptionist and then turned toward the hallway. "I'll be back," he said to Alex.

He followed the corridor signs to the nurses' station and asked for Beth's room number. "I'm her husband," he said, his voice sounding thin.

While the nurse scrolled through records on a computer screen, a middle-aged man wearing a white coat and a stethoscope took note of him. The doctor closed a file and stepped around the huge square desk. He extended his right hand.

"I'm Ben Abrams, your wife's physician. I'm on my way to her room now. Why don't you join me?"

"How is she?" Josh walked beside the doctor down a nondescript hallway.

"Your wife is a very sick woman. I would not ordinarily allow family to visit so soon. However, I understand she hasn't seen you in six weeks." The doctor stopped in front of Room 607.

"Thank you."

"Please keep your visit upbeat and relaxed. Stress, or even excitement, could cause her to have a stroke—or worse."

Josh nodded.

"Let me be frank with you. Your wife should be dead right now. For whatever reason, she has managed to survive. She is still in grave danger." He opened the door and stepped inside.

Josh followed.

"Bethany, I have a surprise visitor for you." Dr. Abrams crossed the small room. "Please don't overdo your welcome. I think he will understand if you don't get up."

Beth began to cry when she saw Josh. "You're here!" she said.

Seeing her like this almost took him to his knees. His wife was surrounded by machines and immersed in wires. But thank God she was alive.

He rushed to her bedside, brushed her hair from her face, and kissed her on the forehead. Then, encircling her unfettered hand with his, he pulled her close to him.

—❦—

Three days later, while waiting for Beth to return from another procedure, Josh fumbled through the cable television channels. His wife had been transferred from critical care into a private room yesterday, a reason for celebration. He was also relieved to have a quiet place to wait. He had done a lot of waiting since arriving at the hospital three days ago. Scheduled tests and the task of keeping up with doctor visits had taken priority over personal needs. Finally, prompted by a growling stomach, he decided to get something to eat while he had the opportunity.

The hospital cafeteria was located on the first floor near the main elevators. Although nutritionally adequate, the food tasted like cardboard. Josh walked to the dessert display and reached for a slice of cherry pie. Then he remembered the cookies he had stashed in his coat pocket. Beth's chocolate chip pizzazz cookies. He had found them on the kitchen counter after arriving home on his first night in town. They were a sweet reminder of his wife's love.

Guilt and doubt overwhelmed him. Was God nudging him to leave the tour, to stay at home with Beth? Dr. Abrams had said she would need around-the-clock care for a while. Neither he nor Beth had family living close enough to help.

Josh purchased a cheeseburger and carried his tray to a table in the rear of the cafeteria seating area, nodding to a table of familiar faces before taking a seat against the wall. He had made several acquaintances in the short time Beth had been in the hospital, and he had learned their personal stories. Some had family awaiting surgery, while others were recovering. Each person's expression changed daily, depending on the condition of his or her loved one. They were all riding the same emotional roller coaster. Except for a group of giggling student nurses, who sat at the corner table. Life went on for those momentarily unaffected by the temporal nature of this existence.

Josh had eaten half of his sandwich when his cell phone rang. It was Beth.

"Where are you?" she asked.

"In the cafeteria. Can I bring you something?"

"No." Her voice quivered. "Dr. Abrams came in a few minutes ago. He wants to talk to us together."

"I'll be right there."

He quickly disposed of his tray and headed upstairs to her room. Beth greeted him with an odd expression.

"What's wrong?" he asked.

"I'm not sure. But the look on the doctor's face scared me."

"It's probably nothing." He took a seat on the side of her bed and stroked her dark brown curls. "Most likely some instructions he's afraid you'll forget," he teased.

She smiled. It thrilled him to see her looking more like herself again.

A half hour later, while Beth was eating a light supper brought by the hospital staff, Dr. Abrams appeared. "I'm sorry to interrupt your dinner. Are you having filet or lobster tonight?"

They laughed.

The doctor's face sobered. "I'll get to the point. We've confirmed that you have a three-centimeter dissection of the carotid artery. As you know, this is a serious condition. However, there is a complication that concerns me even more." He exhaled deeply. "Mrs. Harrison, you're pregnant. Test results came back today."

Josh turned to his wife. Her eyes met his, and then she looked away. She refocused her gaze on her hands, which she held clasped tightly in her lap. When her shoulders began to shake, Josh walked to the side of the bed and put his arm around her, the possibilities of all that could be ahead for them swirling in his mind.

They had hoped for children. Perhaps in the next year or two. But not now, and not under such circumstances.

Finally, turning to Dr. Abrams, he broke the silence in the room. "What does this mean for my wife?"

The physician shook his head. "If you value Bethany's life, you must terminate the pregnancy."

# 4

## May 22, 1969

Isaac Ruben kicked a stone as he shuffled home from the *yeshiva*. Summer break had begun. Unlike most of his friends, who played softball or spent their afternoons in the library, he helped his grandfather at the flower shop each day.

Grandfather wanted him to learn the business, to make it his life's work and to carry it on for a second generation. But Isaac had other ideas growing in his head. Stripping thorns from roses left his hands swollen and sore, and sweeping the floors was a thankless task.

"Watch what you're doing, *eynikl*. Can't you do better than that? A lazy person must do a task twice."

"I'm sorry, *Zayde*. I will do better."

Although he tried, his heart was not in it.

Delivering flowers was the best part of his chores. He would stack three or four bundles in the handlebar basket of his bicycle and set out to explore the periphery of his world. His mind raced faster than his feet could pedal—as free as the wind blowing off the East River.

Sometimes he would sit on the bank of the waterway and look across to the Manhattan skyline, watching the planes take off for places he had never seen. Cities he could only dream about.

Someday he would fly away on one of those big airplanes. And he would never return.

# 5

## Present Day

Shadows and sound darted around the room like children playing tag in a park. In the distance, Beth heard laughter, followed by muffled conversation. The voices ebbed and flowed.

Pain had gone, at least for the moment. Its absence brought freedom. Ecstasy. Almost weightlessness. She drifted on an ocean breeze. Palm trees, caressed by the wind, waved against a cloudless, blue sky. Although distant, the sun's rays warmed her.

Then she realized that something, someone, held her down. She flexed her forearm, producing no movement. A slight irritation rose inside her. Then panic.

Where was she? She tried harder to pull herself up. Heat surged through her body, and she became aware of an intense light surrounding her.

She must escape.

The shadows gathered closer, blocking out the artificial sun, and a sharp object pricked her skin. Numbness began to spread. Was it her body or her mind being anesthetized?

A silent scream sprang from deep inside her. Trapped by flesh and bones, it ricocheted across her soul. Irritation turned to discomfort, then hopelessness. Without warning, a low whine cut through the muffled sound of voices. Life was being pulled away from her.

She heard herself scream.

"Mrs. Harrison, please. Relax."

Beth tried to focus on the woman's face. "My baby . . ."

The nurse stroked her forehead. "Your baby is fine, dear. You've had a nightmare."

Josh rushed toward her. "Is everything okay?"

Beth reached for his hand. "I'm glad you're here."

---

A few minutes later Josh stepped outside his wife's hospital room and approached Dr. Abrams, who was standing in the hallway and scribbling onto a chart.

"What just happened in there, doctor?"

Dr. Abrams motioned for him to walk down the hallway. "Your wife had a morphine-induced dream." They stopped a few steps from the nurses' station, and the doctor looked squarely into Josh's eyes. "It's nothing to be concerned about."

"I have a hard time accepting that." Josh ran his fingers through his hair. "I'm afraid these drugs will affect the baby."

"Any medication can put the baby at risk, but—"

"I've heard the word *risk* way too many times this week. I need facts, reassurances. How long will Beth have to stay on the morphine?" Josh pointed to the clipboard in the doctor's hands. "Or any of these drugs?"

Dr. Abrams studied him. "I don't think you understand. Your wife is in a lot of pain. She needs medication just to get through the day." He frowned. "Her pain is intolerable. Do you understand that?"

"Of course, I do, but . . ."

The physician continued. "We don't dispense morphine, or any narcotic, unless it's necessary. In Bethany's case, narcotics may be required for months." The muscles in his jaws twitched. "If there is no sign of healing after a few months, then we'll discuss surgery, which has its own set of risks."

Josh shook his head. "I'm not challenging your judgment, but . . ."

The doctor heaved a long sigh. "You're emotionally involved. You've chosen to keep the baby." He softened his stance a bit. "Of course, that's your and your wife's decision. But, please, realize that this pregnancy is a complication to an already serious condition."

The doctor's piercing blue eyes cut through the chilled air between them.

Josh steadied himself against the wall, trapped between two difficult choices, and nodded.

"My priorities are with your wife. Her artery is microscopically dissected. It's weak and vulnerable. The more stress on that tiny tear, the more likely it will rupture. Even the smallest complication could cause that to happen."

"Shouldn't she have surgery right away?"

"In many cases, these fissures repair themselves. But it takes time. We should know more in three or four months. In the meantime, I want to give Bethany all of the advantages I can."

"Because the pregnancy adds risk. . . ." Josh heard himself repeat the word he had come to hate. "What happens if her artery doesn't heal in seven months, when the baby is born?"

"Pregnancy is a natural condition, but it puts additional stress on the body," the doctor said.

"Beth could die in childbirth?" It was more a statement than a question.

"Of course, it's a possibility. The trauma of labor will put pressure on her artery and if it hasn't healed by that time, well

. . . we don't know what will happen." He took a long breath. "But you have to understand that just getting to that point is dangerous." The doctor studied Josh's reaction. "It's not too late to terminate, to give your wife every advantage you can."

"Dr. Abrams, Beth doesn't want to do that." Josh chose his words carefully. "I appreciate you shooting straight with me and your concern for my wife's best interests. I need all the insight you can give me." He ran his fingers through his hair. "But Beth is determined."

Josh looked down at the floor and then back to the doctor.

"She has—we both have—a strong faith, and we must ultimately believe that God will get us, and the baby, through this."

Ben Abrams shrugged a shoulder. "I wish you the best, and I'll do all I can to help you. Just understand, I'm not in the business of miracles."

---

Ben Abrams shook his head as he walked away. What was it with religious types always basing their lives on the unseen? The intangible rather than the tangible. How could that kind of thinking help get someone through life much less influence their afterlife, as they all seemed to believe?

Such irrational thinking wasn't for him. It was nothing more than a *bubbe-meise*, a fairytale told on a grandmother's knee. Those days were gone for him, if they had ever really been. He had chosen to live a reality-centered life, one based on science not superstition or spiritual mumbo jumbo. Perhaps his philosophy about life wasn't perfect, but he had helped many more people than religion ever could.

He made a quick stop at the sink to wash his hands before entering his next patient's room. Slathering his hands with liquid soap, he rubbed them together quickly, rinsed with hot water, and reached for a paper towel to dry.

*You can no more clean your soul with prayers than you can clean it with soap and water.*

Ben hoped that Bethany Harrison's religious beliefs didn't play a role in ending her young life too soon. But he had done all he could do.

He wadded up the paper towel and threw it in the trash, disposing of the matter.

⚭

Nashville rush-hour traffic diminished as Josh stood, staring out the window of Beth's seventh-floor hospital room taking in the panoramic view of Nashville in front of him. Looking down onto the flat, pea-gravel roof of the reception building and the vast concrete-and-brick hospital complex to each side, he had a transcendent perspective on the world below.

The ambulance entrance, although quiet now, awaited the next trauma that would pass through the doors and alter a life, a family, forever. The windows of the huge hospital wing across from where he stood lined up like a giant crossword puzzle, twelve stories high and half a city block wide. Some were backlit. Some dark and ominous. Josh imagined a different story playing out behind each pane of glass.

A birth. A fight for life. Perhaps even a battle lost.

He said a silent prayer for those whose lives depended on the bittersweet cocktail of human compassion and sterile technology, with the assurance that God could work through both.

In the distance a church steeple reached to the sky. Beyond it was the beginning of a perfect sunset. Blue and purple clouds swam through streams of orange, as dusk replaced the imperfect clarity of the daylight. Another day ending left hope for tomorrow—hope, and the realization that life could change in an instant.

At this point, Beth and the baby were doing okay. Still, he hated to go. But in a few hours he must leave for his shows in Oklahoma. Beth had insisted he fulfill his commitments, despite his protests to the contrary.

A noise in the hallway outside the door jolted Josh back to the moment. The night staff was coming on duty, greeting each other with eager conversation and good-natured laughter.

Life continued.

⚬⚬⚬

"What are you thinking about, honey?" Beth asked.

"How much I hate to leave you." Her handsome husband turned to look at her. His boyish grin always brought her comfort.

"I'll be fine. Besides, there's not much you can do here except toss and turn on that squeaky old cot all night." She pointed toward the daybed in the corner of her small room.

"My bus bunk will feel great compared to that thing." He leaned over to kiss her. "I'm glad you're better."

She smiled. Having Josh nearby always made her feel better, even if her head continued to hurt as if it might explode at any minute.

"Don't worry about me, Joshua. You go and sing your songs. That's what you're supposed to do. I'll be waiting for you to take me home on Sunday."

"Are you sure?"

"We've been through this a dozen times. Alex will take good care of me while you're gone. Don't worry!"

"I wish your mom could be here."

"Josh, I'm fine." She loved the way he worried about her. "Mom has her hands full with Grandma. I will be fine with Alex here. End of discussion."

"Okay." He drew the word out. "I guess I need to be going. The bus leaves at midnight. I've got laundry to do when I get home."

It was her turn to fret. "I'm sorry, I wish I could—"

He pressed his lips to hers, silencing her protest. Her jaw quivered, and tears welled in her eyes. Despite her putting on a strong front, his leaving tore her apart. With her unfettered arm, she reached up and pulled him closer, wanting to hold him forever. Josh responded with lingering lips on hers, and a dam of pent-up emotions broke inside her. Tears streamed down her face. If only she could tell him everything.

She retreated into his warm, strong embrace, the fragrance of him reassuring her for the moment. Life had been so good. Why had her past come back to confront her?

They held each other until darkness overtook the dusk outside her window. Finally, feigning sleep, she allowed her husband to slip quietly out of the room, leaving her alone with questions, fear, pain—and guilt for what she could not tell him.

# 6

Hey, girl! How are you feeling this morning?" Alex walked into the hospital room carrying a huge bouquet of purple blooms.

"Those are beautiful," Beth said, trying to sit up in bed and reach for the flowers. When she did, she became entangled in the tubes and wires that ran from the medical machines lined up beside her. Without warning she burst into tears.

*Not again.* The thought of crying made her cry even harder.

"Here, let me help." Alex set the vase on the bedside table and began to methodically untangle the tubing that filled Beth's veins with drips and doses of solutions.

Beth wasn't quite sure what kind of *solution* they represented. Her head still hurt and her mental focus fluctuated from zero to obsession in sixty seconds. "I'm sorry," she said, doing her best to regain control.

"Why are you crying, Mama? Everything is going to be okay."

The word *mama* brought a smile to Beth's face. Alex had been calling her that since she found out about Beth's pregnancy a few days ago.

Her neighbor and friend had been a godsend. She had stepped in to take care of everything since Josh left town on Thursday night. Alex fed and exercised Buster at home and then brought food and personal items to Beth at the hospital. Beth was thankful her neighbor had the time to give. If Alex had a family of her own, she might not be able to help.

Beth had often wondered why Alexandra Hayes had stayed single into her early forties. It certainly wasn't for a lack of physical beauty. She imagined the vivacious redhead had left a trail of broken hearts behind her. Today, Alex's copper-colored hair hung in a loose braid over her shoulder, and she looked fit and trim in a white cotton shirt and khaki pants.

"Do you want a tissue?" Alex asked, picking up the box from beside the bed.

"Yes, please." Beth took one with her free hand and wiped away the stream of saltwater that had trickled down her cheek. "I'm sorry. I'm just a little emotional right now."

"Well, I can certainly understand why. It's not like your life hasn't changed drastically in the past week." Alex plumped Beth's pillow and then returned to the task of untangling wires and tubes.

"Thanks for your help."

"I'm afraid I'm not doing a very good job." Alex laughed as she picked at the mess. The freckles on her face knit together while she worked. "I'm afraid I might pull something loose if I apply too much pressure. If I did, do you think you would deflate like a hot air balloon?" Alex offered a wry smile.

Beth laughed out loud. "I'm not too worried about that. But I'm worried about falling asleep and offending my company." She yawned. The sedatives Dr. Abrams had ordered were keeping her down.

"Lie back and relax," Alex said. "You won't hurt my feelings, I promise."

Beth turned away, staring at the ceiling. She took several slow breaths, in and out, while Alex worked. The lines between the ceiling tiles began to blur, and then Beth heard them. Laughing. Talking. Playing.

"I give up. I'm calling a nurse." Alex hit the call button on the side of the bed.

"Do you hear them?" Beth turned to her friend.

"The nurses?"

"No. The children."

"What children?" Alex looked puzzled.

"They're singing now. Don't you hear them?"

"I hear the nurses down the hall—"

"Shhhh."

"Bethany, I don't . . ."

"How can I help you, Mrs. Harrison?" A nurse walked into the room and approached Beth's bed.

Beth stared at her, still thinking about the children.

Alex spoke up. "Yes. These wires are twisted." She pointed to the mass of tangled plastic near the bedrail and then stepped across the room, to the other side of the bed.

"They certainly are. Let me fix these for you, dear." The nurse unplugged one of the tubes that ran to the dispenser, which hung from the pole beside Beth's bed.

Alex settled into the chair next to the window. "Josh will be home tomorrow."

"Oh—that's right! I forgot." Beth perked up at the thought of her husband.

Alex scrunched her face. "I'm sure it's easy to lose track of time in here."

"Speaking of time, Mrs. Harrison, it's past time for your nap." The nurse reconnected the tube. "You need to say good-bye to your guest for right now."

Alex stood and walked toward the door. "Can I bring you something special to eat when I return?"

"No, thanks, I don't have much of an appetite." Beth's words were slurred, another unwelcome side effect of the medication.

"That will change when you get home, dear. Remember, you're eating for two now." The nurse smiled and patted her hand.

Alex waved. "I'll see you in a while, Mama."

A few minutes later, the nurse adjusted the drug dispenser. "You're almost out of morphine. I'll be back with a replacement bag. In the meantime, you settle in and try to get some sleep. Okay?"

"Sure," Beth said, before she dozed off.

<hr />

Beth remembered Alex visiting later that afternoon, but she could only recall snatches of the conversation. The drugs had diminished the clarity she had once taken for granted. At times, fear and frustration overwhelmed her. For years, she had prided herself on being in control of her life. Now she drifted. It was sometimes difficult to discern between illusion and reality.

Knowing that Josh would pick her up in the morning and take her home carried her through the rest of the day, and she slept peacefully until nightfall. About six o'clock, a new assortment of nurses paraded in and out of her room taking care of shift-change duties.

As darkness fell outside her window, her mood shifted, the absence of light provoking unpleasant musings. The antiseptic smell of the hospital room reminded her of another time. An old feeling of shame and self-loathing crept into her consciousness, and the past came closing in around her. She had made many mistakes when she was younger, but only one still haunted her.

God had now given her a second chance. The gift of life. New life.

It was a generous offering of mercy she did not deserve, but she would do everything she could to take care of the precious baby growing inside her. She would guard it with her life. Even if the very act of it killed her.

If it did, she took comfort in knowing that she would have two babies to hold in heaven. The child she now carried. And the child she had aborted.

# 7

**Present Day**

Josh, please slow down."

Beth tried to focus on the solid white line on the road to ease her nausea. Every curve brought a rush of vertigo. Each pothole jabbed her in the stomach.

"Sorry." Her husband shot a quick glance her way. "I'm anxious to get you home." He slowed his Jeep Cherokee and continued to make his way through traffic on Woodland Street, across the river from downtown Nashville.

"That day in the ambulance, I wasn't sure I would ever see home again."

"You had to be frightened."

"That's the amazing thing. I wasn't." There was no way to explain how that day had changed her life. "God's presence kept me at peace. The further I drifted from life, the closer I felt to him."

"Tell me about it," Josh said.

She tugged on her safety belt and settled back into her seat. "I saw my life pass in front of my eyes. You know, like they always say happens before you die?"

Josh stopped at a red light and turned to look at her. The warmth in his brown eyes encouraged her to continue.

"Somehow I understood that he knew everything about me. Everything, yet he still loved me." Chills skittered up and down Beth's spine as she remembered the experience. "I wanted to go with him, Josh. I wasn't afraid."

"I'm glad he let you stay." Josh returned his attention to the traffic ahead.

"Me too." Beth reached across the console, picked up his hand, and placed it on her stomach. "With you, and with the baby."

"Bethany, we need to talk about that—"

"Stop it!" She pushed his hand away. "We've already made that decision. I'm not giving up this child!"

"Beth, I don't want to lose you. We can have another baby some day, when you're well. This is not a normal circumstance. God would understand."

"Understand what? That we don't have enough faith to get us through this? Or that we don't practice what we preach?" She forced a deep breath, willing herself not to cry. "Of course, he would understand that our lives are more important than the one he gave us to protect."

"Beth—"

"No! I don't want to talk about it."

She punched the remote button on the door to open the passenger side window and closed the subject. For good.

They rode in silence, while Beth stared out the window. A lot had changed since she last passed through these streets on the outskirts of downtown Nashville. In one week's time, summer had surrendered completely to fall. The trees, which had once been dressed in red and gold, now stood with their branches almost completely exposed. Fall pumpkins and corn stalks still decorated the front porches and lawns of the beautiful, older homes in their community, but frost had muted the green foliage surrounding them.

East Nashville was a picturesque, peaceful, and convenient place to live. A handful of nearby markets and restaurants made shopping easy. It was also close to the center of Nashville and three interstate highways that connected the city to outlying suburbs and shopping malls. Titans' football stadium and the Bridgestone Arena were just across the river. The accounting office, where she worked, was less than half a mile beyond.

As Josh drove through the streets of their neighborhood, the cool morning air whipped across Beth's face, helping to ease her queasiness. She breathed in the fresh early winter air, remembering she had almost died last week. Yet, today, she overflowed with life.

The glimpse of heaven God had allowed her to see last Sunday would stay with her forever. It had changed her life and was enough to get her through this ordeal. No matter how difficult.

With that thought, the guilt settled in on her again. What would Josh say when he knew everything? When would she tell him about her past sins and the real meaning of this child to her? She feared the truth might send him out of her life forever. A tear slipped stealthily down her right cheek as Josh turned onto their home street.

"We're here," he said, breaking into the silence between them and then stopped the Jeep in front of their small blue cottage, a place she had loved since the first time she saw it. The place they had called home for almost a year, since shortly after they married.

Beth wiped the streaks of moisture from her cheek and returned her husband's smile. "It's good to be here."

Almost immediately, Beth saw Alex step off her front porch and wave. Her neighbor's broad smile was contagious from thirty feet away. She rushed to the curb, as Josh helped Beth out of the Jeep. "Good to see you, girl! How do you feel?"

"Like a bulldozer hit me."

"Are you hungry?" Alex looked from Beth to Josh. "I made chicken salad."

Just the thought made Beth's mouth water. While she didn't care for most of Alex's ultra-healthy cooking, her chicken salad was exceptional. "You know I love your chicken salad."

"Sounds great." Josh slammed the car door after removing Beth's bag from the backseat.

"Okay! I'll bring it over. I made fresh bread, too. See you in a minute."

The perky redhead hurried back to her white clapboard house, one of the most unusual houses on the street. The modified Cape Cod had a deck built over the front porch, a place where Alex often set up her art supplies.

Beth's stomach growled. She hadn't realized how hungry she was. Not only for home cooking but also for home. And time alone to think about how her life was changing.

*Thank you, God, for giving me a second chance.*

<hr>

"Lunch was great," Josh said, before taking a long drink of sweet iced tea. "The best meal I've eaten in six weeks."

"Thanks. But I'm sure anything would taste good, just because Beth is home." Alex smiled and then turned to Beth. "Your release from the hospital is an answer to prayers. Everyone at church has been praying."

"We're humbled by that," Josh said. "It has been too long since I was in town on a Sunday morning. I've missed being able to attend services." He looked at Beth, who was nodding off at the table. "Why don't we move to the living room and talk for a few minutes?"

While Alex cleared the dishes, Josh dug into the bag of prescriptions they had purchased on the way home. He compared the label instructions to the doctor's orders, and then extracted Beth's midday medication. The amount of pills she was supposed to take boggled his mind. He handed his wife a glass of water and two tablets. "You need to take these," he said.

Beth frowned and then swallowed the pills.

When they adjourned into the next room. Josh took a seat in his favorite chair beside the fireplace. Alex sat cross-legged on top of the ottoman near the window. And Beth snuggled into the nearby sofa.

"I'm thankful you're home," Josh said to Beth before turning to Alex. "And I'm thankful you can help her while I'm gone. I'm committed to touring almost until Christmas." He shook his head and stared into the fireplace. "Not great timing, but it will help pay the medical bills."

The expression on Beth's face dropped when he mentioned their extra expenses. Perhaps for the first time she fully understood the impact her illness would have on their finances.

"I guess I can't work for a while, huh?" She studied her hands, which were clasped together in her lap. "I'm sorry."

"You don't need to worry about it, honey," Josh assured her. "I want you to stay home. To get well. I've already called Bob Bradford."

Beth's boss, and Josh's accountant, had promised that Beth could return to her job when she was ready. But in the meantime, everything would rest on Josh's shoulders.

"I'm here to help," Alex said.

"You have no idea how much we appreciate it. You've already done a lot," he told her. "But we don't expect you to do it for nothing."

Alex shook her head. "Please don't worry about that."

"We won't accept your help any other way." Josh hoped he wouldn't offend his neighbor, because she represented the best option they had for Beth's caregiver.

He glanced toward Beth, who was now preoccupied with Buster. The little dog had crawled beside her on the sofa and laid his head on her lap. Josh turned back to Alex. "It's worth a lot of money to me to leave with the knowledge that we have someone capable to watch over her."

"I'm here for you. I'm here for Beth," Alex said.

"It may not be an easy job."

"I understand." She looked from him to the sofa and smiled.

Beth had dozed off.

---

That night Josh fully understood the implications of his words. His wife slept fitfully, so sleep tread lightly across his consciousness. He roused at one a.m. to discover Beth's side of the bed empty. Straining to listen through the darkness, he recognized the sound of running water in the bathroom.

Before he could climb out of bed to check on her, Beth's silhouette staggered through the door. He watched her pick her way across the room, as if navigating a minefield. When she reached the foot of the bed, she collapsed onto the floor. Almost like a building imploding into itself, her legs gave way and her body folded.

Josh threw back the covers and rushed to his wife, gently lifting her upright. Beth's limp body gave in to him without effort. He braced her sturdy frame against his shoulders, holding her with a firm grip.

Without warning, she began to laugh hysterically.

The spark of fear and concern that had been lit in his gut a moment ago ignited into anger. How could she do this to him? To their child?

"Stop . . . Beth. Stop it!" His reprimand crescendoed with each word. His eyes had adjusted to the darkness, and he could see her staring at him, as if in shock. Then, she started to sob. She embraced him with shaky arms and buried her head in his chest. Josh rocked her in his arms, holding and comforting her for several minutes until she had settled down enough for him to lead her back to bed.

For the remainder of the night, he lay awake considering what their life had come to and where they were going. Beth slept without incident for the next few hours. She rested so peacefully he found himself straining to watch her diaphragm rise and fall, assuring himself she continued to breathe. Twice she had nightmares, or presumably so. She muttered irrelevant bits of conversation aloud, and her muscles jerked and flailed against themselves.

Josh considered reaching out to awaken her and soothe the pain of her tortured dreams. But he feared that would only burn the images of the hallucinations into her conscious mind. So, instead, he prayed. He asked God to have mercy on his wife and on their child.

And to help him get through the next eight months.

# 8

## May 30, 1971

Ka-plop. Ka-plop. Ka-plop.

Isaac rolled his bicycle beside him as he walked home from the flower shop. The front tire had gone flat. It was ruined this time, and he knew he had to find a way to replace it. His bicycle represented the only freedom he had.

Grandfather had sent him home early today to help Mama Ruth prepare for Shavuot, the Jewish Festival of the First Fruits. His handlebar basket was piled high with flowers and greenery to decorate the house. Uncle David, Aunt Rachel, and his cousins, Adina and Eli, would be coming over soon for the all-night celebration, a time for reflection on God's gift of the Torah. Shavuot represented both ending and beginning to the Jewish people. It was the time when they had been freed from enslavement, before the giving of the law to Moses on Mount Sinai.

Mama Ruth would serve her usual Shavuot evening meal of roast chicken, noodle kugel, fresh vegetables, cheese blintzes, and fruit. Afterward, they would read the harvest story in the book of Ruth. Then they would play games and spend the night discussing the Torah.

Grandfather would be home before sunset, which meant Isaac had a full hour to convince Mama Ruth to help him buy a new bicycle. For months, he had saved his allowance and the small amount of money he had earned working in the school cafeteria. Yet his savings fell short of the $89.95 necessary to buy the silver Schwinn Manta Ray he had already picked out at Frankie's Hardware.

Isaac had spent hours staring through the front window of the store, two doors down from his grandfather's shop. The five-speed, muscle bike had a Stik-Shifter and medium rise handlebars. All he needed to buy it was eleven more dollars, plus change. He should be able to sweet-talk that amount from his grandmother, given enough time.

He opened the door to their brownstone, the only home he could remember, and rolled his old bicycle into the entryway.

"Isaac, you're here!" Mama Ruth looked up from the hall table where she was arranging a bowl of fresh fruit. She stepped to him, brushed the curls from his face, and planted a kiss on his cheek.

He smiled. His grandmother must now stand on her tiptoes to embrace him.

She held him at arm's length. "You look so much like your mother. I miss her." Moisture filled her eyes. "Ah! Enough sentiment, old woman," she muttered to herself. "Quickly, son, gather the silver candlesticks and cheese platter from the breakfront. We must finish the preparations." She nudged him in the direction of the dining room and resumed her work.

"Yes, Mama Ruth," he said, securing his bike in the far corner of the entry before he set out to do his chores.

Isaac knew in his heart it was his grandmother's love that had kept him here for almost twelve years. Without her, he would have run away when he had been old enough to take care of himself. Grandfather's old-fashioned ways and chilly self-absorption would have driven him out, just as it likely did his mother many years before.

Or, perhaps, the strange religion had drawn her away. Isaac knew very little about his real parents. His father, Michael, his mother, Rebekah, and his brother and sister had been killed soon after he was born. There were times Isaac wished the accident had taken him too. He often wondered what life would have been like with his family.

Mama Ruth still grieved for her daughter. But Grandfather refused to even speak of her. "*Cherem*. She is dead to me. I do not want to hear her name," he would say.

The words hurt Isaac. He never understood how someone could deny flesh and blood. To throw them away like a faded flower on a broken stem.

On a few occasions, when Grandfather wasn't home, Mama Ruth had shown Isaac photos of his family. His mother's beauty took his breath away. He would always do his best to commit to memory the details of her eyes, her nose, and her hair. He tried to imagine her smell, the softness of her voice.

In his favorite picture, his mother glowed. Her beautiful smile lit up her face as she held him, an infant no more than three months old. He saw that he had a striking resemblance to both his parents. His dark wavy hair and olive skin came from his mother, but the blue eyes reflected in the mirror each morning were like his father's. Perhaps too much so and that was why Grandfather was so hard on him. He must have hated the man who took his daughter away.

Or, perhaps, Isaac considered, he was walking in his mother's shoes. Had she endured the same childhood he now lived?

If only she could tell him how well he was doing.

# 9

**Present Day**

Are you sure you don't want to go out to eat?" Josh asked.

"No," Beth growled back at him. "I can do it." She threw a pan into the sink with a loud clatter.

Josh had watched her moods go up and down during the past three days, but this was the worst he had seen. "Honey, I'm not saying you can't. I'm just suggesting it would be easier if we go out."

"I'm sorry my cooking isn't as good as the gourmet food you eat on the road." She shot him a disdainful look. "It works just fine for me when you're gone."

She turned her back to him and wiped her cheek with a dishtowel. Her shoulders began to twitch and heave, and then he heard muffled sobs.

The moods always played out after the tears came, and then a sense of normalcy returned. Although a tired and melancholy version. He hated to see what the prescription drugs were doing to her. She was up one minute and down the next.

He approached his wife and laid his hand on her shoulder. She turned to embrace him, and he stroked her hair.

"Are you okay?"

She nodded, pulled away, and rubbed her eyes. "Yes. But I'm not sure why I, why we, have to go through this."

"We'll make it." He assured her, while trying to reassure himself.

"I know. Somehow." She nodded and pulled away to return to her meal preparation.

Josh walked back to the table and took a seat on the bench. He knew the situation was difficult for Beth too. But the responsibility of it all scared him. He had to be strong for both of them.

He had so many questions. So many doubts, about the kind of long-term damage the drugs were inflicting. God had been gracious to give him Beth when he needed her most, just before he lost his mother to a devastating illness and less than a year before his father passed away from grief and exhaustion.

Josh had hoped for a family of his own since losing his parents. But not under these circumstances. Beth interrupted his thoughts as she set two plates on the table, one in front of him.

"It looks great, honey," he said.

She sat opposite him, and he held her hand across the table while he said grace. The food smelled delicious. Beth had made one of his favorite meals. Meatloaf, mashed potatoes, and corn. He picked up his fork and took a big bite of the meatloaf. He had looked forward to eating Beth's home cooking the entire time he was away.

The mealy texture of the hamburger shocked him back to reality. His first impulse was to spit it out. But Beth was beaming, proud of her accomplishment. He rolled the soggy mixture around in his mouth. It would have been tasteless except for scorched places on the bottom crust. He took a long drink of iced tea and swallowed.

Beth watched him dig into the mound of mashed potatoes on his plate. He smiled back at her. He could make a meal of mashed potatoes anytime. *But not these potatoes.* They were lumpy, which wasn't so bad. But Beth must have salted them twice. They were almost intolerably seasoned. How would he make it through the meal without hurting his wife's feelings?

He took a small bite of the corn. *Sweet and delicious.* Thank God for Del Monte.

"This is great," he said. "Would you please pass the corn, honey?"

She smiled and handed the bowl back to him. He piled more of the golden kernels onto his plate, practically smothering his potatoes and meatloaf.

"You're eating a lot of corn," she said, her expression wavering.

"For some reason I've been craving it." He whispered a silent prayer for forgiveness of his little white lie. "Thanks for cooking for me."

She smiled. "You're welcome!"

His wife had gone out of her way to fix supper when she didn't feel well, and he would fill his stomach with sweet corn. Even though his stomach complained, his heart overflowed with love for her.

<hr />

"Do you think we'll get through this?" Josh asked Alex while they stood in the backyard watching Buster running at warp speed.

The little black-and-white terrier scampered like a streaker at a football game, dodging trees and bushes as he ran. The chilly weather always invigorated him.

Josh too. The clear crispness of the air would have made for a perfect football game day. But, instead of watching his favorite sport on television or at Bryant-Denny Stadium in Tuscaloosa, Alabama, he was discussing his wife's bizarre behavior with their neighbor. Alex had stayed with Beth this morning while he ran errands, and she knew what he was facing.

"God will get you through it."

"Us. You're in the midst of this battle too."

"We can make it a day at a time," she said.

Alex was one of the most positive Christians he knew, even when circumstances didn't warrant optimism. "Nights are worse than daytime. She's had some terrible nightmares. Even getting out of bed and acting . . . strangely." Josh wasn't sure how to describe Beth's manic actions.

"Sleepwalking?"

"Yes, I guess that's what it is."

"It's likely the medication. She'll grow more tolerant after a while."

"That's what I'm afraid of." Josh shook his head. "I don't know the long-term effect of those drugs. On her, or the baby. And I worry she could accidentally take an overdose. I have it hidden so she can't get to it."

"I'll keep everything with me in the spare bedroom while you're away. I'll spend every night, for as long as I'm needed."

"Thank you." Josh heard his voice crack. The thought of Beth being alone in the house terrified him.

"No problem." Alex picked up a tennis ball lying on the ground in front of her. She studied it. "I'll move my things in tonight before you leave."

"I appreciate your help." He inhaled from deep within his diaphragm, trying to calm his nerves. "I don't know what we would do without you."

"I'm glad to do it. I can work on art projects in my room when she's napping. Besides, you're paying me, remember?" She threw the tennis ball to Buster. The little terrier tackled it with a kangaroo bounce and then taunted Alex with a wag of his tail. Dancing on his back legs, he twisted his butt and begged for another game of catch. "Besides, how hard is it to help a friend?" She rubbed Buster on the top of his head and threw the ball again, sending him running off into the yard.

"You don't take compliments well, do you?"

Alex blushed. "I'm just happy to help. It's no big deal. Beth needs someone with her, and I've got extra time on my hands at the moment. God works out the timing in our lives."

Josh's stomach growled out loud. His turn to blush.

"Hey, I made a pot of chili this afternoon. Why don't I bring it over for your and Beth's supper?"

"I wasn't hinting, I promise." He grinned. "But, if it's not an imposition, that would be great. We've been eating my cooking for the last three days." No need to mention the failed attempt at supper Beth had made the night before. "We won't accept, however, if you don't join us."

"Okay, I'll be right back." She turned toward her house and shouted over her shoulder. "Did I mention it was tofu chili?"

Josh frowned.

"You'll love it. Really." She laughed.

*Alex and her health food.* At least it would be better than a frozen dinner or a bowl of cereal.

---

Beth lifted a spoonful of chili to her lips but the smell turned her stomach. "Do we have any Doritos?" She looked from Josh to Alex. "The nacho cheese kind?"

"That's all you've been eating for two days," Josh scolded her.

"I want them. And chocolate milk too. Do we have chocolate milk?"

Alex almost spit out her iced tea. "I hope you don't eat Doritos and drink chocolate milk together."

"What's wrong with that?" Beth growled. She was tired of people telling her what to eat, what to do.

"Withdraw my last statement, your honor. I didn't mean to offend you." Alex suppressed a grin.

"I don't see the humor in any of this. I'm sick of being laughed at—and treated like a child."

"Don't be rude to our guest." Josh glared at her. "Alex is only trying to help."

"I don't need help, thank you very much." Beth tried to stand but her feet became tangled. When she fell back into her seat, the tears began to flow.

*Not again. Why did she always have to cry?*

Josh frowned and offered his napkin.

Alex offered an apology.

"Beth, I'm sorry. Really. I didn't mean to upset you. I was just teasing. If you want to eat Doritos every day, it's up to you. Sometimes I try to mother people I love. I can't help it. I was raised in a Jewish family, you know."

Beth dabbed her eyes with the napkin. Alex could almost always make her smile. "I'm the one who should be sorry. I'm not sure what's happening to me." She took a deep breath. "There's too much going on, too many changes. My illness. The baby. Taking a leave from my job. I feel like I'm out of control."

"We both feel that way, honey." Josh reached for her hand. The warmth of it calmed her rattled nerves. She leaned back into the wooden banquette.

"You both have a lot on you right now," Alex said. "Let me do the dishes while the two of you have some together time." She scrambled out of the booth, picking up utensils, plates, and bowls on her way to the sink.

"No. Let me do it." Josh grabbed the dirty dishes from her hands. "You and Beth go on into the living room."

Beth winked at Alex. "Is he a great husband or what?"

"He even eats tofu." Alex pretended to whisper, but her words were loud enough for Josh to hear.

"Are you sure that was tofu?" Josh asked with a smile on his face. "It was delicious."

"We girls never share our secrets, do we, Bethany?" Alex laughed.

Beth swallowed hard and fought back the realization that, if she wanted to find complete forgiveness, she must eventually reveal one of her most guarded secrets.

Only then could she let go of the niggling guilt inside her.

<hr />

Josh heard the girls laughing and talking in the other room as he cleaned the kitchen. An unexplained peace settled over him knowing that Alex would be staying with Beth while he was away. Family couldn't do it. Alex had been an answer to prayer. Even before those prayers had been prayed.

God had led him and Beth to the house next door to Alexandra Hayes. His perfect plan set in place for the day she would fulfill a special need in their lives.

He ran his fingers through his hair. It would be so easy to become anxious over the circumstances, but he had to stay focused on the knowledge that God would provide.

*Luke 12:31, He will give you everything you need* had been his mother's favorite verse. He wanted to trust the Lord as much as she had. He wished he could share his concerns with her right now, to seek her guidance. She would tell him to pray and to keep his confidence in God.

He hoped he could do that. But something uncomfortable—an awareness of darkness yet to be uncovered—also pricked at his spirit. A drug-induced veil had fallen over his wife and, at times, he hadn't recognized her in the past few days.

Even worse, he wasn't sure he knew who he was anymore. Fear stirred in his heart. Fear that had grown from a mustard seed less than two years ago.

Fear that had been planted the day his father left the ministry.

# 10

**Present Day**

Take a right here." Beth pointed to the street sign ahead. The address matched what she had been given for her new obstetrician's office.

Alex steered her yellow VW Beetle into the lot in front of the large brick building. "Now, to find a parking spot. This place is packed. Is there a run on maternity care this time of year?"

Beth smiled. "Thanks for bringing me today."

"You don't need to drive in your condition."

"Don't remind me. It's depressing being so dependent."

Alex pulled into an empty space and switched off the ignition. "You realize God has given you a wonderful blessing, don't you, girl? Despite the trials?"

"I know." Beth nodded, while searching for a tube of lipstick in her handbag. She flipped down the sun visor mirror to apply the color to her lips, fighting to stay within the lines.

"You're shaking. Are you okay?" Alex asked.

"I'm fine." Beth snapped the visor shut and opened the car door. Alex had no idea how difficult this was for her. Facing death had been easier than the prospects of living on an emotional roller coaster ride, hanging onto the good things and struggling through the bad.

The idea of having Josh's baby excited her, of course. But she also had concerns. She couldn't remember a day in the past two weeks when her head hadn't hurt. Aspirin had never set well with her system. Now, she existed on high-powered prescriptions that challenged her lucidity.

How could she possibly take care of a baby? She had become a child herself. She couldn't be trusted on her own. She'd taken a leave of absence from the accounting office and needed a caregiver day and night. Not exactly what she had envisioned for herself at twenty-nine and a year into her marriage.

If only Dr. Myers would put her primary fear to rest. She could deal with everything else.

Beth stepped outside the car and slammed the door. Alex walked beside her to the lobby of the physicians' building.

"Relax," her friend said. "Practice your deep breathing."

Beth took a long, deliberate breath. She held it for a few seconds and then exhaled in short bursts. Alex scanned the building directory before pushing the call button on the elevator. They stepped inside the lift and rode, without speaking, to the third floor.

Once in the waiting room, Alex took a seat while Beth filled out preliminary paperwork at the front desk. She found Alex rifling through parenting magazines when she joined her in the sitting area.

"You'd think they would have pity on us single girls," Alex said. "Look at the cute babies on the covers of these things."

"You'll be a godmother soon and, trust me, you can have all the cuddle time you want," Beth assured her. "Diaper time too."

Alex's broad smile connected the freckles on her creamy complexion into a soft blush. She adjusted her sweater and continued to dig through the pile of magazines, finally pulling out an old issue of *Town and Country*.

Beth looked around the crowded room. She might as well settle in for a long wait. She wondered what circumstances had brought each woman—and sometimes her male companion—to see the doctor. Perhaps circumstances worse than her own. An unwanted pregnancy, a questionable test result, or even a scary symptom she had discovered at home.

A few women wore business suits and fidgeted with their cell phones. Each seemed more concerned with other things than medical issues. Several mothers with young children juggled their crabby offspring.

"Tori . . . quiet!" A pretty, blonde woman repeated over and over while the child ignored her.

One couple, sitting in the corner of the room, whispered together nonstop and focused their attention on the baby bump under the young woman's clothes.

Nurses crisscrossed the charcoal-gray carpet that ran from one reception area to another. The room had been decorated to the nines and could easily have been mistaken for a home decorator's office, except for the photos of babies and toddlers adorning the walls.

Light gray dots peppered the luxuriously thick floor covering and coordinated with the stripes on the upholstered chairs. Dusk-colored draperies hung at oversized windows. The fabric fell into puddles on the floor.

Flamingo pink lamps provided the decorating *pièce de résistance*. They sprouted from translucent glass side tables and reached toward the ceiling. It was medical-office chic done to excess, but it kept Beth's mind off her problems for a while.

After a twenty-minute wait, a nurse called Beth to the prep area. Entering the inner sanctum, they walked past black-and-white portraits of mothers holding babies. The nurse led Beth to an intermediate examination area, where she underwent basic testing: weight, height, urine sample, and blood pressure. Once Beth was seated, the nurse asked about current medications. Beth gave her the printed list that Alex had prepared in advance, along with a folder from Dr. Abrams's office.

The older woman glanced through the paperwork. "You're having a rough time right now, sweetie. When did you learn about your dissected artery?"

"About two weeks ago."

"How are you holding up emotionally?"

"I'm concerned, you know, with having to take the morphine and other drugs."

"I can understand." The nurse patted Beth on the arm. "You will do fine. There are no perfect pregnancies. Dr. Myers can help you manage everything, and that includes having a healthy baby." She smiled. "This is your first visit, right?"

"Yes, ma'am."

"Well, don't worry, you're in good hands."

The nurse asked Beth to follow her down a long hallway. They stopped at the door to a small, cubical-shaped exam room. Inside, she gave Beth a crisp cotton gown. "It ties in the back. Make yourself comfortable. The doctor will be in soon."

The nurse shut the door behind her, leaving Beth in the midst of another designer's utopia, this one inspired by Pepto-Bismol. Fitting. Her stomach turned just thinking about the physical exam.

The faux-painted, pink walls featured more baby artwork. Except for the standard medical amenities, Beth could have been inside a plush hotel suite. After undressing and slipping on the gown, she took a seat on the examination table. Then she covered her legs with the pink sheet that had been provided.

Why were doctors' offices always so cold? A chill traipsed up and down her spine while she sat, waiting, inside the frigid cubical. She pulled the sheet tighter to herself as shadows from the past danced around the room. Despite the luxurious accoutrements, the surroundings weren't all that different from those almost ten years ago. The old memories came rushing back. Memories she had tried to forget. Her heart pounded when Dr. Myers knocked on the door and, right on cue, tears rolled down Beth's cheeks.

The tall, dark-haired physician, who wore her hair in a pixie-cut, entered the room, the nurse one step behind her. "Hi, I'm Nicole Myers . . . "

When she saw Beth's tears, she frowned and handed her a tissue. "Bethany, what's wrong?"

"I'm sorry. How embarrassing." Beth shook her head and dried her eyes. "I'm just a little emotional." She could feel the heat creeping into her face.

"Not that uncommon, my dear. You have a few extra hormones floating around in your system right now." Dr. Myers offered a reassuring smile and then rolled the chrome stool from the corner of the room closer to the examination table.

Beth watched the slender woman, who was probably ten years older than her, take a seat on the stool and begin to read through her chart. "You have a lot going on. I can understand why you're concerned. But," she smiled, "you know what? We can get you through this. You and your baby can get through this."

The doctor's words raised Beth's spirits. "Thank you, Dr. Myers."

"How much morphine are you on right now?"

"Twenty-five milligrams."

The obstetrician made a written notation. "Okay." She set the papers aside. "Let's do the exam." She spoke over her shoulder to the nurse. "Alisha, I want to draw an extra vial of blood before Bethany leaves. I'll need to run some additional tests."

The gray-haired woman nodded and prepared a syringe, making quick work of the task, before rejoining the doctor at the exam table. While doing Beth's physical, Dr. Myers chatted about baby names, nursery furniture, and mother-child portraits.

The latter amused Beth in light of the wall art throughout the doctor's office. The woman was obsessed with baby photography. But Beth liked her a lot. Her hopes soared. Perhaps her baby would survive this high-risk pregnancy after all. Only one question remained.

"Everything looks good. Let's talk." Dr. Myers once again took a seat on the stool and picked up Beth's chart. "What concerns you the most?"

"What do you mean?" Beth tried to swallow the lump in her throat.

"You were upset when I came into the room earlier. Fill me in. I want to know how I can help you." The doctor looked squarely into Beth's eyes.

Beth took a deep breath and exhaled slowly. "I've never shared this with anyone. But I know I need to tell you. I want to give my baby the best chance possible." Her voice trembled. "I had an abortion when I was in college, and I'm concerned it will affect my pregnancy."

"Was there anything unusual about your abortion?" The doctor asked. "Was it late term?"

"Oh, no. I was only about eight weeks."

"Good. Did you have complications? Uncontrolled bleeding? Infection? Perforation?"

"No . . . no. I don't think so." Beth struggled to remember the details she had tried to forget.

"That's all good. Complications with an abortion can create problems with future pregnancies."

Tears threatened again, but they were tears of joy.

"How about gastronomical problems?" The doctor asked.

"What do you mean?"

"Have you noticed any unusual digestive symptoms lately? Lower stomach or abdominal pain?"

"Not really. I'm on strong painkillers now, so I don't know." Beth thought back. "I might have had some pain before going to the hospital."

"Where?"

"Here." Beth placed her hand over the right side of her lower stomach.

"I didn't feel anything unusual," the doctor told her. "How about dizziness, light-headedness—"

"Oh, yes. A lot of that now. But I thought it was from the drugs."

"It could be, and I don't want to alarm you," Dr. Myers said. "But there is a higher rate of ectopic pregnancies in women who have had abortions. I'm sure you know, that's a very serious situation, dangerous for both mother and baby." The doctor jotted more notes on her chart. "I want to run a couple of tests. Let's try to rule this out so we can move on in a positive direction."

Beth clutched her hands to ease the shaking. "How do we do that?"

"We can be relatively certain with two simple procedures. One is a hormone test, the other is a specific kind of ultrasound."

"Yes, please, Dr. Myers. Let's do them. I have to know."

"Alisha, let's schedule her as soon as possible."

# 11

**Present Day**

The sky was overcast in Milwaukee when Josh stepped off the bus for his hotel room. The others would be leaving soon for the concert hall, where they would do a sound check and spend the afternoon.

He had several hours to get in a two-mile run, eat lunch, and then relax before he showered. A staff member from the hall would be picking him up at five p.m. so he could join his band and crew for dinner.

Josh had never liked exercising, but after ten hours on the bus, he had to admit it would feel good to stretch his legs. And he always enjoyed seeing areas of the various cities they worked that he would not have ordinarily seen. Once in a while he would come upon a good place for lunch or a shop that interested him. On a really good day, he would be able to run next to the waterfront, in a park, or even on a school track that was open to the public.

He didn't expect to be so fortunate today, because the outside temperature was hovering around the thirty-two-degree mark. Not bad for this area, but chilly enough to get his exercise done and then hurry back to the hotel for a hot lunch at the restaurant.

The road life wasn't a bad life. In fact, it could be fulfilling and quite interesting. He saw new places, met new people, and experienced things he never dreamed possible when he was a young man growing up in central Alabama. But things were beginning to change. If all went well, he would be a father this time next year. And there would be two reasons to want to stay home.

He hurried to his hotel room and changed into his jogging clothes. He was halfway to the elevator when he realized he had forgotten his cell phone. He heard it ringing as he was opening the door to his room but didn't get to it in time. The call went to voicemail.

He dialed his number, entered his code, and listened. It was Beth. She was crying so hard he could barely understand her. She said something about an ectopic pregnancy. Tubes . . . uterus . . . more tests. He heard enough to understand the bottom line. They might lose the baby. She asked him to call her back right away.

*Oh, God, I don't know if I can handle this.*

Josh hit resend to return the call, praying for the right thing to say to his distraught wife. Yet, just as he hadn't found the right words to comfort his father eighteen months ago, he doubted he would find them today. How would he even find comfort for himself?

Beth answered after the first ring. "I'm so glad you called me right back. Dr. Myers said my pregnancy could be ectopic." Her words came in a torrent, and then she paused. "I'm afraid this is all my fault."

"How could any of this be your fault, honey?" Josh feared that paranoia could be another side effect of the painkillers Beth was taking. "You're doing the best you can. . . ."

"But our baby could be in trouble already, and not even have a chance." She whispered the words into the phone, as if saying them out loud would seal the child's fate. "I-I . . ." She began to cry. "It's my fault, and I don't know what I can do."

⚬≈≈⚬

The evening meal at the hall in Milwaukee reminded Josh of his mother's cooking. Fried chicken, mashed potatoes, white gravy with just enough black pepper and grease cooked into it, and buttery, homemade yeast rolls.

Catering was provided by someone different in every city. Each show promoter hired a local company. Most days they served spicy ethnic food, dried out hamburgers, or cardboard chicken. A lot of cardboard chicken, which was usually accompanied by instant mashed potatoes and a broccoli medley. Josh winced at the thought. He hated broccoli.

But meals today were courtesy of a local church. At the moment, Josh could think of no better mission work than to serve good food to a bunch of home cooking–starved musicians who needed the comfort. In reality, the show promoter had traded catering for a section of seats in the back of the auditorium.

Josh helped himself to seconds of the fried chicken and grabbed a piece of chocolate cake before sitting down with his road manager, Ryan Majors. Ryan rarely took time to eat crew meals with the rest of the band. Instead, he ate on the run or very little at all—one reason for his lean physique. But Josh had asked Ryan to join him tonight for a conversation.

"I need your help." Josh wiped his face with a paper napkin.

Ryan listened while picking at his salad. "Is it just me, or is this meal the worst we've had in a while?" He scowled. Evidently boys from Arizona didn't grow up on fried chicken.

"I need your help." Josh said again. "I need to free up some personal time. I'm dealing with Beth's insurance paperwork and medical bills."

Ryan nodded but never looked up.

"I'm putting you in charge of the merchandise accounting. Mitch will report directly to you, and you'll report to me."

This time he got his road manager's full attention. Ryan's blue eyes sparkled, the reaction Josh had expected. Ryan thrived on responsibility. No doubt he also hoped his new duties would add pay to an already well-padded salary.

"I'll be upfront with you, man. I can't pay you extra. I'm operating on a tight budget. But I promise I won't leave the job on you forever."

Ryan nodded with a little less enthusiasm. He popped a cherry tomato into his mouth. "I'll take care of it."

"Thanks. I'll talk to Mitch. We'll go over everything on the bus in the morning."

"Works for me." Ryan snatched his fedora from the tabletop, stood up, and collected his salad plate and utensils. "See you in a while. I have to pick up the performance check."

Josh lingered over dessert and reconsidered his decision. Giving up control of merchandise accounting didn't feel right. But he had no option. He had to give up some of his responsibilities. Merchandising could be delegated.

His personal issues could not.

# 12

Isaac shifted from one foot to the other as he contemplated the risk of his actions. Grandfather wouldn't be home for another hour, and Mama Ruth had gone to the grocer's. If he had the courage, he had the time.

He pressed his nose to the thick glass pane of the dining room window to check again. No one was in sight. No time to linger. He crossed the room to the gigantic breakfront that anchored the sidewall of the room. The wooden floor creaked when he kneeled to pull open the bottom drawer of the massive mahogany heirloom.

The large piece of furniture held a number of family treasures, some from places and times he could scarcely comprehend. Fine silver and linens from his grandparents' grandparents had been meticulously packed and brought over from Europe. Yellowed newspaper clippings from the Great Holocaust had been handed down to enlighten future generations. And an antique ram's horn *shofar*, as well as a *tallit*, from Mama Ruth's great-grandfather.

But it was remembrances of his parents, brother, and sister that drew Isaac to the aged china cabinet today. Family birth certificates, medical records, and photos lay tucked beneath a black velvet *kippah* that had belonged to his mother. The skullcap was nestled among a number of his mother's personal items, which Mama Ruth had saved for years.

Isaac set aside baby shoes, a prayer shawl, and a bat mitzvah dress to dig deeper. The photographs were his favorite indulgence. He had once spent hours looking through them with his grandmother, her face radiant when she spoke of her daughter and other grandchildren, his brother and sister. She had told him stories he would never forget.

Yet Mama Ruth, too, must pick her time to sift through these memories, the only tangible reminders of the family she had lost. Grandfather had threatened to destroy everything if he caught her sharing the photos with Isaac. So, only once or twice a year, she would wait until Levi Ruben left the house and then summon Isaac to her side.

He now carefully folded back the aged lace, which hid a dark blue, velvet-covered box at the bottom of the musty-smelling drawer. He opened the lid and sorted through the photos with care. The aged paper was as fragile as his connection to the people they revealed.

Isaac stopped at his favorite photograph. His mother smiled at him through the quickness of time. He took in every detail of the photo, trying to piece together the life he would have had. Soon he lost himself in the daydream that his family still lived.

"Isaac! *A broch!*"

Grandfather's voice snapped Isaac back to the present reality.

He turned to see Levi Ruben standing at the entrance of the room. His fiery, dark eyes sparked with anger. "You disobey me?" The old man picked up momentum, rushing closer. His face was as red as a cup of spicy borscht and his arms flailed the air.

Isaac's first instinct was to cower, to hide in the gap between the giant wood bureau and the corner of the wall. But something inside him clicked. Whether from courage or foolishness, a calm strength descended upon him. He was a man now, nearly sixteen. He chose to no longer live in terror. He would take the blows his tormentor was about to deliver, but this time he would land a few of his own.

"Let me have the photos. I will destroy them once and for all." Grandfather shouted when Isaac stood to confront the older but sinewy man.

Grandfather's cheeks puffed in anger, the skin stretching tautly from ear to ear. He looked like he might explode. "You think you can fight me?" He lifted his hand to strike Isaac. "Justice is mine."

Then, without warning, his grandfather froze. His face contorted and constricted, one side up and the other down. Isaac watched the man stagger forward before he fell backward, landing on the floor, deadly silent.

"Levi!" Mama Ruth screamed as she ran into the room. "*Oy gevalt!* Isaac!" She turned to him. "Run. Fetch the doctor!"

# 13

**Present Day**

Beth waited all day for Dr. Myers to call with the test results. At 6:35 p.m., the phone rang, and Alex noted the number on the caller ID.

"Doctor's office." She passed the phone to Beth.

Beth squeaked out a hello, her lungs barren of air.

"Bethany, it's Nicole Myers. I have good news for you." The doctor's smile radiated through the phone. "There is no ectopic pregnancy. Your baby is developing fine."

"That's great." Beth inhaled in deep bursts. "So, where do we go from here?"

"I want you to track your blood pressure. Do you have a home monitor?"

"Yes. Dr. Abrams asked me to do the same thing."

"Check it three times a day and keep a written record. Bring it to your next appointment."

"Okay."

"Do you have any other questions?"

"What about the effects of the morphine on the baby?"

There was a heartbeat of silence. "It's not optimum, but," her voice smiled again, "babies are survivors."

"Thank you for helping me, Dr. Myers."

"That's why I'm here, to help babies and their moms."

Beth smiled.

"Your child's health is most dependent upon your health. We'll keep a close watch on you during the next seven months," Dr. Myers assured her. "May I give you one more piece of advice?"

"Yes, ma'am."

"Don't overdo it, but try to get out of the house once a week or so. It will keep your spirits up."

"I will," Beth promised. She hung up the phone and then squealed. "Everything is normal."

Alex reached to hug her. "God is good. He will get you through the next seven months, just like he's brought you to this point."

"I'm not sure I'm deserving of so many blessings."

"None of us are, girl. But he watches over us from the time we are conceived. He knows our name before we're born . . ." Alex stopped midsentence. "Wait! I'll be right back."

Moments later Alex returned with a large, white gift bag. It had been decorated with ivory-colored lace and tiny, creamy white bows. "I couldn't wait to give this to you."

"That's too pretty to open." Beth took the bag from her caregiver. "Did you make the gift bag?"

"Yes." Alex blushed. "Go ahead, open it."

Beth tugged on the ivory-colored tissue, revealing a large, white organza pouch inside the bag. "It's soft," she said. After loosening the drawstrings on the fabric sack, she pulled out a pashmina baby blanket. "Oh, my . . . it's beautiful." She looked up to see Alex's eyes moist with tears.

"I wanted you to have something to hold. Something tangible to remind you of the gift growing inside you, of the child God will reveal in his perfect timing." Alex wiped her eyes and handed Beth the phone. "Why don't you call Josh and give him your good news?"

—◦◦◦—

Sitting on the side of the bed as she prepared to tuck herself in that night, Beth caressed the luxurious cashmere and silk baby blanket. She ran her fingers over the satin-wrapped edges. The materials were exquisite. But even the finest fabrics couldn't assuage her guilt.

Josh had been relieved to hear the good news that her pregnancy was normal and tried to reassure her, yet there was also sadness in his voice. He'd sounded like he was exhausted. They were both dealing with almost more than they could handle, and not just physically but emotionally.

Her conversations with Dr. Myers and Alex this morning had triggered a range of emotions within her. Although she had hope for the future of the child she now carried, her happiness was detoured by the pain of the past.

"Babies are survivors," Dr. Myers had said.

*When given the chance.*

That thought kept replaying over and over in Beth's mind, and she groaned with the knowledge that her first child's life had been cut short because of her own selfishness.

—◦◦◦—

The hotel coffee shop buzzed with activity. Dishes rattled, the phone rang, and people milled about, talked, and laughed. Josh wasn't in the mood for people, but his stomach was empty. He sat across the table from Danny, who was buttering a piece of half-burnt toast.

"So you received good news yesterday?" Danny asked.

"Yes, finally. Beth called last night."

"So her situation is a lot better?"

"Are you kidding?"

"I wasn't. But, obviously, I hit a nerve," Danny frowned. "What's wrong?"

"I'm sorry." Josh dug deep inside himself to mean it. "I'm not in a good mood today."

"I can tell. I've never seen you like this. You're always the positive one."

"Beth's problems are getting to me," Josh said, his voice matching his mood. "I don't want to bore you with my worries."

"Like I haven't shared mine with you." Danny shook his head. "Get it off your chest. I'm listening."

Josh leaned back into his chair. He might as well talk. His hamburger was tasteless. "It's hard, isn't it?"

"What do you mean?" Danny salted his eggs.

"Living your faith through the difficult times. It's hard."

"We're only human." His driver looked up. "Is your wife worse than what you've told me?"

"No. Just not better."

"I don't understand."

"I just wish Beth didn't have to take the painkillers."

"So it's the drugs you're concerned about?"

Josh nodded. "The baby may be fine right now, but I'm worried about the long-term effects." He measured his words. "And I'm just not sure Beth cares one way or the other."

"Of course she does." Danny stirred two packets of sugar into his coffee. "My mom took morphine after her surgery. She wasn't thinking straight for a while," Danny said. "She got through it, and Beth will too."

"But will the baby?"

"I'm no expert, but I have to believe the doctors are doing what's right for both Beth and the baby. You have to trust them, as hard as that may be. Dad and I have had to do that in Mom's situation."

"How is she?" Josh was ready to change the conversation.

Danny took a sip of coffee. "Actually, she had a good visit with her doctor yesterday."

"That's great, man."

"My dad's cautiously optimistic—"

Dishes crashed to the floor just beyond where Josh was sitting. He turned to see a young waitress on the verge of tears. Scattered shards of glass lay at her feet.

Ryan Majors, who was seated nearby, jumped up to assist her. "Let me help you, sweetheart."

"No, thanks," she told him. "I can do it."

"It's not a bother." Ryan bent to gather the broken cups and plates, piling them, along with soiled utensils, onto a plate that had remained intact.

The young woman seemed to be more upset about Ryan's intervention than about her mishap. Had Ryan provoked her discomfort?

"So what's a beautiful girl like you doing working in a coffee shop?" Ryan asked, appraising every curve of the young girl's figure.

The young blonde blushed deeper. "I'm working for college money." She stiffened and turned, clutching an armload of dishes to her breasts, and then walked quickly to the back of the dining room.

"Are there any other hot dishes in the kitchen?" Ryan called after her.

The waitress ignored him, disappearing behind the swinging metal door.

A smile lingered on Ryan's face until he saw Josh watching him. Ryan nodded and returned to his seat.

"That was embarrassing," Josh said to Danny. "Everyone in the room saw it. It looks bad for all of us."

Danny just shook his head. "Anyone who would cheat on his wife would cheat on his friends."

"I hope you're not right about that," Josh hoped he hadn't made a mistake putting Ryan in charge of thousands of dollars of merchandise money.

When he finished eating, Josh glanced at the digital display on his cell phone. 2:40 p.m. He had enough time to grab a bottle of water from the cooler in the front of the bus before a courtesy car from the local radio station picked him up for a midafternoon interview.

As Josh approached the black Prevost coach, Mitch opened the airlock door and stepped off. The band and crew had begun to gather to leave for the venue and the afternoon sound check. Josh would meet them there after his interview.

He nodded silently to Mitch and then stepped up into the driver's compartment landing. The privacy curtain between it and the front lounge was drawn, and Josh heard several members of his crew talking and laughing behind it.

"So what's the deal with Josh's crazy wife?" He heard Ryan ask.

"She's sick." Shane came to Beth's defense.

"She's a junky," Ryan scoffed. "He needs to get over his obsession with the possibility that she will ever get well and get on with his life."

# 14

**Present Day**

The throbbing in Beth's temple pounded out an ugly rhythm. Would the pain ever stop? She had awakened with a headache each morning since returning home from the hospital more than two weeks ago. Her clothes no longer fit and, at this point, she looked fatter than she did pregnant.

Tugging at her bra did no good. It wouldn't stretch enough to fasten. She took it off, hurled it into the dirty clothes basket, and then stomped across the room to the antique chest of drawers where she kept her workout clothes. Digging through a stack of multicolored shorts and several pair of sports socks, she found the gray athletic bra her mother had given her last Christmas. It had been a full size too large.

Beth pulled the spandex halter over her head and adjusted it around her newly formed curves. It fit perfectly. *Yes!*

Her mood took a nosedive when she stepped into her favorite pair of jeans. The curves she had welcomed in her bosom were unwelcomed at her waistline. An inch of flesh stood between button and buttonhole. She shimmied out of the faded blue Levi's and flung them across the room. They missed the dirty laundry container and landed on top of the dog, who had been investigating alien smells in the corner of the walk-in closet.

Buster fought his way out from under his attacker and in true Boston terrier style decided to launch a counterattack. Beth's jeans flew through the bedroom as fast as little legs could carry them. She laughed, despite her headache.

Searching through another drawer, she found a pair of pink sweatpants and a matching sweatshirt. She donned the comfy clothes and caught up with Buster. He had finally tired and stood panting over his prey. She snatched the jeans from his mouth.

"Are you ready for breakfast, Budder?"

The black-and-white terrier yipped and spun around before bolting toward the front of the house. His paws slipped and slid across the hardwood floors in an effort to get traction. Beth straightened the wrinkled throw rugs he left in his wake.

"Slow down, Mr. B.," Beth said, following him into the kitchen. He ignored her admonition and headed straight for the dog food pantry.

"First things first," Beth said. "I have to take a pill before I fix you something."

The dog plopped down on the rug in front of the kitchen sink, not happy about waiting.

Beth reached across the counter for the Lortab Alex had agreed to keep in a bowl for Beth's breakthrough pain. She tried hard not to take the extra medication, but even Dr. Myers had said it would be necessary at times.

Popping the pill into her mouth, she gulped a glass of water from the faucet. A surge of fatigue sidelined her when she turned to continue her chores. She leaned against the kitchen cabinet to gather strength and mental acuity. Just getting dressed this morning had taken a lot out of her.

She glanced at the clock. She might as well feed Buster while she waited for Alex to return from home to prepare their breakfast.

The little terrier danced in circles on his back feet, eyes sparkling, as Beth poured brown nuggets into a stainless steel bowl.

"You're hungry, aren't you? Me too. I wonder what's keeping Alex."

While the little dog ate, Beth carried a bowl of fresh water to his feeding mat near the back door. With shaking hands, she bent to place the bowl on the floor. The world around her began to spin, and she braced herself against the back of the banquette.

Her balance had been off since coming home from the hospital. The handful of pills she took each morning was most likely the cause, but her blood sugar was also dropping. She needed to eat something soon.

Still holding on to the banquette, she maneuvered her body onto the cushiony seat of the handmade bench. The breakfast booth, tucked away in a cozy nook of the kitchen, was her favorite place in the house.

Beth ran her fingers along the beautiful finish her husband had applied to the premium oak wood. He had chosen each board with care and then stained it to perfection. He took pride in his carpentry. Few people knew that Josh had the skill to craft fine wood as well as songs. She smiled thinking about her husband. He had a knack for putting things together, whether it was words or lumber.

The finish he had chosen for the benches matched the antique dining table that stood between them. The table had once occupied Rose Harrison's kitchen. Beth allowed her eyes to wander. Many reminders of family filled their home. From the table to the pie safe that stood in the corner of the butler's pantry. Josh had refinished it with Williamsburg blue milk paint and replaced the old tin with beveled glass. Beth loved the way it had turned out.

She had lined its shelves with crisp, white fabric runners and displayed colorful jars of canned fruits and vegetables from Josh's mother. Rose Harrison had packed the Mason jars with love and high-quality ingredients from her personal garden.

Josh and Beth ate the contents only on special occasions, because it was the last Rose Harrison had put away before her health deteriorated. A simple woman, church and family had been her life's priorities.

Beth owed Rose Harrison more than she could ever repay. His mom had encouraged Josh to cherish home and family. After he and Beth had bought their house, Josh had worked for months, building, sanding, and refinishing. Beth admired her husband's talent, as well as his determination. Nothing seemed out of reach in Josh's mind. He set his sights, and his standards, high. And he worked hard to achieve his goals.

Family had been important in Beth's life too. She studied the old wooden bowl now sitting in the middle of the table. The aged vessel was a McKinney family heirloom. It had been handed down through several generations on her father's side. Today, the solid hickory bowl held more than a dozen, delicious looking Chartreuse apples. She and Alex had bought them yesterday on an excursion to the Farmer's Market.

The scent of the spicy green apples flooded Beth's consciousness like an exotic perfume. The pain pills, at times, seemed to heighten her senses. Her tummy rumbled, and she looked at the clock for the third time. Where was Alex? Perhaps she should call her.

Beth was usually finished with breakfast by now. Hunger pangs would soon turn to nausea if she didn't put something in her stomach. Frustration replaced anxiety. It would be easier to fix something than to call Alex.

Josh and her caregiver sometimes treated her like a child. She was a grown woman and could do some things for herself. Even if she was shaky, she could surely fix her own breakfast.

Beth got up quickly, too quickly. Steadying herself with one hand on the back of the bench, she waited for the dizziness to subside before she walked to the kitchen cabinet. She pulled open the utensil drawer and picked out a paring knife. Then she spun a couple of paper towels off the roll on the counter.

The pattern on the black-and-white tile floor made her dizzy as she crossed it to take a seat again in the breakfast area. Plucking an apple out of the wooden bowl, she cut the first slice. Juice ran between her fingers. Her mouth watered.

Buster had long since finished his breakfast, so he ran to the table to investigate. The little dog had a bottomless pit for a stomach. Beth ignored him, and he jumped at her arm, landing a bump as she quartered the apple. The knife slipped.

"Ouch!"

Blood oozed from Beth's index finger. The blade had sliced about an inch of flesh. She knew it was deep, because she had felt the blade against the bone. Panic set in. This was not what she needed while taking blood thinning medication.

The bright red blood trickled onto the Chartreuse fruit. The sight caused a swell of wooziness. She dropped the knife, wrapped a paper towel around her finger, and rushed to the kitchen sink. Within a few seconds, the crimson beads of liquid had saturated the paper towel. Beth turned the faucet on, tore away the messy paper, and shoved her hand underneath cold, running water. The blood flow stopped temporarily.

She eased her hand out of the water to check the wound. Huge droplets again oozed from her finger like a rising tide, forming a pool of red lifeblood in the white porcelain sink below.

She knew she was going to be sick.

A rush of darkness filled her head and her knees buckled.

# 15

July 29, 1975

Grandfather's stroke changed Isaac's life. Levi Ruben could no longer walk or speak. Short of a miracle, Isaac would be running the flower shop and providing for his family's day-to-day existence for the rest of their lives.

His hope of attending college, of living on his own, had been stalled, frozen in time. Isaac could not, would not, leave Mama Ruth on her own in such dire circumstances.

If there was anything positive about his situation, it was that he was now in charge. No longer would he have to listen to Grandfather's constant yapping and complaining. He could make the decisions and even try some ideas that had been brewing in his head for a while.

He was grateful to have the help of his Cousin Roi, the youngest son of Levi Ruben's brother Moshe. Grandfather and Uncle Moshe had worked together since the late 1940s. Moshe and his three sons, Eli, Chaim, and Roi, cultivated the flowers, plants, and greenery that Grandfather sold in the shop.

Although each operated his business independently of the other, their partnership had, on occasion, created contention in the family. When all was said and done, however, family blood—and the need to survive—kept them together during the difficult times. For that reason, Uncle Moshe offered his youngest son's assistance to Isaac.

Tall, lanky, redheaded Roi worked hard. In ordinary circumstances, Isaac would have enjoyed the companionship of a boy close to his age. Yet, business was brisk, and many days the responsibilities overwhelmed them both. Although three years older, Roi had no problem taking orders from Isaac, even doing the dirty work Isaac had once done.

"Roi, I need the roses stripped and cleaned as soon as possible. I have lots of orders to fill this morning." Isaac pointed toward the pile of multicolored flora in the back corner of the shop that Roi's oldest brother, Eli, had delivered a few minutes before.

Isaac was thankful he could now delegate his least favorite chore, dethorning the spiny stems. Roi considered it simple work compared to the hours he often labored in the hot sun working for his father, watering and pruning plants each day.

No job in the flora business was easy. You would tear your flesh stripping flowers, and then need nimble fingers to design delicate bouquets.

While Roi stripped the roses, Isaac prepped the design table. He cleaned his workspace before organizing his tools and replenishing his supply of glass containers, floral paper, tape, and wire.

The heat from the late July morning had filtered into the shop, and Isaac welcomed the rush of chilly air when he opened the door to the large cooler. Grandfather and Uncle Moshe had built the closetlike structure into the back wall of the shop the year Isaac was born. Three years ago, he had helped his grandfather install a commercial chiller. The chrome box with its beveled glass doors now displayed fresh arrangements.

Isaac chose blooms for his first few orders of the day and transported them to the worktable, the way he had watched his grandfather do every morning for the first sixteen years of his life. Levi Ruben was a master at floral arrangements. He created living works of art from the blooms in season, adding twigs and leaves to complete his masterpieces.

Grandfather's work was renowned within their multi-cultural community. People from all walks of life came to the shop to purchase bouquets and centerpieces for gifts and special occasions, such as birthdays and anniversaries. Some even used Grandfather's creations as conciliatory offerings to end a lovers' quarrel or pledge their lifelong love.

Isaac had come to understand a lot about humanity during his years of working at the shop. Many people lived a lie—and flowers were sometimes used to perpetuate their fraud. Men and women alike purchased Grandfather's beautiful arrangements to bridge the gap between truth and desire, to conceal their indiscretions, and to hide the real agenda in their relationships. Complete strangers walked into the shop daily to reveal secrets about themselves, laying bare privileged information that belonged on a psychologist's couch.

"Young man, I need your help. I want to send a dozen roses to, *ahem*, a friend. Here is her address—and cash. Of course, you won't keep a record of the transaction?"

"Never, Mr. Stein. I understand. And how is Mrs. Stein, by the way?" Isaac enjoyed watching the cheaters squirm.

Although he would never reveal to anyone that Mr. Stein had a mistress, he thoroughly enjoyed the irony of the situation. If Mrs. Stein should eventually learn of the affair, chances were good that her husband would return for amnesty flowers. It was a never-ending game of human chicanery with flowers as the pawn.

Of course, greenery and blooms were also used in ritual worship, for funerals and celebrations of religious holidays.

Religion was, perhaps, the biggest illusion of all.

If there was a God, and man was made in his image as the Torah taught—from what Isaac had seen of human motives—he would have a hard time trusting him.

# 16

**Present Day**

The back door opened, and Alex ran to Beth in time to catch her fall.

"What's wrong?"

"I cut my finger," Beth muttered. "I need to sit down."

"Let me help you." Alex grabbed a clean dishtowel from the cabinet drawer, threw it over her arm, and half-dragged, half-carried Beth to a bench at the kitchen table. She pulled up a side chair for herself and sat down. "Let me see the damage you've done."

"It's bad." Beth's hand trembled as she held it out for Alex to examine. Red globules continued to ooze from the cut.

"Hold this towel around the wound," Alex directed. "I need to clean the blood away so I can see it better." Seconds later, Alex returned with a bowl of warm water and a roll of paper towels. She cleaned the wound, while Beth explained how she had injured herself.

"This is all my fault. I thought I had time to do a few things at home while you were still sleeping."

"I could have fixed cereal." Beth did her best to smile, although her finger now throbbed more than her head.

"Keep holding your hand up," Alex said. "I've got to get this bleeding stopped."

"I'm sorry I was so stupid. I can't do anything for myself." Beth fought back tears.

"Relax, girlfriend." Alex stroked Beth's hair. "Everything will be okay." She removed the damp towel to see if the blood was clotting. "We're making progress." Alex reapplied pressure to the wound. "Where do you keep your first-aid kit?"

"In the hall bathroom." Beth started to get up. "I'll go—"

"Whoa . . . you stay put. Hold your arm up and keep pressure on this. I'll be right back."

Beth held the towel firmly until Alex returned with a bottle of antibacterial spray and a box of bandages. She disinfected the cut and wrapped a large bandage around Beth's index finger.

"Is this too tight?"

"No. Feels good."

"You know you're going to need stitches on this? It's deep."

"Please, no. I don't want to go to the emergency room again," Beth pleaded.

---

Josh dragged his tired body up the steps of the bus entrance. One more show, and then he could take a few days off for Thanksgiving. He tossed his black carry-on bag onto the jump seat and greeted Danny. The look on Danny's face told him something was wrong.

"Is everything okay?"

"No," Danny said. "I just talked to Daddy, and my mom's back in the hospital." His driver's massive shoulders trembled. "I'm worried about her."

"Keep your chin up, man. I'm praying. For your daddy too."

"I appreciate it."

"Do you need to fly home? Mitch can drive us the rest of the way."

"My dad told me to finish the trip. We'll be there in forty-eight hours." Danny offered a weak smile. "Are you ready to roll?"

"Everyone here?"

"Yup, in their bunks. Except for Ryan. He's working in the back lounge."

"Let's go. Keep us safe, man." Josh slapped his driver on the shoulder and turned toward the rear of the bus.

The bus transmission engaged as Josh entered the bunk-room hallway. He prepared for a slight bump forward, readying his bus legs, a term seasoned road warriors used to describe the ability to stay balanced on a forward-moving, sideways-swaying bus.

He opened his closet door and dropped his bag onto the floor. The space wasn't much bigger than a broom closet, but he had just enough room to squeeze in a small bag and a couple weeks' worth of hanging clothes.

Josh walked past seven identical closets and four curtained bunks on his way to the back lounge. He opened the door and stuck his head inside.

"Hey, you planning to work all night?"

"Just finishing up with the merchandise reports," Ryan said, shuffling papers.

"How's it going?" Josh stepped fully into the room.

"Fine. No problem. If Mitch—" Ryan's words were obscured by the squall of air brakes. "What in the deuce is that driver doing now? I'm going to give him a piece of my mind." Ryan set his papers aside and made an effort to stand. When he did, the bus lunged forward throwing him back into his seat. He cursed and started to get up again. "He's the roughest driver I've—"

"Stay here," Josh ordered. "He's in heavy traffic."

Ryan's jaw tightened. He threw his hands up in disgust and, with mock compliance, settled back into his seat, again picking up his paperwork.

"Try to get some sleep. You're tired and grumpy." Josh turned to leave and then had a second thought. "By the way, if I ever hear you mention my wife's name in a bad light again, I will fire you immediately."

Ryan's face turned a deep shade of red. He choked out an unintelligible response.

"I'm glad we understand each other." Josh closed the bunkroom door and walked toward the front of the bus. Running his fingers through his hair, he pondered the distance between his driver and his road manager.

The only rub Josh had ever seen between Danny and anyone on the road had been with Ryan. Everyone seemed to like Danny. Although he was large enough to push his weight around, he chose to temper himself. He was a gentle giant in all aspects of his life, including his faith.

Ryan, on the other hand, was lean and fast with a runner's body and an aggressive nature. He was an extraordinary musician, who held a degree in business, and was an excellent multitasker. Ryan had the charm of a politician when he wanted to use it. But it seemed that he chose to use it less and less lately.

Perhaps more than anyone here, Josh understood that road managing was a thankless task. That was one reason he tried to go easy on Ryan, despite complaints from everyone he worked with.

Coordinating a tour required a laundry list of skills. Most musicians focused on creative things and needed help getting from point A to point B. Ryan was a take-charge guy. He was like a good doctor with a bad bedside manner.

Ryan was a cattle herder, but his position ultimately required a shepherd. Josh hoped he could learn to see the difference. A good attitude could always accomplish more than sarcasm and arrogance.

After changing into a pair of running shorts and a T-shirt, Josh crawled into his bunk. Two more nights and he could sleep in his own bed for a few days. He pulled the bunk curtain closed, shutting out the world the best he could, but his mind kept churning. He couldn't afford to lose his road manager or his driver in the middle of a major tour. He needed Ryan, even if he wasn't perfect.

Too many personal issues required Josh's time right now. He had a lot to do when he got home. Alex needed a break from caregiving. And the baby's room had to be painted before Beth could start the decorating she had planned.

For now, he would relax in his bunk and pray for God's help with all the strength he could muster. He would pray for Danny's mom, and for Beth, and for the baby. He had to believe that everything would be okay. God answered prayer. He had to believe that more now than ever. He had to trust that everything would work out.

# 17

**Present Day**

Josh ran his hand along the smooth, perfectly restored, antique table in Alex's kitchen. "We appreciate the invitation to Thanksgiving dinner."

"Glad to have you," Alex said before turning to Beth. "Some people will do anything to avoid cooking."

"Actually, I'm just too busy visiting the emergency room." Beth returned the joust.

"That's not what you told me Sunday." Alex lobbed one back.

"Ouch." Beth laughed.

"The two of you are having way too much fun while I'm on the road." Josh said. He hadn't seen his wife this relaxed in weeks. "I'm sorry I've missed it."

"Oh, lots of fun," Alex said, stirring a pot on the stove. "It was hilarious walking into your kitchen and seeing Beth on the floor in a pool of blood."

"It wasn't that bad," Beth winced.

"Okay, maybe not a pool of blood. But you scared me."

"It's my hobby. Scaring people." Beth winked at Josh.

"Well, you're good at it." Alex dumped a bowl of cranberries into the hot pot.

"So what happened, exactly?" Josh had heard the story over the phone, without the details.

"It was my fault," Alex said.

"No, it wasn't. It was Buster's fault." Beth stroked the black-and-white terrier snuggled in her lap. "Of course, I had some liability in the matter too." Her face clouded over. "It's just that I wanted to do something for myself for a change."

"You need to relax and enjoy the pampering while you can," Josh told her.

"Read a book or two," Alex said, still stirring the pot of cranberries.

"Great idea, but I can't focus enough right now to read." Beth blushed and averted her eyes to the dog.

Josh studied his wife. She appeared childlike, vulnerable. More so than when he had first brought her home from the hospital.

"Just do your best, Mama. That's all you can do." Alex walked over to the table with a paté knife, celery, and cheese spread. "Can you fill these stalks with pimento?"

"As long as it's a dull knife." Beth smiled and pushed the dog off her lap. "Scoot, Buster. I need to wash my hands so I can help with dinner."

Josh watched her disappear down the hall. "I've been concerned about her."

"I can understand why," Alex said. "She's having a tough time. One minute she's on the top of the world, and the next she's sobbing uncontrollably. I never know which Beth I'll find when I get her up in the morning."

He nodded.

"I feel terrible about Sunday, you know? She usually sleeps in until I wake her."

"You're doing a great job. Don't worry about it."

"Oh, no!" Alex froze.

"What's wrong?"

"My contact slipped out." Alex poked around on her face with her index finger. "Josh, can you help me?"

"Sure." Josh tripped over the dog when he scrambled out of the chair to assist her. "Sorry, Buster." The dog groused, walked to the edge of the room, and lay down. "Where did you lose it?"

"That's the problem. I don't know." Alex grinned. "I'm hoping it's still on my cheek." She stood perfectly still. "Do you see it?"

"Turn your face to the light," Josh told her. "And hold your head up."

Alex readjusted her position.

"No. Like this." Josh gently tilted her chin while searching among the freckles for the lens.

"Can you see it? I hope I didn't drop it into the food." Her body shook as she squelched a chuckle.

"I'm not sure what you two girls have been drinking today, but you're both in a mood. Hold still." Josh moved his face closer. "I see it."

"Ouch!"

"What's going on?" Beth asked, as she walked into the room.

Josh and Alex were laughing so hard, tears streamed down their faces.

"Josh . . ." Alex couldn't catch her breath. "Josh . . ." She tried again to speak. "Sorry. Give me a minute." She fanned her face.

Josh wiped moisture from his eyes. "I was trying to find Alex's contact lens." He looked at Alex and grinned, and then back to Beth. "And I . . . I almost had it." He chuckled. "Until I stepped on her foot."

He held his stomach and doubled over with laughter.

"I don't get it," Beth said.

"That's not the best part." Alex regained control of her speech. "The funny part is when the dog farted."

"Poor Buster, are they picking on you?" Beth cooed.

Josh smiled. The girls had had him in stitches all afternoon.

A ringing phone interrupted the mood. He reached into his back pocket and pulled out his cell phone. Danny Stevens's name appeared in the viewer. "Hey, man, happy Thanksgiving."

"My mom passed away." His friend's voice faded into silence, broken only by heavy breathing.

"Oh . . . no. I'm sorry." Josh tried to find the appropriate words. "Is there anything I can do?"

"We're not sure what we are going to do yet." Danny sniffed back tears. "You know, with the funeral and all. We don't have any plans."

"Let me know when you do, and I'll get the word out to everyone," Josh said. "Are you okay?"

"Yeah, I guess. Just pray for us. That's the main thing. Just pray."

Josh hung up the phone. Why did the idea of praying seem unsettling to him? Hadn't he prayed for Danny's mom for months? Now she was gone.

Just when he had begun to believe that everything would be okay, he had more soul searching to do.

# 18

**Present Day**

The parking lot had already begun to fill up when Josh and Beth arrived at Faith Chapel. The small country church rested snugly in a grove of trees near the north side of Wilson County, thirty miles outside of Nashville. Josh recognized several of the cars in the gravel lot as those of his band and crew. Shane's red convertible, Mitch's old pickup truck, and Ryan's black Mercedes with vanity plates that boldly proclaimed his "superstar" status.

Josh backed his Jeep Cherokee into a space alongside the church. He nodded a greeting to an older couple as he walked to the passenger side to open the door for Beth. She looked stunning in the black dress she had purchased yesterday on a quick shopping excursion with Alex.

This was Beth's first real outing since her hospitalization. He was concerned if she would have the stamina to sit through a funeral and a graveside service. But she had said she wanted to be supportive of Danny and his family, and to him.

Josh had agreed to sing one of Nell Stevens's favorite hymns, accompanied by Shane on the guitar. Shane and he had run through the song last night at the house. Singing at funerals had to be the worst gig in the world, but it was something all singers were asked to do at one time or another.

Singing to a grieving family wasn't easy. But it was a gift that remained with the family for years to come. Music left an indelible impression on people's lives, memories that would be relived every time they heard the song.

As he and Beth walked arm-in-arm toward the front of the church, Josh spotted Danny standing on the concrete stoop outside the entrance. Danny's skin appeared as pale as the early patch of snow lying in the shadows of the bare oak trees around them.

"Danny looks nice in his suit. I don't think I've ever seen him so dressed up," Beth whispered in Josh's ear. "But he still reminds me of the Pillsbury Doughboy." Her eyes danced with mischief.

"And you remind me of my wife, the funniest and prettiest girl in the world." Josh winked at her, and she blushed. He loved her lack of self-absorption. "I'm glad you're feeling up to this today."

She took his hand in hers. "Me too."

They walked from the shadow of the tall oak grove into the sunlight.

Sometimes it was easy to see where life was heading. At other times, the path disappeared behind a wall of doubt. Perhaps it was good to be reminded occasionally that this life will one day end, because Josh didn't want to fail to fully enjoy the present. His wife could be taken from him at any moment, and he was determined to enjoy every minute he had with her.

He tried to wipe the negatives from his mind and think about tomorrow's plans to announce Beth's pregnancy to their church family. In a few weeks, they would be celebrating the end of her first trimester. A good sign, the doctor had said, that the baby was tolerating the morphine. No doubt, good things were intermingled with the bad.

"It's all good." Beth stopped and turned to him.

"How do you always manage to read my thoughts?"

"You're too quiet," she said, pushing a strand of chin length, dark brown hair behind her ear. "I know you. You're under a lot of stress." She paused to reflect on something in the distance. "Most of it's my fault, and I'm sorry for that," she said. "But there's not much I can do about it."

"It's not your—"

"Shhh." She put her fingers to his lips. "Let's forget about our problems and try to bring some peace to Danny and his family."

"I love you," Josh said. "Nothing could ever change that."

———— ∞∞∞ ————

The church was crowded by the time they found the seat reserved for them up front, near the family. Beth slid to the inside of the bench so Josh would have access to the aisle.

"Good morning." A well-dressed, older woman greeted Beth as she settled in.

"Hi, I'm Bethany Harrison."

The woman stuck out her hand. "Nice to meet you. I'm Pamela Morris, a friend of Nell's."

"I'm very sorry for your loss," Beth said. "I didn't know her, but her son works with my husband."

Pamela leaned forward to take a look at Josh. "You're a nice-looking couple."

Beth felt heat rise in her face. "Thank you."

"Do you have children?"

"Oh . . . no. Not yet. But we're expecting our first." She patted her tummy.

"How exciting, dear!" The woman's blue eyes sparkled, and then she teared up. "I'm sorry." She dabbed a tissue to her face. "I know Nell would have loved to meet you. She loved babies. I would expect she's doting over all of the little ones in Heaven right now."

"It's a shame she will never see her grandchildren," Beth said, nodding toward Danny, who was seated two rows in front of them.

"Her daughter Susan, Danny's sister, has two. But Nell would have loved to see Danny married with children."

"How did you know Mrs. Stevens?" Beth asked.

"We met through our volunteer work."

"That's nice," Beth said. She could visualize this beautiful, gray-haired woman looking dapper in a Red Cross smock or delivering food to the elderly. "What kind of volunteer work?"

"Abortion clinic." Tears welled again in Pamela Morris's eyes. "Nell and I worked together as street counselors. There are so many young women taken in by the lie that unborn babies are not viable human beings."

Beth swallowed hard to keep down her lunch. *Dear God, what are you doing to me?*

"I'm sorry, Mrs. Morris. I need to find the restroom."

"It's through that door and to the right. Are you okay, honey?"

"Just a bit of morning sickness still hanging around." Beth did her best to smile as she nudged Josh to let her by.

<hr>

The funeral was inspirational and uplifting. A celebration of a life well lived. Josh wished he had known Danny's mother better. No doubt she had played a big role in honing the character of her son. Some of the stories that were related about Mrs. Stevens reminded Josh of his own mom, a woman full of humor as well as faith.

After they had gathered around the grave, Jim Stevens motioned for everyone to move in closer. He would be giving a personal and, most likely, tearful tribute to his wife.

"This is from Proverbs 31," he said and then cleared his throat, gathering his composure.

"Who can find a virtuous and capable wife?" He began. "She is worth more than precious rubies." He wiped a tear.

"Her husband can trust her, and she will greatly enrich his life. Her children stand and bless her. Her husband praises her." His words came in bursts of emotion.

"Charm is deceptive, and beauty does not last. But a woman who fears the Lord will be greatly praised." The Reverend Stevens looked up to the sky and smiled.

"Reward her, Lord, for all she has done. For all she has been. Let her deeds publicly declare her praise." He wiped his face again, pulled the rose from his lapel, and placed it gently on the casket.

"Amen."

A few minutes later, the smell of dirt filled Josh's nostrils. An involuntary twitch spread throughout his body, a shudder that could easily be attributed to the late autumn chill. But he knew better.

He had been here before, standing at a graveside while a broken and questioning man eulogized his wife. This time it was Jim Stevens. Almost two years ago it had been his own father, paying tribute to his wife of thirty-five years.

From all appearances, Danny's dad had managed to hold onto his convictions, to make peace with them, and to reconcile his spiritual beliefs with the untimely loss of his wife. But Josh's father had died in spirit the day he lost his wife.

Samuel Harrison had mustered the strength to see her through to the end. But after she passed away, his trust in God had been shoveled into a four-by-six-foot hole and covered with dust.

# 19

A buzz of activity surrounded Beth as she and Josh prepared to leave their Sunday school classroom. They had announced her pregnancy to the class this morning, and everyone wanted to offer congratulations.

Men slapped Josh on the back and shook his hand. "Good going, man!" Women gushed, giddy with excitement.

Sarah Gilmore grabbed Beth's neck and squealed. "You'll be the best mom!"

"I'm so happy for you, hon," Rachel Monroe drawled.

"Is this your first?" A new member of the class asked Beth.

She shook her head, almost indiscernibly.

"Oh, yes! Isn't it exciting?" Sarah replied on Beth's behalf and then added, "Congratulations, Josh. We're happy for you both."

Beth glanced sideways to her husband. His face reflected the enthusiasm of the well-wishers. He also seemed to be relaxing more now that he'd had a few days off the road. Beth knew that the weight of the world rested on his shoulders, and she could do little to help.

"Are you okay, honey?" Josh grabbed her arm and walked her toward the sanctuary.

"I have a headache, but I'm okay."

"If you're feeling up to it, I'd like to stay for the service." His brown eyes entreated.

"I can handle it," she said halfheartedly, hoping he would pick up on her lack of excitement.

"Great!" Josh opened the door to the main worship area and, placing his hand on the small of her back, ushered her to their usual seat near the front of the large auditorium. They always sat three rows back, to the right of the pulpit, and in front of the piano. It was a habit Josh had formed as a child in his family church. His mom, the church pianist, would finish playing and then sit with her son while Josh's dad preached the sermon.

Beth scanned the room. Friends, acquaintances, and visitors streamed through the doors on each side of the pulpit platform. Their church was home to a growing fellowship. Young people, singles, married couples with children, recent retirees, and a considerable number of seniors made up the congregation. Gloryland Temple had something for everyone, including a Saturday evening service that catered to those with interest in learning about Messianic worship.

On the rare occasions when Josh was home on Saturdays, he and Beth would attend the Messianic service and then return for the regular worship the next morning. They had met Alex, not yet their neighbor at the time, at the Saturday evening service.

Alex had been born into a Jewish home and converted to Christianity in college, and she had taught Beth a lot about the traditional Jewish faith and lifestyle. They had baked *challah*, a sweet, braided egg bread; decorated Alex's house for

Hanukkah; and stayed up all night studying the Old Testament on *Shavuot*.

Beth enjoyed the celebration of Christ through the old sanctities, but it was the old-fashioned, Sunday morning service that kept her centered on a Christian journey.

Despite the disparity in size—Gloryland Temple was much larger—something about it reminded Beth of her grandparent's small, country church in Southern Illinois. It was at their church she had made a childlike commitment to Christ when she was in junior high.

The choir doors opened, bringing Beth back to the present. Dozens of men and women dressed in flowing purple robes filed into the loft directly behind the pulpit. Josh reached for her hand, helping Beth to her feet. She leaned into his embrace during the opening prayer and Scripture reading. They sang two hymns before the congregation was seated.

Beth sat in awe while the choir performed a stirring rendition of "Amazing Grace." The lyrics washed over her with a sweetness that calmed her tired soul, even easing her headache. She found solace in the great, old hymns, and this was one of her favorites. She pulled a tissue from her handbag and wiped her eyes. How much better could the salvation experience be expressed?

> Amazing grace! How sweet the sound
> That saved a wretch like me!
> I once was lost, but now am found
> Was blind, but now I see.

After the choral presentation, Pastor Brandon stepped up to the podium. His message today was on Christian living. "In Matthew 10:21, we are told that brother shall deliver up the brother to death, and father the child. When we look around our world today, we don't have to look far to see that Jesus was

**111**

right." Pastor Brandon's eyes swept the room. "These things are prevalent, even in our own neighborhood.

"Perhaps the best—and worst—example is the abortion-on-demand thinking in our society." He paused and shook his head. "Mother turning against child. Does it get more hideous than that?"

A familiar rush of guilt swept through Beth. When the minister looked in her direction, she decided to take a bathroom break. Before she could excuse herself, Josh reached for her hand, placed it on his thigh, and covered it with his warm palm.

Feeling like a wanted poster tacked to the post office wall, Beth calculated mentally the bounty on her head. It was there for the taking by the first person to expose the truth about her life. Josh squeezed her hand. Her heart went out to him. Her near-perfect husband had no idea about the sin she struggled to put behind her.

During the closing song, he whispered in her ear. "Let's go forward to ask for prayer for your healing and the baby." His eyes glistened with moisture from the anointing of the service. She nodded, with no real reason to decline.

The minister gave the closing invitation, and Josh led her to the front of the auditorium, where they knelt in front of the massive acacia wood altar. It had been carved to represent the ancient Jewish Ark of the Covenant. Draped with a cloth of purple velvet, the great table was adorned with gold-colored candlesticks and a ceremonial, leather-bound Bible.

Josh whispered into Pastor Brandon's ear, and he smiled at Beth. After the final verse of "Just as I Am," the minister waved his hands in the air to quiet the congregation.

"Everyone, please be seated. We have a special request this morning." The pastor urged Josh and Beth to stand close to him. "Two of our special young people, Josh and Bethany

Harrison, have asked for your prayers. Many of you know about Bethany's recent illness, but I am happy to also announce, for those of you who don't know, that Josh and Bethany are expecting their first child."

The congregation applauded, and the pastor clasped Josh and Beth's hands in his as a few of the elders gathered around.

"Please join me in prayer for the Harrisons and their unborn child."

During the prayer, many of the church membership murmured in the background.

"Yes, Jesus"

"Thank you, Lord."

In closing, Pastor Brandon proclaimed, "And everyone said . . ."

"Amen." The congregation recited in unison.

Within a few minutes, more than half of the four hundred or so in attendance surrounded Beth and Josh. Each person offered his or her best wishes, a hug, or a commitment to pray for her pregnancy.

"Children are not an accident," one elderly woman told her. "You have been truly blessed."

—————

Beth rolled her weary body into a fetal position, curling up in the corner of the small, blue-tiled shower stall.

*Liar. Deceiver. Who do you think you are? Forgiven? A good Christian? I don't think so. You're a fraud.*

She rocked back and forth as the water poured down on her. Despite the powerful stream, no soap, no scrubbing, and no amount of convincing would make her feel presentable. It was impossible to clean the inside, the dirty part.

She had allowed herself to believe a lie for all of these years. Perhaps God could forgive her, but she would never forgive herself. The steaming hot liquid ran down her face, stinging with its accusations. *God may love you, but he can't like you very much. How could he? You've lied to Josh since you met him.*

No, I haven't.

*Ah, but deceit is the same thing as lying. When he finds out what you've done, he will leave you. You might as well get it over now. Make plans for your future. Alone.*

I'll tell him soon. He'll understand.

*Even if he does, your baby will suffer for what you've done.*

But that's not fair.

*Not fair? Are you kidding? An eye for an eye.*

I've already repented for that . . . many times over. God has forgiven me.

*Why should God show you mercy? You put your own child to death. You must be punished. Baby killer.*

Liar.

*No . . . you're the dirty, rotten liar, woman.*

She held her hands over her ears to shut out the sound.

"Bethany. Bethany. Beth-a-ny!"

Josh called to her.

She wiped the water from her face. He must not see that she had been crying again. At this point, he had reason enough to question her sanity. The pills. The emotional tirades. And now, a total breakdown in the shower.

# 20

**Present Day**

I can't eat this." Beth pushed her plate of stir-fried vegetables away.

"What's wrong?" Alex gave her a sideways glance before opening the refrigerator door and reaching for a bottle of spring water. "You need to drink more water too. You didn't finish your second liter yesterday."

"I go to the bathroom enough the way it is. I'm sick of it!" Beth protested.

"You're not in a good mood today, are you?" Alex plopped the bottle of water on the table and took a seat on the bench opposite Beth.

"My mood is fine, you're the one with the prob—" Beth stopped midsentence, remembering her manners and how much Alex had done for her. "I'm sorry. I am in a bad mood. If my head doesn't hurt, I have no energy. Or I'm dizzy. It's one thing after another. I'm tired of being on this medication."

"Let's do something to take your mind off the bad stuff. I saw a neat project idea in one of those parenting magazines when I was waiting for you at the doctor's office the other day."

"What kind of silly project?"

"You document your weekly baby progress through photos. You can send them to Josh and use them for your baby book."

Beth stared at her caregiver. Well-meaning or not, she could sometimes be irritating. "No, thanks. Remember those nude photos of Demi Moore on the cover of *Vanity Fair*? I don't want to go there."

"No, silly. Not nude. You would wear your workout leotard."

"You're truly unrelenting," Beth said, trying to work up a speck of excitement about the idea. "Tell you what, I'll make a deal with you. If I do it, I can have a glass of chocolate milk and Doritos for lunch instead of this health food."

"You drive a hard bargain. But chocolate milk does have calcium." Alex threw her hands in the air in mock indignation. "So much for my nutritional counseling."

After lunch, Alex began setting up photo equipment in the freshly painted nursery, and Beth retreated to the bedroom to find a black leotard. It took a few extra tugs, but she managed to make one fit.

Glancing at her profile in the mirror as she left the room prompted a heavy sigh. She had already started to gain weight. But she could see a small baby bump. A shiver of excitement ran down her spine. This baby was real.

*Thank you, Lord.*

"Your black outfit will contrast perfectly with these pastel walls," Alex told Beth when she walked into the nursery. "Stand over here, next to the window, so I can get natural lighting on your face." Alex nudged Beth by the shoulders and placed her where she wanted her.

"Thanks."

"For what?"

"For being such a good friend," Beth said, giving Alex a spontaneous hug. "I know this isn't easy for you, giving up eight months of your life."

"You're paying me. . . ."

"Not what you deserve. You're neglecting your artwork so you can stay with me."

"Bethany, these eight months will go quickly for you, for me, and for the baby. I'm excited to be enjoying it with you." She smiled mischievously. "Besides, this is going to be a real artsy shot. I may have to ask permission to put it in my portfolio."

---

The roads were clear on the way to Detroit. The Triumphant Tour concluded tonight at the Joe Louis Arena. More than twenty thousand fans would be packed into the venue to listen to five hours of praise and worship songs from five separate acts, the two headliners and three opening acts, which included Josh. It would be a spectacular ending to the seven-month tour, which had grossed more than fifty million dollars in ticket sales alone. That figure didn't count merchandise sales, a sizable amount on its own. The average artist sold at least ten dollars a head each night.

Josh's portion was miniscule compared to the star bands. But he couldn't complain. He was earning a decent living. Entertainers usually made more money selling merchandise than they received in record sales or even performance fees. Unfortunately, his merchandise income had been down for the last two months. And he needed every penny to make up for the loss of Beth's salary.

She had taken a leave of absence from Bradford Associates, but Josh hoped it would be permanent. Although they missed her income, he saw it as a good exercise in streamlining their lifestyle. After the medical bills were paid, and they didn't have the extra expense of Alex's salary, they should be able to afford for Beth to stay at home with the baby—at least for a while.

They wouldn't be able to fix up the house like they had originally planned. But they already had the basics, except for nursery furniture. Beth had promised to shop at outlet stores and garage sales for furniture while he was away. He had managed to get the room painted during his Thanksgiving break.

He would be on the road now almost straight through Christmas. God had blessed him with an opening slot on another tour, which would provide an additional twenty days of income this year. He had almost turned it down six months ago, thinking he would enjoy having that time to relax. He made the decision to accept it for the sake of his employees. His band and crew were paid a day rate rather than a salary, so being off for a month at the end of the year would make it hard on them and their families. As it turned out, it had been a blessing for him too.

The familiar ping of a message-waiting alert urged Josh to check his inbox. It was an e-mail from Beth. He skimmed the four or five sentences to make sure she was okay, and then he reread each word. Just knowing her day was going well brightened his.

She'd had some bad days this week, based on the e-mails he had received from Alex. If only he could be there to help more. Rolling satellite made life on the road more tolerable, but it also reminded him of what he was missing.

A while back, Alex had helped Beth upload the baby's sonogram video. He had been able to count ten fingers and ten toes and even look into his baby's eyes. Life was good, especially when things were going well at home.

Another message from Beth appeared in his inbox. This one had an unidentified attachment. Josh clicked the file, and a photo popped onto the screen. It was Beth standing in profile, holding her hand on her stomach. Her smile was radiant. He picked up the phone to call her.

"Hi, honey!" she said. "Where are you?"

"On our way to Detroit. It's the last day of the tour. The Christmas shows start tomorrow."

"Oh, right. I remember now."

"Thanks for the photo. When do I get another one of those sexy poses?"

"Don't make fun of me."

"I wasn't making fun, honest. You're the hottest pregnant mama I know."

"I hope you don't know any other hot pregnant mamas."

"Nope. You're the only one." He smiled into the phone. "So what are you doing for the rest of the day?"

"We might drive around to a few consignment shops and look for baby furniture. If not today, we'll go Monday after my doctor's appointment."

"Good. Do those shops deliver? Remember, I won't be home until almost Christmas."

"I'm sure they do. If not, I'll put it on layaway for you to pick up when you get home."

"Have fun. And watch the budget."

"I wish you were here to help me."

"I wish I was too. But the next three weeks will pass before you know it. I'll talk to you tomorrow, okay?"

"I love you."

"Love you too."

On Monday, after stopping by the hospital for a routine scan ordered by Dr. Abrams, Beth and Alex scoured three consignment shops in the Green Hills area.

Beth flopped down into the passenger seat of Alex's car. "I'm disappointed," she said. "I'm not sure I know what I want, but I know I didn't see it today."

"There's plenty of time." Alex assured her and turned the car in the direction of home. "You'll find the perfect thing if you just keep looking. Maybe we should hit the garage sales again on Saturday. It would be a good excuse to get out and walk."

"I suppose." Beth's energy had all but faded away. "Hey, look! There's Maison de Reve Furniture. Let's check it out."

"I don't think so. That's a designer store," Alex frowned. "It's not wise to shop over your budget."

"Why not? We'll get some good ideas, and then we can improvise inexpensively from yard-sale finds. You're the best at that kind of thing. Come on. Turn in here." Beth tugged at Alex's sleeve.

"Okay," Alex said, making a quick right into the parking lot. "But I don't like this idea. It's too easy to . . ."

Beth bolted out of the car almost before it stopped, her energy renewed.

"It's amazing how shopping can pep up a girl." Alex caught up with Beth in front of the massive glass entrance of the high-end showroom.

Beth took a deep breath and stepped inside. "This place smells like money."

"Burning money," Alex grimaced.

"Don't be so negative." Beth spotted a drop-dead good-looking salesman walking their way. "This should be fun."

"How may I help you beautiful ladies today?" The young man flashed his gorgeous green eyes.

"We're just looking." Alex grabbed Beth by the arm and dragged her toward the opposite direction.

Not easily deterred, Green Eyes followed them like a new puppy.

"Great. What's your main interest?"

"Nursery furniture." Beth pulled away from Alex.

"My name is Lane." The salesman stuck out a manicured hand. "What's yours?"

"Bethany. And this is Alex."

"Bethany, we have the highest-quality infant furniture in Nashville. Let's walk this way." He stepped aside to allow the girls to pass. "Straight ahead. I'll follow you."

"Do you believe this stuff?" Beth whispered to Alex as they strolled past vignettes of designer living rooms, dining rooms, and bedrooms. "Look at that chair. I love cabbage rose print."

"Me too." Alex said, finally starting to get into the spirit of the shopping trip.

"That would look great in the baby's room." Beth pointed to a chaise lounge in one of the front window displays.

"Remember why we're here." Alex gave her a gentle push.

"Look at that . . . oh, my." Beth raced toward the next vignette. "This is exactly what I was hoping to find." She caressed the top of the baby changing table and dresser combination. "I love this color."

"It's called Cherry Mocha," the salesman said. "And, of course, it's 100 percent lead free. Some lower-end lines don't maintain our standards of quality. We want parents to be confident in the safety of our products. We feel children are worth the difference in price."

"I hadn't thought about that," Beth said, nodding in agreement.

"Do you prefer the sleigh style bed or the classic?" he asked. He had a beautiful smile.

"Definitely the sleigh. It's perfect."

"It has a lot of personality, doesn't it? One of the best things about this model is that it grows with your baby." He directed her attention to the vignette across the aisle. "That is the same crib, once it has been converted to a full-size bed. Your son—or daughter—will be taking this set to college with him or her some day. No box springs are necessary."

"Wow. That's great."

"Yes. A real money saver overall. You pay more upfront, but less in the long run."

"This guy is good," Alex whispered into Beth's ear. "Of course, you need to tell him that you will have to look around."

"I don't know . . .", Beth hesitated. "I think I've found what I want." She spoke loud enough for the salesman to hear.

"Do you want the four- or six-drawer changing table?" he asked.

"Definitely the six."

"Good choice. Now . . . if you buy the collection rather than buying each of these pieces separately, we can give it to you for an exceptional price."

"Really?"

"Let's talk about it over a cup of coffee," he suggested. "Please, follow me to the conference table."

<hr/>

"Can you believe he gave me a dozen roses?" Beth stuck her nose into the bouquet of pale pink buds and settled comfortably into the passenger seat of Alex's car.

"He should have given you a rose garden considering the price you paid for that furniture." Alex glared at her.

"I don't think it was that bad," Beth argued. "I may have spent more upfront, but it will pay off as the baby grows. And it's 100 percent lead free."

"You sound like the salesman." Alex pursed her lips. "But Josh may not be so happy with you—or me—when he finds out."

"Why would he be mad at you?" Beth gave Alex a hard look. "It was my decision, not yours." She thought about it for a moment. "And don't tell him. I'll let him know soon enough."

"Don't worry. I'm not saying a word." Alex promised. "This is between you and Josh."

"Thanks." Beth inhaled the sweet scent of rose petals. "I'll tell him about it when he comes home for Christmas, after he sees the furniture."

# 21

Isaac threw his Torah and skullcap onto the bed. He'd had enough. He and his grandfather had done nothing but argue since Levi Ruben returned to the flower shop last month.

Grandfather could have his antiquated way of doing business. It was his problem if he didn't appreciate that Isaac had doubled the profits in the past two years. Isaac would bide his time until he could work out his personal plans. Then, he would be out of here for good.

He had applied to Columbia University, and when the acceptance letter came—and it would come because he had scored in the top ten percentile on his national exams—he would use his inheritance money to finance an education.

Isaac had been grateful to learn this spring about the trust fund his parents had left. Without it, he wouldn't have the chance to break free. Certainly not the opportunity to attend college. He might not have known his parents, but he would have a better life because of them.

Columbia was a prestigious school, attracting the best students from all walks of life. There, he would meet others like himself. People his age, who understood the value of science and modern medicine. People who didn't rely on old-fashioned religion to heal their bodies or numb their minds. Ironically, his grandfather's health had improved because of advances in science. But the old man still clung to his ritual belief system.

Grandfather saw the world as black and white. Like a skull-cap lying on a chenille bedspread.

Isaac understood the nuances of gray, of compromise. That there was much more to life than a dirty flower shop on an out-of-touch corner on Long Island. He hated to think about leaving Mama Ruth. But she had chosen her life's sentence with Grandfather. Isaac Benjamin Ruben—or whoever he was—had done his time.

# 22

**Present Day**

Boss, I hate to bother you." Josh's bunk curtain shook, and he heard Danny's muffled whisper. "But we have a problem."

Josh glanced at his watch. A quarter past four in the morning. The bus motor droned. They must have stopped at a truck stop for refueling.

"Boss."

"Yeah, man." Josh's words came out little more than a grunt.

"I'm sorry to wake you, but I need your help with something."

Josh ran his fingers through his hair, unsnapped the bunk drape, and slid it open. "What is it?"

Danny's voice croaked. "My credit card won't work. It was denied. I thought you might know what to do. Sorry to bother you."

*So much for sleep.* Josh grabbed his street clothes. "I'll be right there. Give me a minute."

"Sure thing." Danny straightened up, turned, and walked toward the front of the bus, closing the galley door behind him.

A few minutes later, Josh stepped outside the bus. The bright lights of a truck stop on a frosty morning never failed to amaze him. It was a scene he had experienced many times, and it represented his way of life, even more than screaming crowds, hotel restaurants, and endless interstates. It was the world that turned while others slept.

Big, eighteen-wheel rigs in fueling bays. The smell of coffee and fried eggs. Pure Americana that most Americans had never experienced, or even knew existed. Air brakes squealed. Tired voices yelled hellos, good-byes, and last-minute instructions. There was a common respect among those on the road that went beyond CB radio conversations about speed traps and weigh stations. No matter what time or what mood he was in, Josh always took a moment to enjoy this scene. To soak it in.

Danny met him outside the bus. "I'm sorry to put you through this. I didn't know what else to do."

"It's not your fault. Did they tell you why the card was rejected?"

"Over the limit."

Josh pondered that thought. "I'm not sure how that could happen. Bradford pays the bills every month. Let's go check it out."

Danny followed him into the truck stop. They took a place in line behind a burly truck driver.

"Let me look at the card while we're waiting,"

His driver handed him a thin piece of plastic. Josh turned it over in his hands, hoping to find an answer to their problem. Nothing seemed out of order.

The man in front of them walked away, and Josh stepped to the counter.

"May I help you?" A sleepy looking clerk asked.

"Yes. We are fueling on . . ."

"Bay five," Danny said.

"Yes. We're fueling on bay five, and it seems my credit card doesn't work. Would you mind trying it again?"

"Sure." She grabbed the card and swiped it through the machine. The clerk drilled her fingers on the counter and looked around the room while the machine gurgled, popped, and finally regurgitated an answer.

"Sorry, sir." She gave Josh a passing look. "It doesn't work."

"Okay, let me use my personal card." Josh pulled his wallet from the pocket of his jeans. "Do you take Visa?"

"Yes, sir." The clerk exchanged the cards and initiated the authorization process another time. The machine churtled through the same irritating motions, and then spit out its response.

"Sir, this card doesn't work either. It's telling me it's also over the limit."

Josh ran his hand through his hair. How could that be? He had just paid the balance on the account. Beth and he charged very little on their personal credit cards. In fact, they always paid everything off in full each month in order to avoid finance charges.

"Are your computers working okay?" Josh asked.

"Yes, sir. Working fine this morning," the clerk said. "What would you like to do now?" She sighed, pointing to the line of people standing behind him.

"I'll pay with cash," he told her. "Will two hundred dollars get us through the next leg of the trip?" He asked Danny.

His driver nodded.

Josh pulled out the last two bills in his wallet. "Please, set us up for two hundred on bay five. Sorry for your trouble."

The cashier took the bills, held them up to the light, and flipped the switch that activated the fuel pump. "Thank you, sir. Here's your receipt. Have a nice day."

Danny mumbled something to her before following Josh into the predawn morning.

"Thanks, boss. They must have a problem with their machines."

"Appears so," Josh said. "But I'll call my accountant's office when they open this morning to make sure the problem is not on our end."

*I'd better call Beth too.*

<hr />

"Bethany, do you have any idea why our business credit card would be maxed out?"

"I don't, but I can check with Bob Bradford."

"No need. I have a call into him already."

"How about our personal Visa?" Josh asked.

"Ummmm. No, I can't think of anything." The furniture company was supposed to wait until delivery day to run the charge. Surely they hadn't—

"Is everything okay there?" he asked.

"Just fine."

"All right, talk to you later." Josh hung up.

The sinking feeling in the pit of Beth's stomach told her she had made a big mistake.

<hr />

Josh stepped out of the dressing room and turned left. His steps were much lighter now that he had spoken with Bob Bradford a second time. Bradford had duly chastised the credit card company, and they had offered their apologies. The tour account had never been over the limit, and there should be no more problems for the rest of the tour.

He followed the signs on the wall that pointed toward the catering area. Like most of the venues he had worked during the past seven or eight months, a network of corridors ran underneath the building like a giant, underground spiderweb. Yards of whitewashed concrete block walls, broken only by ominous, dark green metal doors, stretched in all directions.

Mint green and beige-speckled tile floors, and artificially chilled air, gave the place a clinical feel. These same halls would be stifling after the show, when sweaty musicians and crew members rushed through them with instrument cases and production cargo in tow.

Snippets of conversation from earlier in the day ran through Josh's head, and anxiety increased the pace of his steps. Beth had been short with him when he called to let her know that everything was okay with the business account. Ryan had almost bitten his head off when he tried to talk about the lacking merchandise sales. Perhaps the camaraderie of the crew meal would bring some needed relaxation.

Josh heard music in the distance. A few feet ahead, it surrounded him. He had stepped into a musical garden retreat in the midst of a manmade jungle. Sweet strains of "A Mighty Fortress Is Our God" wafted through the corridor, causing him to redirect his steps and leading him to a door at the end of an extraneous hallway.

Josh peeked through the small, vertical window in the door. He could see the familiar shape of a grand piano, inside what was likely a rehearsal room. It was impossible from his vantage point to see who cajoled such unearthly music from the earthly elements of wood, wire, and ivory.

It was, most likely, the keyboardist for one of the main acts on the tour. Josh hadn't met everyone yet. This was only the second day of the Christmas tour. The pianist's touch was light, but the style, although unfamiliar, was reminiscent of old-style Gospel piano.

Perhaps this was a local musician, or even a tuner, who had wandered into the hall to practice. No matter, Josh wanted to express his awe and appreciation for such talent, which had obviously been honed through hours of dedicated practice.

He urged the door open, the locking mechanism releasing with a slight click, and entered the rehearsal room. The pianist, whose face was still hidden behind the lid of the behemoth instrument, never stopped playing. Josh hesitated, wanting to listen to the music for a while longer before introducing himself. But to stay for more than a few moments without making his presence known would be eavesdropping.

"Hello," Josh called out.

The music stopped, and Josh stepped around the side of the piano, his right hand extended to greet the stranger.

"Hey, boss."

"Danny?"

The big man blushed.

"I didn't know you played piano."

Danny ran his hands gently over the tops of the ivory keys, caressing them like a familiar lover.

"I knock around on it a bit."

"Man, you weren't just knocking around. That was some incredible playing."

"Thanks," Danny said. He appeared to be at a loss for words and started to get up.

"Sit." Josh motioned for his driver to return to his seat on the cushioned bench. "Please."

Danny acquiesced.

"I would love to hear more."

"Really?"

"Yes." Josh looked around for a folding chair. Finding one, he pulled it closer. "Please, continue."

Danny stared at him for a few seconds, shook his head, and then turned again to the instrument. He picked up where he had left off.

The music carried Josh away to a time and a place he hadn't been for a while, transporting him to an old, country church in Alabama, listening to his mother play. This song reminded him of the invitation she often played at the end of his daddy's service.

> A mighty fortress is our God,
> a bulwark never failing;
> our helper he amid the flood
> of mortal ills prevailing.

At the end of the song, Danny turned to him, met his eyes briefly, and then directed his gaze to the floor.

"Why have you been hiding your talent from me?" Josh asked. "I had no idea."

"I didn't think it mattered. You know, I'm not as good as Shane." Josh's keyboard player Shane was one of the best in the business.

"Not as good? Man, you're great."

"Thanks."

Josh stared at the man he had never seen before. "Play something else."

Without speaking, Danny returned his fingers to the keyboard. His touch was as light as air as he played song after song, hymn after hymn. After the third or fourth song, Danny turned back to him. "Would you like to hear one of my original tunes?"

"You write too?"

"Well, not lyrics. Just melodies." He smiled wryly. "I can't sing a lick. Couldn't carry a tune in a wooden bucket."

"I'd love to hear something you've written."

A few minutes later, after listening to the composition, it was Josh's turn to be at a loss for words.

"I guess I lost you on that one, huh?" Danny laughed. "Can't win them all. I'll stick with old hymns."

"Are you kidding?" Josh smiled. "I loved it."

"Really?"

"Do you have more?" Josh asked.

"Lots. Would you like to hear a tape I put together?"

"Yes. I would love that," Josh told him. "What else are you keeping from me?" He laughed. "Can you cure cancer too?"

"No. Just drive. That's about all I know. Driving and a little bit of piano playing."

# 23

**Present Day**

Josh sat with his legs propped up, relaxing in the jump seat. He stared mindlessly at the highway that stretched before them. The asphalt ribbon narrowed to a glistening alabaster strand in the distance as it rose and fell beneath the bus on this cold Minnesota morning.

Danny's Christmas CD streamed through Josh's earbuds, providing him an appropriate soundtrack while they plowed through the fresh snow. Josh could tell by watching his driver's grip on the wheel that the big coach was traversing as much ice as snow. A treacherous combination. But he had confidence in Danny. He had never failed to get them safely, or on time, to their destination.

Josh tapped his toe while he listened to a rousing rendition of "God Rest Ye Merry, Gentlemen." Every song on the CD—from "Ave Maria" to "What Child Is This?"—had been done well, and in Danny's unique style. There was no doubt that his friend had other talents besides driving.

The music carried Josh back to his childhood in Alabama, where snow had been scarce on Christmas. His mom always played Elvis's music on the stereo while they decorated the tree, strung popcorn, and sipped hot cider. On Christmas Day, after their family meal, they would always gathered around the piano, singing carols while his mother played.

A lot had changed since he lost his mom, but his life was still set to music. Somehow, the soundtrack had already looped back around. Was he destined to repeat the mistakes of his father? Was his faith strong enough to make it through Beth's illness or the loss of his child?

All he could do was take it a day at a time. He picked up the phone and called his wife, just to hear her voice.

―――∞∞∞――――

Beth hung up the phone. Josh would be home in ten days, and she couldn't wait. It would be their last holiday together, alone, as a couple. She wanted to make it special for him.

She glanced around the living room, taking in everything she had done in preparation for his return. Alex had helped her with the decorations, and the house looked beautiful.

The fresh-cut white pine stood six feet tall in front of the large, double living room window. Alex had dragged it into the house and set it up. Then they had covered it with hundreds of soft, white lights, and tied ivory-colored, linen bows onto the tips of the branches.

Strings of cranberries crisscrossed the evergreen needles from top to bottom. An antique, hand-punched tin star sat at the top. Covering the bottom was an embroidered, burgundy red tree skirt, a gift from her Grandmother Randall.

With everything now completed, Beth had time on her hands. Alex had gone home for a while. Perhaps she should put Buster out for a few minutes and then take a short nap.

"Want to go outside, Budder?" She asked the sleepy-eyed terrier.

The little dog grinned and raced to the back door. "Good boy. When you come back, we'll snuggle on the sofa for a while."

When she opened the door, he took off running and barking to the far end of the backyard. Beth looked up into what, an hour before, had been a clear-blue sky. Steel-gray clouds now gathered into a brewing storm. The wind, taking advantage of the open door, shoved its way inside with a whiny howl, blowing her Farmer's Almanac calendar off the mudroom wall.

When she bent to pick it up, the realization hit her in the gut, almost knocking her to the floor. December 13. She braced against the kitchen doorsill. How had she let today slip up on her? Especially this year.

And then she remembered the bear.

She turned and walked purposefully through the house, down the hallway, and into the guest bedroom. She knew exactly where the box was stored. On the top shelf of the closet, safe and nondescript, just like the memories she held of this date ten years ago.

She tugged the heavy green wooden chair from her antique desk in the corner of the room, dragging it across the carpet and placing it in front of the closet. Then, standing on the tips of her toes, she clawed her way through the quilts and pillows that obscured the benign, brown shipping carton.

*He had been relegated to a box.* Among other things that no longer applied to her life, like a high school letter sweater and college term papers.

She stretched her arms high above her head, with the ball of her foot resting on the edge of the chair, but could still only touch the box. Although the chair began to tip, Beth was determined to wrap her hands around the container and pull it out. When she finally grasped it, the box responded too easily. It released, throwing her off balance. She caught her breath, steadied herself, and then scrambled down from the chair with the carton in her arms.

Beth placed the box on the white flokati wool rug near the bed and lowered herself to a cross-legged position in front of it. With adrenaline-induced strength, she popped the tape that sealed the carton. An excess of emotions tumbled out when she lifted the lid. Her elementary school class photo. A piggy bank filled with silver dollars her grandfather had given her. And her high school diploma.

The rust-colored bear lay in the corner of his cardboard tomb, covered with dried flowers from an old corsage. She lifted him—or was it her?—gently, stirring up the smell of dust and deceit. Beth realized that he represented everything she withheld from her husband. The life she had lived before him. The lives she had extinguished, her own along with her child's.

She thought back to the woman in front of the abortion clinic that day. The one who had pleaded with her to reconsider her actions. But the women inside had told her it didn't matter, and she had chosen to believe the lie. Now, just like Eve, she had come to understand the price.

Beth hugged the lifeless bear and cried. Its button nose and dark eyes reminded her of what she had lost. And what she had to look forward to, if God granted her the child within.

"Bethany, are you okay?"

She had been facing the wall and had not heard Alex come into the room. Beth ran her hand over her eyes and turned, still clasping the bear in her arms.

"What's wrong?" Concern swept across Alex's face.

Beth hoped her eyes didn't give away the tears. "I'm fine. I was just—"

"Crying." Alex stepped toward her. "Have you been crying?"

"Yes. I was just—"

"Worried about the baby again?" Alex asked, staring at the stuffed toy.

Beth swallowed hard. "Yes. I guess I was."

Her secret was safe.

"Let me fix you some hot tea."

Alex reached out to help her up, and Beth took her hand.

"I saw Buster sitting by the door for a long time, and I got worried about you. That's why I came back early. I hope you don't mind."

"Of course not. Thanks for checking on me."

# 24

**Present Day**

For as long as Beth could remember, her family had driven to Southern Illinois to celebrate Christmas Eve with her grandparents. She had never broken the tradition. Even during her rebellious, college years, she would drive on her own from Nashville or meet her parents halfway, at their home in Kentucky, and ride with them the rest of the way.

This year would be no different. Josh had finished his tour in time for them to make the trip together on Christmas Eve morning. They would return tomorrow for an intimate Christmas on their own.

In the meantime, Beth couldn't wait to see her family and share the excitement of her pregnancy. Christmas was one of those rare occasions when everyone—including aunts, uncles, and cousins—from her mother's side of the family got together. Her parents; her brother, Scott; Grandpa and Grandma Randall; and Uncle Jim and his family would fill her grandparents' small house with lots of love, laughter, and controlled chaos. Josh had joined the festivities for the first time three years ago, shortly after they had started dating.

The Randall clan tradition was to gather for a big meal and a small gift exchange on Christmas Eve, and then everyone would attend worship service at her grandparent's church the following day.

Grandma, Aunt Jean, and Beth's mom contributed to the holiday feast each year. Beth looked forward to the food, the fellowship, and the worship. The tradition touched her heart in a special way. It also left her stuffed and determined to diet after the New Year.

She couldn't imagine what it would be like when her grandparents were no longer able to host this special occasion. Each year, Beth's mother, her aunt, and now Beth and her cousin Mandy, contributed more in the way of food. Even though her grandmother had relinquished some of the responsibility, she remained determined to prepare her signature dishes, especially those she knew her grandchildren enjoyed. Beth's mother and Aunt Jean always prepared haute cuisine made from the latest recipes they had seen on the Food Network or in a food magazine, and there was often two of everything— the old-style fare and its gourmet cousin.

Grandma's staple menu included a spiced, pineapple-glazed ham and marshmallow-covered, candied sweet potatoes. Beth's mother always baked a prime rib roast of beef cooked medium rare and served with garlic mashed potatoes. Grandma's green bean casserole was made with mushroom soup and French fried onion rings. Beth's mom prepared Green Beans Almandine.

Grandma Randall served chilled jellied cranberry sauce from a can, sliced and presented on a special, silver server, while Beth's mom made a fresh cranberry-orange peel relish served in a glass compote. Although Beth would never tell her mother for fear of hurting her feelings, she preferred the old-fashioned style of her grandmother's cooking.

This year, despite having been recently hospitalized, Grandma managed to contribute many of her regular foods, including homemade dinner rolls she served with butter and honey. The bread by itself would have made the meal special.

Grandma's kitchen, although small and only semimodern, smelled like culinary heaven at Christmas. Grandma covered the table with a white linen cloth, one she used only on rare occasions. She set out her Spode Christmas Tree Grove pattern dinnerware, which had been a Christmas gift from Beth's parents many years ago. The dishes would one day be passed along to either Beth or her brother, Scott.

An old wooden buffet that had belonged to Beth's maternal great-grandparents, held a variety of desserts. Homemade cherry pies, Aunt Jean's coconut cream pie, and Beth's mom's special Burnt Butter Bundt Cake. Her cousin Mandy always made a cheesecake. In recent years, Grandma had added peach cobbler to the menu because she knew it was Beth's favorite.

The Randall family's perspective on Christmas set the tone for the coming year. They celebrated the presence of family and food, exchanged small gifts, and ended the weekend worshiping together. This year was especially meaningful because Beth's brother, Scott, had been given furlough from the military base where he was stationed in Germany.

The cousins, all in their late twenties or early thirties now, still brought their sleeping bags for the overnight stay. After the older family members went to bed, the younger set commandeered a corner in the main part of the house and talked for hours. It was their one time each year to catch up with one another.

A list of concerns crowded Ben Abrams's consciousness as he drove away from his house on Christmas Eve morning. Frost clung to the corners of the windshield of his new Mercedes G550 SUV, a direct result of last night's decision to avoid the cluttered garage. Something he would tackle on Saturday.

The weekend wouldn't come soon enough. His office was closed today. But, as the doctor on call for the Christmas holidays, he would have an erratic schedule for the next four days.

Ben switched on his headlights as he wound his way out of the Belle Meade neighborhood where he had lived for more than a decade. The morning fog hung low, eliciting a subtle and much-needed peace. He had combined a recent business trip with a short visit to his grandmother, and seeing her frail condition had provoked a dreaded dose of reality. The knowledge that he might be losing her soon weighed heavily on him.

He had tried to convince her to move to Nashville, to stay with him. But she had adamantly denied the need, as she always had. Forcefully uprooting her from her home of more than fifty years didn't seem right.

The desire to be independent was something he understood. He was thankful he had found a way to use the self-discipline that came with it to help others. Working as a physician had brought him much fulfillment. And, despite an early distrust of people that had come from his unorthodox upbringing, he had grown to love the kinder side of humanity.

Some of his patients made a deeper impact on him than others. Bethany Harrison came to mind. He had honed his skills, and he was adept at the most innovative of procedures, but microsurgery, which might be required in her case, was still challenging. He would hate to see the life of such a vivacious young woman cut short because of her religious beliefs.

On Christmas morning, Beth's stomach churned as she and Josh returned to her grandparents' house after church services. She had plans to tell him about the abortion on their drive back to Nashville, and the dread had begun to set in.

Less than an hour later, while Josh carried their luggage to his Jeep, Beth hugged her family and said her tearful good-byes.

"We'll see you in a month or two, honey," her mother said, with a worried look on her face. "Sooner if you need us."

"I'll be fine, Mom," Beth said. "Really. Alex is taking good care of me."

"I love spending time with your folks," Josh told Beth, as he held the car door open for her. "They make me feel like part of the family."

"You *are* part of the family." She crinkled her nose at Josh's humble personality.

While they were stopped for fuel and a bathroom break in Paducah, Kentucky, Beth worked up her courage. If she was going to talk to Josh, now was the time.

She pulled the seatbelt over her ever-widening midsection and snapped the buckle securely. Her husband laid his hand gently on her tummy. "Maybe we should talk about names on the way home."

The happiness in his voice broke her heart. "I need to tell you about something first," she said, watching as he merged the car into traffic on I-24 East.

"Let me guess." He winked. "You're pregnant?"

"No, silly."

"It's twins?"

"No!" She laughed.

He tensed. "Triplets?"

"No. It's not about our baby. She—or he—is doing fine." Beth took a deep breath. "It's about what happened when I was in college." The tone of her voice changed the mood in the car.

Josh gave her a sideways glance. "I don't understand."

"This is not my first pregnancy. I should have told you before now."

"What do you mean?" His mouth twitched, as if wanting to smile but holding back for a punch line.

"I made a mistake when I first moved to Nashville. I ran with the wrong crowd. Not bad people, but not believers."

Josh's potential smile faded.

"I began to doubt some of the things I had been taught. You know, that everything your parents say is best."

"I think we've all been there," he said.

"But I decided to act on it. I was lonely. Feeling different than everyone else. My friends partied into the night. Some even experimented with drugs. I started to feel like the last good girl on earth, like I was setting myself up to be better than everyone else."

Josh shook his head and ran his fingers through his hair. "Honey, don't—"

"No, I have to tell you . . . should have told you a long time ago."

*God, why do I have to tell him?*

She composed herself. "I know now that it was just an excuse, a lie I told myself." She folded and unfolded the tissue in her hands, trying to pick her words carefully. "Unfortunately, it wasn't the only lie I told myself. I made the biggest mistake I've ever made in my life. I got pregnant."

She studied Josh's face for a reaction. His jaw was set, and he kept his eyes straight ahead.

"So you miscarried?" he asked.

Beth's bottom lip trembled, as she stared into the distance.

"No. I hadn't dated the guy for long. And, the truth was, I didn't want to spend my life with him. I knew he didn't care about me, not beyond having a good time. We were both nineteen, and we had our lives ahead of us."

"So you put the baby up for adoption?"

Beth crossed her arms tightly around her stomach, hugging the baby in her womb. "No. I had an abortion." The guilt and pain that had been buried inside her for years burst to the surface, erupting hot and ugly like lava from the depths of the earth.

Josh took his foot off the accelerator and eased the Jeep to the side of the road. He stopped the car and turned to her, his dark-brown eyes full of confusion, pain, and anger. "Why didn't you tell me?"

"Because . . . I was ashamed."

A psychologist would have a fancy name for what she had just done. Probably even congratulate her for finally getting it out. Surely it would be cathartic. She could now make peace with her past. Maybe even realize it wasn't as bad as she had thought. The light of day would now bleach her sins.

Or she could make excuses. The same ones she had told herself for years.

*It was only a fetus.*

*I had to do it. There was no real choice.*

And, of course, *it was best for everyone, especially the baby.*

Beth stared at the dirty, dry underbrush beside the four-lane highway. A few remaining Jack-in-the-Pulpit berries decorated the winter wasteland, like red blood clinging to the dying grasses, and a rush of nausea filled her throat. She opened the car door and stumbled across the scrub grass in the right-of-way. Then, falling to her knees, she began retching up the remains of the secrets from her past.

After she returned to the car, they rode in silence. The look in Josh's eyes, and his body language, told her everything she needed to know. All she had done was transfer her pain to him. What she had thought would be the path to complete forgiveness had sent her in the wrong direction.

If she could take back the words, she would. But then again, there was a lot in her life she would like to take back right now.

As they approached the I-24 and I-65 intersection outside of Nashville, Josh spoke. "Don't tell anyone else about this. I can't imagine what it would do to my career." His voice was dry and empty.

"Please, don't hate me, Josh. I never wanted to hurt you. Try to understand my pain."

He glanced at her with disgust. "I understand I don't know you," he said. "I always thought you were honest with me. I guess I was wrong."

<hr />

Bethany ached to get home. Maybe if she gave him some space, his mood would improve before bedtime. When she walked in the door, she knew that wasn't going to happen. Their living room floor was covered with white, fluffy, pillow stuffing from inside Josh's favorite chair, and the dog was lying in the midst of it.

"Buster! You're a bad, bad boy!" She rushed to the little terrier's side. Although she was angry with him, she feared Josh's reaction would be worse.

"What's this?" he asked, standing frozen in the entryway.

The little terrier cowered.

"You stupid . . . " Josh raised his hand to strike as he crossed the room.

"No!" Beth gathered the shaking dog in her arms. "Don't hurt him. He doesn't know any better."

"Doesn't know better? Are you kidding me?" Josh turned his anger on her. "We've taught him from the first day to do the right thing."

"And he made a mistake."

"A mistake? My chair is ruined."

"What's wrong with you, Josh? Are you so callous you can't forgive anyone of anything?" Beth held back her tears. She wasn't about to give her husband the satisfaction of seeing her cry.

"The world is a rough place," he scowled. "You have no idea what I have on my shoulders right now. My work. Taking care of you."

Beth bit her lip. "I can take care of myself just fine, thank you very much."

"You're positive everything will work out, aren't you? Well, we don't live in a fairy-tale world, Princess Bethany." He pointed toward her stomach. "That's a real baby in your womb. If you would stop taking so many prescription drugs, maybe you would understand that."

"Stop it!" Beth screamed.

"No. You stop it," he said. "You've killed one baby, and I don't want you to kill another."

# 25

**Present Day**

The phone rang, and Josh shouted a hello to the unknown caller. Most likely a telemarketer.

"Josh?"

It was Beth's Grandpa Randall.

"Is everything okay?"

"Yes, sir." Josh's conscience pricked. "I'm sorry. I was just yelling at the dog before you called."

"I don't mean to bother you. I was just checking to see if you kids got home okay."

"Yes, sir." Josh looked around for his wife, who had left the room. "Would you like to talk to Bethany?"

"No. In fact, I'm glad you answered." The older man said. "I want to thank you for taking such good care of my grand-daughter. I meant to say something while you were here but never got the chance."

Guilt grabbed Josh by the throat and held his words hostage. "I do the best I can," he managed to say.

"It can't be easy, son. You have a lot to handle right now, but you're doing a good job."

"Thank you, sir. I'm not always perfect, but we'll get through it." Josh tugged at the collar of his shirt, which was beginning to feel like a noose around his neck.

"With God's help you will." Beth's grandfather's voice was shaky. "My wife and I aren't able to help you much from way up here, but you're both in our prayers. Give Bethany our love."

"I will. And thank you again for the Christmas gifts."

Josh placed the phone back in its cradle and a few minutes later went in search of Beth. She was already in bed asleep. Or pretending to be.

---

Josh awoke to silence the following morning. Beth must have gotten up early, something unusual for her these days. The drugs usually kept her asleep well into the day.

No doubt she wanted to be as far away from him as possible. A twinge of guilt nipped at him for the way he had acted last night. In the light of day, he felt somewhat like the bully who had picked on the smallest kid at school.

He had probably overreacted. But what was he supposed to do? Praise her for her dishonesty? She should have told him about the abortion before they were married.

But it wasn't just that. Josh assuaged his conscience with the reminder that he was carrying the financial load by himself. Beth had no idea what he had to deal with right now. He had been out on tour for almost nine months straight, and weariness ached in every muscle. Since her illness, he had to deal with medical bills, insurance forms, and making sure that every aspect of their lives ran smoothly.

No doubt, she didn't appreciate him as she should. She had only been thinking of herself. She wasn't even trying to back off the drugs. Alex had told him last week that Beth's tolerance to the morphine had increased, requiring her to step up to a larger patch. She now took more than twice what she did when she left the hospital in October. What was that doing to their baby?

Josh heard the click of Buster's toenails on the hardwood floors. The little dog jumped into the bed, grinned at him, and then rolled over for a belly rub. Dogs had the forgiveness thing down pat. Much more so than humans.

It was time to put the past behind him and Beth.

Josh threw back the covers, put on his robe, and set off for the kitchen to find his wife. The smell of fresh coffee aroused his senses when he walked into the living room, meeting Beth in the hallway. She gave him a questioning look. He smiled, and her face brightened.

"Good morning," she said, shortening the distance between them.

"Yes, it is." He reached out to pull her to him, and the door-bell rang.

Her expression changed from acquiescence to panic.

"What's wrong?"

She pulled her blue pinstriped robe closer to herself, fiddling with the sash. "It's the furniture deliverymen. I'm not ready—"

"It's no problem," he told her. "Get dressed. I'll take care of it." He tucked a lock of her dark brown hair behind her ear. Perhaps they could start today off better than last night had ended. "I'm anxious to see what you found at the consignment shop."

"Josh . . ." Her voice faded.

"What?"

"Never mind," she said, before hurrying down the hallway to the bedroom.

When Josh opened the door he saw the truck from Maison de Reve Furniture. *What had Beth done?*

An older man in tidy blue coveralls stood on the front porch. He held papers in his hand. "Good morning, sir. Is this the Harrison residence?"

Josh nodded.

"We're here to deliver some bedroom fur—"

Josh stepped forward. "I believe there's been a mistake. My wife isn't—"

A younger man quickly joined his co-worker. "Hey, aren't you Josh Harrison, the singer?" He stuck out his hand. "I'm thrilled to meet you."

*What were the chances?*

"I'm sure you hear it all the time, but your music really changed my life." The younger man pointed to the sky. "Really helped change my relationship with the guy upstairs, if you know what I mean." His cheeks colored slightly. "And with my family too."

Josh shook his head. "That's great to hear." He opened the door wider.

The first man looked from his co-worker to Josh. "So, you said there was a mistake, Mr. Harrison?"

Josh stepped backward. "It's not a problem. We didn't expect you this early, but we'll work it out. I'll show you where the furniture will be going."

---

By the time she slipped out of her pajamas and into jeans and a sweatshirt, Beth had decided to stand up for herself. So what that Josh thought she'd spent too much money? Hadn't she made the decision that was best for the baby? If her husband couldn't see that, it was his problem.

When she walked into the nursery, the deliverymen were unpacking the combination dresser–baby changing station. Josh had parked himself next to the window. He stood with his arms folded against his chest and a gruff expression on his face. He gave her a sideways glance as she entered the room.

"You must be Mrs. Harrison." The younger of the delivery-men greeted her. "You've picked out a beautiful set for your baby." He pointed toward Josh. "I'm sure your husband and you will enjoy it."

She offered the man a thankful smile, and cast a cynical nod toward Josh. "Thank you. I'm sure we will."

"I was just telling your husband how much I appreciate his ministry," the man continued. "It has really blessed me."

"Really?" Beth turned to Josh. He shook his head and paced to the corner of the room.

"Billy," the older deliveryman interrupted. "Let's quit talking and get this finished before dark." He turned to Beth. "Where do you want the bed set up, ma'am?"

Less than an hour later Josh accompanied the men to the front door, while Beth stayed in the nursery to admire the fur-niture. She ran her hand along the rich dark cherry finish of the dresser and dared to hope that everything would work out, for the baby as well as for her marriage. If Josh would drop the issue of cost, they could move on with life. Maybe she'd spent too much, but they would pay for it somehow. She held her hand to her ever-expanding tummy. Just as long as the baby didn't pay for it—for her mistakes.

Before she could finish the thought, Josh returned to the room, waving a paper in his hand. "How much did you spend?"

"Josh, please." She pleaded for his understanding. "Could you give me a break, just once?"

Anger filled his dark eyes, and his body stiffened. Beth braced herself for his words.

"Why don't you give *me* a break," he shoved the paper in her face. "I'm the one paying for all of this."

"Yes." She said almost under her breath. "You're the perfect one. Always the perfect one, aren't you? Just like that man said." She pointed toward the door. "Well, I've got news for him. You may minister to others, but you sure don't bring it home."

# 26

**Present Day**

The following Wednesday Josh switched on the small television in the bathroom before getting ready for a meeting at his accountant's office. He was grateful to have the appointment. Anything to take his mind off personal problems.

He and Beth had hardly spoken earlier. Then she'd left with Alex for a grocery-shopping trip. Since arguing last week, they'd said very little to each other, with Beth staying in one side of the house, mostly in the baby's room, and he in another.

Maybe Bob Bradford would have good news to share.

Josh flipped through television channels, stopping on the morning news. Sometimes it helped being reminded that others led imperfect lives, that everyone struggled from time to time. The news certainly substantiated that. War ravaged half the world. Pandemics threatened. And the economy had taken a bite out of the American lifestyle, including the entertainment business.

With less discretionary income, people downloaded less music, purchased fewer concert tickets, and bought less souvenir merchandise. Another issue Josh had to address with Bob Bradford today, waning merchandise sales.

In many ways, God had continued to bless the Christian music industry. People sought to be uplifted and reassured that problems of this world were exactly that: of this world. Christian music celebrated eternal life. Yet, Christians still expected their favorite entertainers to minister about contemporary issues. Hadn't the deliveryman said just that last week?

Josh's stomach turned at the thought of having to share his faith during the upcoming tour. He wasn't sure he had enough to share. Of course, he believed in God and the promise of salvation. But the past few months had drained his spirit. He was no longer confident he had chosen the right path for his life. As a Christian entertainer, he was expected to encourage and edify others.

That was difficult for him to do from where he stood right now.

He washed his face and splashed on cologne while the Wednesday morning news ran through a laundry list of global problems. Financial scandals, celebrity infidelities, and the disgusting story about a mother who had strangled her four-year-old son so she could keep up with the party crowd. How could a mother kill her own child for convenience?

The pit in Josh's stomach moved into his throat. That thought was too close to home. He turned off the television, walked out of the bathroom, and closed the door behind him.

Leaving early for the meeting gave him time to stop for breakfast. He pulled his Jeep into a metered slot on Church Street in front of the Haute Bean Coffee Shop across the street from Bradford's office. The familiar surroundings of the coffee shop brought back memories. Many times, when he and Beth were dating, they had shared a cup of coffee or a sandwich here. Their usual table, now empty, sat in silence, just as he and Beth had done lately.

He was scanning pastries in the glass case, when a man with an accent of unknown origin greeted him. "How can I help you, sir?"

"I'd like a muffin of some kind."

"We have double chocolate chip, apple streusel, cranberry lemon, and low-fat pumpkin."

"Chocolate chip. And a small coffee."

"Regular, decaf, or today's special, Jamaican Almond Mocha?"

"Regular, please." Josh handed a five-dollar bill to the clerk. There were so many choices in life. And they all came at a price.

A few minutes later, he found a seat at a highboy table in the front of the shop. The coffee tasted better than any he'd had lately, and the chocolate worked to improve his mood. He checked his cell phone. It was time to head on over to Bradford's.

Large flakes of snow began to fall as Josh stepped out into the cold morning. The white stuff was already sticking in the shadows between buildings. If the temperature kept dropping, traffic would be a mess by the time he drove home.

He pulled his wool scarf—the one Beth had bought him for Christmas—tighter to his neck and crossed the street. He swung open one of the massive lobby doors in the red brick building which housed Bob Bradford's suite of offices. Bradford's business provided financial management for many of Nashville's hottest stars and occupied the entire third floor.

The nicely appointed, but nondescript, reception area reassured clients that Bradford Associates was a fiscally conservative operation. Their company slogan, "Our business is making your business a priority," was posted below the company logo on the copper-colored wall behind the front desk.

Josh hadn't been seated long before Bob Bradford's assistant, Marcia, ushered him to the conference room. Bradford and a few other staffers were talking among themselves as he entered. A stack of paperwork was piled high on the eight-foot mahogany table.

Bob Bradford stood and greeted Josh. After a quick introduction to those he didn't know, and a few words to acknowledge those he did, Josh took a seat next to Bradford, who got straight to the point.

"I wish I had better news for you." He squinted his eyes. "But we've found an irregularity in your books."

It seemed that no one in the room breathed.

"I don't understand," Josh said.

"Someone in your organization is keeping two books, son." The accountant cleared his throat and sat back in his chair, never taking his eyes off Josh. "If you know anything about it, you should level with me now, so we can talk about the tax implications and resolve the matter quickly."

"I don't know anything about it," Josh said, studying his accountant's face. *Was Bradford implying he could be behind such an impropriety?* "But I hope you will explain it to me."

Bradford leaned forward. "Good. That's what I thought. So let's find out who is stealing from you."

Because Bradford insisted on going over every detail, the meeting lasted more than two hours. Bradford explained to Josh that the perpetrator had been clever, but not as clever as the experienced firm of Bradford Associates. There was little doubt that merchandise profits were being manipulated.

Bob Bradford reminded Josh that, when he had initially signed on to use their services, they had insisted he request duplicate merchandise purchase orders from his suppliers. "It's good business in case we need backup," Bradford had told him. Now, it appeared he had been prophetic.

"It's a tempting situation," Bradford said. "Anytime you're dealing with a cash business, there are otherwise honest people who can't resist fudging a little here and a little there."

Josh nodded.

Bradford continued. "After they get away with it, they become more daring. But the truth is always uncovered, either by us or by the IRS. You're not the first musician to have this happen. But the figures are high in your case, almost reckless."

According to Bradford, someone had mismanaged almost $50,000 in funds during the last quarter of the year. "We noticed a small discrepancy in the third quarter," he explained. "We initially wrote it off as error, but something to watch. These year-end figures substantiated motive not mistake. No one makes a $50,000 error. No one deserving of having the responsibility for that much money."

Josh's heart went to his throat. The facts were certain. He had been riding the bus with a thief. Someone who pretended to be a friend had acted otherwise.

At this point, they couldn't be certain who was responsible. Mitch, his merchandise manager, had the most obvious access to the books, but Ryan was now Mitch's supervisor. Could it be both of them working together or one acting alone? Or were the merchandise suppliers setting someone up?

Josh kept thinking back to what Bradford had said initially. The problem, at least on a small scale, had started before Ryan took over the accounting, back when Josh was still managing the books. Could Mitch have been testing the waters?

Only time would tell as they prepared to set the trap.

—◈◈◈—

Beth and Alex hurried through their grocery-shopping list in hopes of making it home before the snow completely covered the streets. Alex scoured the organic aisles, while Beth gathered up chips, soft drinks, and cookies. They met in the dairy section. Beth grabbed two cartons of chocolate milk, and Alex picked out a bottle of pomegranate kefir and a carton of plain yogurt.

"Do we have everything?" Alex asked, marking items off a list. "How about dog food? Does Buster need anything? From the looks of this weather, we may be staying home for a few days."

"I'll grab the dog food and meet you at the checkout," Beth said.

When she arrived at the cashier stand, Beth saw shoppers pouring in through the front door. Some scowling, some laughing, as they brushed the wet, sticky snow off their shoulders. Snow didn't fall that often in Middle Tennessee, so when it did, it was a special occasion.

Whether they enjoyed it or not, Nashvillians always prepared for such storms. Before sunset on any given snowy evening, the milk and bread shelves of local supermarkets were virtually bare. Everyone joked about how the big grocery store chains sponsored the weather alerts.

The girls shrieked with delight at the assault of large, icy snowflakes on their way to Alex's car. After piling groceries into the backseat, Alex dusted off her windshield. Settling into the warm car, she rubbed her hands together. "I think my freckles are frozen to my face. It's cold out there."

Beth laughed. "It's pretty, though, isn't it? I always feel like a little girl again when it snows. Maybe we can build a snowman."

"Let's warm up first," Alex gave her a disdainful look. "I'll make mugs of hot milk with honey when we get home."

"Sounds delicious."

Within a half hour of getting home, they had the car unloaded and were sitting at Beth's kitchen banquette enjoying a steaming cup of honey-scented milk. Buster lay beside Beth, his head on her lap. The little dog was always content to sit quietly beside her, enjoying her company. Something she and Josh no longer seemed to do.

"This is relaxing," Beth said. "I may take a nap and reconsider the snowman project."

"I like the way you think." Alex cracked a smile. "While you do that, I'm going home to organize what I bought today."

Alex got up from the table and carried her mug to the sink. She looked out the window. "It's getting bad out there. Do you think you should call Josh? What time are you expecting him home?"

"I'm not sure," Beth said. "I'll give him a call before I lie down."

"Okay, girl. I'll see you tomorrow. If you need anything, let me know. I'll leave you two lovebirds alone this evening."

Yeah, right. Beth stifled an honest comeback. "Okay. Thanks for your help today, as always."

After Alex left, Beth pulled the cell phone from the pocket of her jeans. She dialed Josh's number. No answer. So she left a message saying she had made it home safe and would be taking a nap. She placed the phone on the sofa table in the living room and walked to the large windows where the Christmas tree had stood until a few days ago.

She spent a few minutes daydreaming about the fun she'd had as a child, building snowmen and sledding down the big hill in her neighborhood. Good times before the responsibility of adulthood. She wrapped her arms around her stomach, feeling sentimental, while she watched the accumulation pile up outside. Even now, slow moving cars slid sideways trying to traverse the street in front of the house.

Something at the end of the sidewalk caught her eye. It was the newspaper. She should pick it up before the snow covered it completely. Josh enjoyed reading the news when he was home.

"Mr. B., do you want to help me get the newspaper?"

The Boston terrier jumped and twirled beside her. "You're always ready for a party, aren't you, little guy?"

Beth scanned the room for the leash but didn't see it. "Do you think you can walk out there and back with me without a leash?"

He responded with a yip.

"Okay, let's hurry. It's cold out there."

Beth pulled her cable knit sweater close to her body and opened the door. The brisk wind blew snow in her face, the icy crystals stinging as they hit her skin and dissipated.

"Come on, boy." She urged the dog to stay beside her.

Buster scampered to the end of the sidewalk, keeping his nose to the ground. He coughed and snorted when he reached the newspaper, inhaling the scent of it. Beth patted him on the head as she bent over to pick it up. Thankfully, the flimsy plastic covering appeared to have kept the paper dry.

She called Buster to walk with her back to the house, and he followed willingly. But when they reached the front door, the little dog started barking.

"What is it, Budder?"

Oh, no . . . a cat.

Beth grabbed for the little dog's collar but it was too late. He bolted off toward the neighbor's yard and disappeared around the corner of their house. She dropped the newspaper beside the front door and took off after him.

# 27

**Present Day**

Josh picked up the newspaper from the stoop as he approached the front door of the house. When he turned the knob, he found that Beth had left the door unlocked again. How many times had he cautioned her about that?

He dusted the snow off his shoes and then tiptoed into the house so as not to wake his wife. She had left a voicemail message that she would be napping. No need to disturb her. Besides, he would be happy to have time alone. It would be great to relax and read the paper in front of the fire. Next week, he returned to the road. Might as well enjoy himself while he could.

He took off his gloves and rubbed his hands together to warm them up. It was freezing outside. The weather matched his mood. The low temperatures had stolen his comfort the way an unknown thief had taken his peace of mind. He'd lost something more important than money in the past few months. He'd lost a friend and employee who would be found out eventually.

Although he was tired and anxious right now, he was determined to fight back. A short nap would do him good before he figured out how. He propped his feet up on the couch and settled in for a while.

———— ∞∞∞ ————

Beth called for Buster, but the wind blew her words back into her face. The little black-and-white terrier was nowhere in sight. In the twenty or so minutes she had been searching, the weather had gone from bad to worse. She protected her eyes with her hand, while looking around for the dog. It would have been nice to have on gloves and a coat. Perhaps she should return to the house for them and solicit help. Or maybe she should just wait for Buster to return on his own.

She saw movement in her peripheral vision. It was him.

"Buster. Buster. Come here. . . ."

The little dog glanced at her and then, as if driven by demons, took off running in the opposite direction. They had already crossed several neighborhood yards and now approached the street that ran behind the houses. She watched him run, barking, into the street and directly in front of an oncoming car.

"Noooo!"

Thank God, Buster cleared the front wheel of the car and kept running. The black cat he chased managed to stay a few yards in front of him.

There was no way she could risk leaving the little dog to the elements. She had to figure a way to coax him to her before he crossed another street.

Perhaps she could corner the little guy. *Please, God, help me get to him.*

A few seconds later, the cat lured Buster into a vacant lot. One that had been partially fenced. The nimble feline scrambled up the rough wood planks and hopped to safety on the other side. Her pursuer stopped briefly, inhaled the air above him, and considered his options.

Beth had only seconds to make her move. She rushed across the wet grass, now covered in two inches of fluffy, white snow, and grabbed for Buster's collar. Mentally calculating the space between them, she lunged forward with one final push, and her foot slipped out from under her.

Her fall played out in slow motion, leaving time for her to contemplate whether the landing would be soft or hard. Beth juxtaposed her body to protect her baby the best she could, but when she hit the ground the pain was excruciating.

---

Josh awoke from his nap with the nagging feeling that something wasn't right. He sat up on the sofa and listened for a clue. Only silence filled the air. He should check on Beth.

When he opened the bedroom door, he found the room just as he had left it. The bed was made, and there was no sign of Buster. Either Beth had taken a nap and remade the bed, or she had never lain down after returning with Alex. Perhaps the girls had started chatting and time had gotten away from them. He picked up the phone to call next door.

"Alex, is Beth with you?"

"No. I dropped her off about two hours ago. Maybe more. Why?"

"I can't find her."

"What do you mean?" Panic fractured her usually calm voice.

"I haven't seen her since I got home. And Buster's gone."

"That doesn't make sense. I'll be right over."

While waiting for Alex, Josh walked through the house again, checking every room and calling Beth's name.

Nothing.

"Did you notice any tracks in the snow when you came home?" Alex asked, rushing through the back door.

"I didn't really look, but . . . no. I didn't."

"Surely she wouldn't have taken Buster for a walk. Not in this weather." Alex peered out the front window. "Her car is still here."

"I'm worried." Josh stepped to the hall closet, put on his heaviest jacket, and pulled on his gloves. "The weather is too bad for her to be outside. But I don't know where else she could be."

"Maybe at a neighbor's house?"

"Not likely. But I'll check." He opened the front door. "You stay here in case she calls."

"Will do." Alex picked up the cell phone from the sofa table. "Look, it's Beth's phone." A worried look crossed her face.

"Stay here anyway. Someone needs to stay at the house. If she shows up, call my phone." He patted his jacket pocket. "I've got it with me."

"Okay. I'll be right here."

Josh walked from door to door, and up and down the street. Few of their neighbors were home. Those who were said they hadn't seen Beth or Buster. He looked around, uncertain about what to do next. He prayed she was somewhere safe, and that he could scold her later for being so unthinking as not to tell him where she'd gone.

The temperature had dropped considerably since he had come home. A light sleet was now falling, making it harder to walk on the ice-crusted surface of the snow. If she was outside, she could freeze to death in no time.

He had to do something. But what? He took his phone from his pocket and started to dial the emergency code. Then he remembered what he had always been told: that the police wouldn't take action on a missing person unless they had been gone for more than twenty-four hours.

Josh put the phone back in his pocket and called Beth's name. Then Buster's.

No answer.

He heard only the icy tic-tic-tic of the sleet hitting the ground and the crunch of the snow underneath his feet as he picked his way through the neighborhood.

Josh detoured from the sidewalk into yards and vacant lots, looking behind every bush and around every fence. He continued to shout. "Beth! Buster, here boy. Beth-a-ny."

Only silence and fear responded.

—⋙⋘—

Beth pulled Buster close to her. If she had anything to be thankful for, it was that she had fallen next to the old, wooden fence, which helped to shelter her from the wind. The temperature was cold, but the wind chill was agonizing. The fence also helped to block the icy rain that had begun to fall.

She rubbed her swollen ankle. When she tried to move, the pain proved almost intolerable. All she could do was wait. And hope that Alex or Josh would find her soon. She wasn't that far from home. Although, she reasoned, she might as well be in Antarctica, if they didn't know to look for her.

The number of cars passing on the street several yards behind her had diminished since darkness set in. By listening to the thump-thump of the tires, she could decipher that the state of the road was bad.

What if Josh hadn't been able to get home? If not, Alex would have no way of knowing that Beth had left the house—until tomorrow.

She shouted for someone's attention, but the wind carried her voice into the darkness without a response.

Fear seized her heart. How long did it take to freeze to death?

*Lord, please don't take my baby and me.*

The words surprised her. Until now, her brush with heaven almost four months ago had anesthetized her from this world.

Josh had been right all along. She hadn't been thinking straight.

Heaven had seemed incomparable to any kind of life on earth, especially one where she had to face the problems she had created for herself. She had been hiding her guilt behind the painkillers and her illness. And she had let her relationship with Josh deteriorate.

Nothing had held her here until now, when death threatened again and she realized that she and her child were in this together. The bond between them could not have become more real than at that moment. They were fighting for life together.

A frozen tear lodged in Beth's eye.

*Dear God, was that a kick from my baby?*

It was the first time she had felt the child growing inside her womb.

She had to get them out of here alive.

Buster wiggled next to her.

"Be still, boy. We need to hang close if we're going to make it through this."

The little dog looked up to her, his black-brown eyes conveying perfect love. Love without fear. Love that rested on trust.

He cocked his head.

"What is it?" Beth asked, and then she, too, heard something. Her hopes rose, and she listened.

There it was again, but it was just the wind howling through the rickety, old fence.

―――∞∞――――

"Bethany. . . . Beth. Can you hear me?"

Josh had wandered for twenty minutes, not sure where to go or what to do. He dialed Alex as he continued to walk.

"Any word?" She answered.

"Nothing. Can you call a few people from the church and ask them to come over and help me search?"

"I already have. A half dozen or so are on their way, but the roads are near impassable. It will take a while."

"Thanks. . . ." Disappointment lodged in his gut.

"What else can I do?"

"Pray. Just pray."

"I'm already doing that." Her voice cracked. Not what Josh needed to hear right now. Alex was always the optimistic one in the group.

He hung up the phone and exhaled, his warm breath turning to steam. Guilt stabbed him in the chest. What if he was too late?

He had so many things to tell Beth. First, that he loved her but also that he would stand with her through the trials and the pain she had been facing alone.

*Oh, God. Please let me tell her I'm sorry for the words I said in anger.*

His throat now hurt from the constant shouting, but he kept it up.

"Bethany, where are you?" He drew out the words. "Hello . . . Bethany. Please answer me. I know you're—"

"Josh, I'm here!"

It was Beth. But where?

"Where are you?" He called to her, looked frantically around, and listened.

"Next to the old fence."

Buster barked, and he saw the little dog running toward him, shaking his nub of a tail. Josh grabbed him up and retraced the tracks he had left in the snow. Then he saw Beth curled up on the ground.

"Josh, honey." Her cries were a mixture of tears and relief.

He released the terrier and ran to his wife's side, wanting to grab her into his arms and hold her forever. He took her hand in his, trying to assist her in standing.

"No," she said. "I can't do it. My ankle is hurt, bad."

Josh looked around to get his bearings. They weren't far from the street behind them.

"Okay. I'll have Alex bring the car." He reached into his pocket for his cell phone. "Are you okay otherwise?"

"Cold," she said. Her face looked taut from the abuse of the freezing wind and chilling temperatures.

He took off his jacket and covered her with it. Then he called Alex to explain where they were. "Drive my Jeep," he said. "The keys are on the sofa table."

A few minutes later, Alex found them. Josh picked Beth up and carried her to the car. He helped her into the back seat and lifted Buster up beside her.

Beth clutched his jacket closer to her body. "The heat feels good."

Buster crawled closer to her and whined.

"You did a good job, Mr. B." Josh patted the little dog on the head.

"Well, actually it's his fault," Beth said. "But I forgive him. He stayed with me when I fell."

Josh put his arms around her shoulder. "I hope you can forgive me too."

"For what?"

"For everything. I've been a jerk lately."

Beth started to protest, but he stopped her.

"No. I want to say this now. I was so afraid I wouldn't have the chance." He swallowed hard. "I'm sorry for being so insensitive to you about the abortion. I'm glad you had the confidence in me to tell me about it. I'm just sorry I didn't have the maturity to handle it. I hope you will forgive me."

"Of course." She reached out to touch his face with her hand and shivered.

"We're going straight to the hospital," Josh told Alex as she slid into the driver's seat.

"No," Beth protested.

"I'm sorry," Josh insisted. "I'm not taking any chances. We'll drop Alex and Buster off at the house on the way."

———— ∞∞∞ ————

Beth was the first to notice Ben Abrams as they wheeled her from the emergency room triage.

"Hi, doctor," she said, embarrassed to see him.

"Baking cookies again, Bethany?"

She grinned. "No, sir. Chasing the dog this time."

He crossed his arms over his chest and smiled. "Mind if I take a look at you for good measure?"

"Not at all."

"We're glad you're here," Josh said. "I was concerned she might have set herself back. You know, with her dissected artery."

"It's doubtful," Dr. Abrams told him. "But you did the right thing, bringing her in."

**170**

After a thorough exam, he pronounced his patient to be in excellent condition, considering her circumstances. "Don't I see you again in the next few weeks?"

"Yes, I believe so," Bethany nodded.

"Great. We'll hope for a better scan this time."

# 28

**Present Day**

Beth wasn't sure if she could carry it off, but she was determined to cook Josh's favorite meal as a surprise for his thirtieth birthday. She had been banned from the kitchen since the green-apple fiasco, and she still walked with a slight limp from her sprained ankle a few weeks ago. But with a bit of advance assistance from Alex, she should be able to fry the meat and finish the rest of the meal on her own.

Cut-up pieces of chicken had been marinating in buttermilk since last night, just like Rose Harrison had taught Beth to do. Alex had peeled and cut up the potatoes and left them to soak in cold water in the refrigerator. Beth would cook and mash them this evening. That left only making biscuits, warming up corn, and stirring up gravy. Beth could stir up chicken gravy in her sleep. She had fixed it many times at her husband's request.

This afternoon, Alex was helping Beth prepare one of Josh's favorite desserts while he attended a meeting. His favorite Peanut Butter Pound Cake recipe had been passed down from his great-grandmother.

Alex shook her head in amazement. "I can't believe there are two sticks of butter in this recipe."

"We don't eat it every day." Beth teased her health-conscious neighbor. "Although . . . it does make a great breakfast snack."

Alex puckered her face.

"Wait until you see the recipe for chocolate sauce I serve with it."

"Great. More fat and sugar." Alex sighed and cracked a second egg into a mixing cup. "Can you make that on your own tonight?"

"I can if you will cut up the dark and milk chocolate bars for me."

"No problem. That takes less time than rushing you to the ER."

Beth mock-grimaced.

Alex placed the egg carton back in the fridge. "You're feeling better, aren't you?"

"I suppose I am. I have less pain. I think I'm acclimating to the medication too."

"That's good and bad news."

"I know. I can only hope I'll have the strength to get off this stuff when I'm healed."

"You will," Alex said. "You will. But it may take time."

———— ∞ ————

The look on Josh's face when he learned Beth had cooked for him made her extra effort worthwhile. The meal turned out just as she had planned, and so did her choice of gifts.

She had known better than to spend a lot of money so she put extra thought into her selection. She had found just the right thing while shopping at a craft store with Alex.

**173**

"It's great." Josh admired the simple, wood plaque that read: *Any man can be a father, but it takes someone special to be a daddy.*

"You'll be a perfect daddy," she told him. "I know, because you're a perfect husband."

Josh shook his head. "Not sure I deserve that. I've let you down in the past few months. I hope I don't do that again." He leaned over and kissed her on the cheek. "I just want you to be well."

"We'll get through this a day at a time," Beth said. She placed her chin in her hand and looked into his eyes. "Why didn't you tell me about your accounting problems on the road?"

Color drained from her husband's cheeks. "I didn't want to bother you with it. How did you find out?"

"Bob Bradford called to check on me this morning when you were out."

"Did he tell you how much money is missing?"

"Yes. Almost $50,000. That's a lot of money. What are you going to do?"

"I'm not sure yet." Josh ran his fingers through his thick, brown hair.

"Didn't you just hire that merchandise guy? Mitch something?"

"Mitch Raider. I'm not sure he's the problem."

"Who else could it be?"

Josh hesitated. "Ryan is his supervisor."

"You don't think—"

"I'm not jumping to conclusions. I need time to think it through. We're working on a plan to get to the bottom of it."

Josh's cell phone interrupted their conversation. He appeared to be puzzled by the caller ID. "It's Langston Wheeler from the record label." He punched the *on* button.

"Hey, man. What's up?" Josh asked, fiddling with the napkin in his lap, a blank expression on his face.

Beth watched her husband talk. She'd forgotten how handsome he was.

"Good. We're good. No, no problem. We've just finished supper." Josh winked at her.

*What a flirt.*

"The tour is going great." He drummed his fingers on the table.

Beth remembered why she had fallen in love with him. Even now, she could lose herself in his thick, Southern accent. It was a drawl that put Kentucky boys to shame.

"Okay, give me the good news first." Josh ran his fingers through his hair. "Really? No kidding? Man, that's great!" He stood and then paced back and forth while chatting with the record label executive.

Beth readjusted her position, trying to get comfortable.

"Thanks for letting me know," he said, and then remembering how Langston had begun the conversation, he asked, "So what's the bad news?"

A few seconds later, he laughed.

*What a great laugh he had.*

"Seriously? That's awesome." Josh stared into her eyes in anticipation of sharing his news. "Okay. Thanks, man. Thanks!"

He punched the end-call button and took a deep breath. "I've been nominated for three Noah Awards." A big smile spread across his face.

"Josh . . . that's wonderful!" She jumped up and hugged his neck. "God is so good."

"Yes. He is. Even to those of us who don't deserve it."

"You deserve it many times over." She kissed him on the cheek. "You've worked hard, and you're a good man. I'm proud of you." She settled back into her seat. "So what's the bad news?"

He sighed. "Langston said I didn't make the cut for female vocalist of the year."

"That's bad." She laughed. "Ouch! The baby kicked me!"

"Really?"

"Here." She placed his hand on her stomach.

He waited, staring into her eyes. "I feel it!"

"I love you, honey."

"I love you too," Josh bent toward her and placed his mouth on hers.

His kiss reassured her. All of the feelings she'd had on hold for the last few months returned. The fear and depression, the worries and the pain, now faded into the distant past.

She smiled, took him by the hand, and led him down the hallway to their bedroom.

---

The next day, Josh stared at the black and white tiles lining the hallway outside the CT scan room. The unlit "in use" light above the door reminded him of those that hung in a recording studio. While an important medical evaluation could never be compared to the process of recording, each had its own significance, as evidenced by the hundreds of letters he received each month from people who said their lives had been changed by his music.

While his work was far less critical than the doctor who would read Beth's scan results, a special lyric in a time of need could soften a heart or soothe a soul. He had heard once that all music was of God, but some had been modified to exalt man. Something about that made sense to him, and he took pride in the kind of music he wrote and sang. He had done his best to praise God with his tunes, with his life. Until recently, he had believed that he had succeeded.

A technician walked by, her sneakers screeching on freshly washed floors. It was just another workday for her. But it was a critical one for his wife. If Beth's artery didn't show improvement soon, she could be facing surgery.

Josh gazed down the long hallway that led to another part of the imaging facility. The tiles twisted around the corner, forming a new pattern where they shifted directions to places unknown.

The light over the scan room door began thumping. Off. On. The rhythm annoyed him. The simple pulse of it mocked his concern for what the machine might find.

About ten minutes later, the imaging room door opened and Beth walked out.

"How did it go?" He handed her the sweater he had been holding.

"She wouldn't say," Beth told him. "But I hope it's good news, so I can cut down on the narcotics."

<hr />

A week later Beth watched Alex remove a morphine patch from the package. She peeled off the protective strip and applied the patch to Beth's upper arm.

"All set," Alex said, before tossing the waste paper into a nearby trashcan. "I need to wash my hands. Make yourself comfortable and try to relax."

Beth stretched out on the bed, the warmth of it drawing her in. She'd had little energy since trying to step down her morphine last week, and her headaches had worsened. While she didn't want to renege on her promise to Josh to taper off the drugs, fear and doubt now pounded in her temple. Things had gone well the week of his birthday and, at first, her goal had seemed attainable. But she had become less enthusiastic as her symptoms multiplied. She'd battled serious bouts of depression, dizziness, and fatigue, and she couldn't stop sneezing.

But it was the pain that affected her the most.

Once in a while, when the pounding was relentless, or despair left her feeling out of control, she again wished that God had taken her to be with him that day in the ambulance. She had felt so free and at peace. Something she hadn't known since that time.

She could close her eyes and almost go back to that place now. Yet, the responsibilities of this life always called her back. She must fight for her child, if not for herself. This baby represented God's gift of a second chance in so many ways.

She had been blessed with a husband who loved her, provided for her, and shared her faith. For far too long she had lied to him. A sin of omission.

Beth had much more to tell him, when it was time. How she planned to make up for the sins in her life. How she loved him beyond comprehension. And how much she appreciated him standing by her through all of this.

But for now, especially with the fluctuation of narcotics in her system, it was impossible to express her feelings about anything related to the abortion. Thoughts tumbled in her head like children playing in a space ball: erratic and out of control.

Hopefully, one day, she would be able to talk about her experience, maybe even have a positive impact on other women—those who had chosen an abortion. Or those who could still be stopped from believing the lie . . . as she had done so long ago.

The nurse stepped into the room. "Bethany McKinney?"

Beth swallowed hard, looking around, scared once again. A calendar on the wall reminded her that Christmas wasn't far away. Her twentieth birthday wouldn't be far behind. *A birthday this child will never see.* Bethany squeezed her eyes shut for a second, pushing back the horrible reminder. She should have asked a friend to come with her. Encourage her. But this way, no one would know. The truth would never be revealed.

"Bethany?" This time, the nurse's voice was more tender. "Are you OK?"

She stood and straightened to her full five feet, six inches. Her parents had raised her to be independent, to think for herself. She could do this.

So what if they wouldn't agree with her decision? Besides, it wasn't really a pregnancy. At seven weeks, the fetus was only a cluster of cells, an inconvenient cluster of cells at that.

That's what the counselor had said.

She had reminded Beth that it was a woman's right to do what was best for her. To plan her own life. To have children when it was time.

Beth wanted a career first and a family later. Everything had to come in the right order. First comes love. Then comes marriage.

Whatever. She was long past childish nursery rhymes and childlike guilt.

Besides, this was better for the baby.

Children need a good start in life. Two parents. A stable home.

Of course, she was doing the right thing.

"Yes," she said firmly. "I'm ready." She sucked in her breath and followed the nurse into a sterile hallway, pulling the door closed behind her. No more indecision.

She was ready to get this done and move on.

The sound of Josh's voice roused Beth from her lifelike dream. She sat up and looked around the room. Why was he here? Panic set in. Something must be wrong. Josh should be on the road.

Then she heard music. Followed by static.

It was the radio. Alex must have turned it on, tuning in to her favorite Christian music station.

Josh's new song, *Listen to Me*, was playing.

> Listen, O Lord, to my cries for mercy
> As David prayed so long ago
> Listen, O Lord, to my call for freedom
> From my sin that only you can know
> Listen, O Lord, to my plea for forgiveness
> That only you can bestow
>
> I worship you for all your greatness
> And thank you for your promises given
> You keep your word forever and ever
> And send your Son to heal our nation
> Then you bless, restore, and heal my soul

Beth pulled the covers closer to her shivering body. *Thank you, Lord, for your promises. And for putting this man in my life.*

"Here you go." Alex set a steaming cup of milk in front of Beth.

"That smells delicious. Thanks."

"I made it with rose syrup."

Beth picked up the sturdy mug and took a sip of the aromatic liquid. "It smells like a rose garden. You didn't . . ." She thought back to the beautiful floribunda bushes in Alex's backyard last summer.

Alex grinned. "No. I didn't make the syrup from my personal stock of petals. But it's easy to do, if you ever want to try it. It's just organic sugar, water, and rose petals steeped together."

"I'll put that on my to-do list," Beth said. "Right after finding a cure for the common cold and achieving world peace. Maybe I should figure a way off these drugs too," she scowled. She'd had to go back to her original dose of morphine yesterday.

"You'll get there, sweetie. Your body just wasn't ready. No one expects you to tolerate the pain."

"Thanks." Beth forced a smile. Alex always reassured her, always calmed her frazzled nerves. She fiddled with the handle of the mug. "I need to tell you something."

"What?" Alex settled back onto the bench opposite Beth, taking a sip of hot tea.

"I've been carrying a load of guilt around, and I need to share."

"I'll help if I can," Alex said.

Beth studied her friend's face and gathered her words. There was no easy way to say it. "I had an abortion when I was nineteen."

Alex's expression didn't change so Beth continued.

"I was caught up in the party crowd, away from home for the first time. And I was in a meaningless relationship." She clasped her hands and placed them on the table to keep them from shaking. "Neither he nor I wanted the responsibility of a baby."

Tears began to flow at the realization that she had not wanted her own child. *God, how could you ever forgive me?*

Alex started to say something, but Beth held up her hand. "No, please, let me continue. This is difficult." She swallowed the lump in her throat and brushed away a tear.

Alex waited quietly.

"I can't believe what I just said. It's something I've needed to admit to myself for a long time." She blotted more tears. "I turned on my own flesh and blood because I wanted an easier life for myself. I didn't want to accept the consequences for my actions. Or, for that matter, the blessing of life that God had given me—"

"God forgives," Alex said softly.

"I know. I just have to forgive myself."

Her caregiver handed her a napkin, and Beth wiped her eyes.

"Every year I think about how old he or she would be. Sometimes, when I look out in our backyard, I can imagine this beautiful child running and . . . " Tracks of sadness trickled down Beth's cheeks. "If only . . . "

"Bethany, you can't think about the if onlys. You have to think about today, and today only. God has given you another child—"

"That's what I'm worried about." Beth's tears returned. "I'm afraid he will punish me by taking this baby away." She wrapped her arms around her stomach and embraced the child inside her womb, the child who had just recently begun to show, despite her maternity clothes.

Alex remained silent. Beth feared it was because she agreed with her assertion.

After a long silence, Alex spoke. "Our God is a God of mercy. He takes no satisfaction in punishing his children. Instead he delights in giving life to those who repent."

Beth stared at her hands, which were clutched together on the tabletop.

"This baby is a sign of God's blessing not his punishment." Alex reached across the table and covered Beth's hands with her own. "Let's thank him."

They bowed their heads, and Alex prayed.

Beth awoke from a sound sleep that night, the bed wet beneath her. She turned over to scan the clock. Blurry numbers read 3:06 a.m. It took her a minute to remember that Josh wasn't home. He wouldn't return until Tuesday morning.

She reached toward the bedside table to switch on the light. Stretching toward the lamp provoked a dull pain in her lower abdomen, almost a cramping. Something didn't feel right. She threw back the covers and stumbled out of bed. Fear and nausea rushed through her when she saw the red stain of blood on the bedsheets.

"Alex!" she screamed and ran into the bathroom.

Within a few seconds, Alex stood by her side. "What's wrong?"

"I'm bleeding." Beth said, her body quaking with fear. "Look at the bedsheets."

"Try to relax. I'll call an ambulance."

"No. Just drive me there." Beth grabbed her robe.

# 29

**Present Day**

The emergency room nurse sat down next to Beth while making notes on a chart. "How far along are you?"

"Twenty-four weeks. I'm due in June." Beth reminded herself to breathe.

"Have you ever had a miscarriage?"

"No."

*Please, God.*

"Any family history of miscarriage?"

"None."

"Have you ever had an abortion or multiple abortions?"

Beth glanced at Alex, who sat in the chair in the corner of the exam room, and then back to the nurse. "One. In 2002."

The nurse never looked up. "Only one?"

"Yes, ma'am." Beth fought back tears.

"Do you know what kind of procedure you had?"

"I believe it was called an aspiration."

"Any complications?"

"I don't think so."

"Good." The nurse patted Beth on the arm and offered a reassuring smile. "Try to relax. We're only being cautious.

Some abortion procedures can leave damage, which may cause an unstable pregnancy later."

Beth's stomach churned. She braced herself, knowing she couldn't hold back. She threw up all over the floor. The nurse grabbed a basin from the cabinet and held it for her.

"Miss." The nurse called to Alex. "Can you hold this for your friend? I'll be right back. I'll order medicine."

Alex rushed to Beth's bedside, taking the small plastic bowl and holding it. "Try to relax, Mama. God will get you and your baby through this."

"No," Beth told her. "I'm being punished for my past sins."

❦

"Bethany, are you feeling better?"

She opened her eyes to see Dr. Myers standing beside her.

"What are you doing here?"

"I was on call. You picked a good night." Her doctor offered a reassuring smile.

Beth grabbed her doctor's hand. "I'm scared."

"Hey, relax, kiddo. This may not be so bad. Your bleeding appears to have stopped. I want to do a physical exam, and then we'll run an ultrasound to check on the baby."

About an hour later, after the exam, the doctor questioned Beth about her physical activities during the past twenty-four hours. She scribbled notes on her chart and then took a seat on the stool beside the bed.

"Your bleeding may very well be normal. A sizable number of women deal with it during their first or second trimester. I didn't see any abnormal dilation, although I'm a bit concerned about the amount of blood you say you lost. I want to keep you in the hospital for a day or two as a precaution. However, if your ultrasound looks okay, there's no reason you can't go

**185**

home after that." Dr. Myers gestured toward Alex. "Is this a friend?"

"Yes. Alex. She's helping me while my husband is out of town."

Alex nodded her acknowledgment.

"I'm glad you're here," the doctor said to her. "Will you be able to stay with Bethany for a few days? She'll need bed rest for a while after returning home."

"Absolutely. Whatever is needed."

"Great." Dr. Myers said in her always-upbeat manner. The she turned back to Beth. "So, when does your husband return?"

"Next Monday. Then he'll be leaving again on Thursday."

"I'm not sure how you two found time to make this baby," Dr. Myers teased.

Beth blushed and grinned, while the other two women laughed.

<hr/>

The following afternoon, after an encouraging ultrasound report, Beth waited to be discharged. Alex had just arrived to take her home when Dr. Abrams walked into the room.

"Well, look who's here. Do you have no other friends, or do you just like to visit us?"

The doctor startled Alex, who had been tending to Beth's dinner tray when he entered the room. She turned and ran straight into him, spilling the contents of the Beth's unfinished plate onto the doctor's crisp white coat.

Alex's face turned as red as the pickled beets Dr. Abrams now wore.

"Oh, I'm so sorry," Alex said.

Dr. Abrams studied her for a few seconds and then grinned. "Bethany, please tell me this beautiful woman is not your caregiver. If so, I'm a bit worried about your life."

He winked at Beth.

She smiled, enjoying a side of Dr. Abrams she had never seen. A much more human side.

Alex blushed again and shoved a lock of thick, red hair behind her ear.

Beth noticed that her doctor and her friend couldn't stop staring at each other.

"Dr. Abrams, this is Alex Hayes. She's my caregiver. And she's very good at—"

"Ben Abrams. Nice to meet you." The doctor extended his hand, ignoring the remainder of Beth's comment.

Alex wiped her right hand on her jeans and reciprocated. "Likewise. But I'm sorry about the beets." She grabbed a towel from the vanity to blot his jacket.

"I don't think a towel, or water for that matter, will help this too much." Ben Abrams blue eyes sparkled. "Don't worry about it. I keep a change of clothes in my office."

"Okay." Alex gave Beth a sideways glance. "Would you please excuse me? I should probably step out of the room and let the two of you talk." She offered another smile to Dr. Abrams before turning toward the exit.

"Miss—"

"Please, call me Alex. Short for Alexandra."

"Alexandra. Lovely name." The doctor paused to reach into his pocket. "Here's my card."

The freckles on Alex's face danced when she took the card from him.

"Please call me if you have any questions about Bethany's care."

"I will." Alex backed out of the room and closed the door behind her.

The doctor adjusted his coat and his composure, refocusing his attention on Beth and stepping closer to the bed. "So what brings you here?"

Beth sobered at the reminder of her situation. "Bleeding. I was afraid I was having a miscarriage."

"Is everything okay now?"

"I think so. Dr. Myers says the baby is fine but that I need to be on bed rest for a week or two after I get home. Later today . . . I'm going home today."

"How are your headaches?"

"They come and go. Maybe a bit better overall."

"Don't I have you scheduled for an office visit soon?"

"Yes, sir. It's next week."

"Great." He smiled. "Call me if you need anything in the meantime. Okay?"

"I will. Thank you, Dr. Abrams."

He placed his hand on her arm. "Feel better."

---

Josh's timing had been off all night. He couldn't stop thinking about Beth's hospitalization. It was impossible to shake the fear that his own selfish desires had contributed to his wife's current situation—and just when things seemed to be going better.

Their time together had sparked the hope that life had returned to normal. Or would soon. But, with a new crisis at hand, the same nagging doubts plagued him. His baby's life continued to hang in the balance, and Beth's latest scan had shown no improvement.

He had to remind himself that whatever happened would be God's will. Yet that phrase no longer comforted him. How strong did he have to be? How much did he have to be tested, to endure, before God moved in his favor? The spiritual struggles of Job came to mind. Unfortunately, so did his father's failed attempt at reconciling his wife's—Josh's mother's—death. The latter scared him the most. Would he follow in his father's footsteps?

"Thank you for coming tonight," he told the sold-out audience as he stepped up to the microphone. "God bless you all for being here. You are in for a special evening with R. O. S. and Fast Train to Glory coming up soon."

The audience applauded. Their clapping echoed across the multithousand-square-feet building. A sound that used to stir him. He had once felt at home in this situation, but now he felt inadequate to minister.

He was tired, and he feared that neither his faith nor his music had the edge required to motivate others. He needed motivation of his own.

Although most people chose not to admit it, showmanship was as important in Christian music as it was in secular. What set them apart was the reason they performed.

All musicians shared a love for music. But secular acts went onstage each night for personal gratification. Christian musicians performed to draw attention to God. Or at least that was the way it should be.

By Josh's standards, he had violated his own tenet for the past several months, and the very thought of that shamed him. He was not the person he professed to be on stage each night. The spotlight hid more than it revealed. The brightly colored lights masked the jester inside a costume of faith.

He longed for the days before life had become so complicated. But the show must go on, and he kicked into automatic gear.

"Let's worship!" He shouted to the crowd. "He has come. . . ."

Thirty minutes later, Josh walked offstage.

"Good set." Andrew Slaughter of R. O. S., an acronym for Rock of Salvation, slapped him on the shoulder.

"Right."

"What's wrong, man? You sounded great out there."

"Thanks." Josh knuckle tapped his fellow musician.

Maybe he was fooling everyone else, but he wasn't fooling himself.

# 30

Ben Abrams secured his helmet and mounted his Lynskey titanium road bicycle. It was his second excursion since the arrival of his new, custom-made bike from the manufacturer in Chattanooga. The crisp March air reminded him of his childhood.

Even though he no longer raced, cycling had been a lifelong pastime. Riding on a road of glass allowed him to see through his problems in life. And, as he had always said, he could ride faster than his troubles could chase him.

This new bike was lightweight and lightning fast. He couldn't have dreamed of such a high-performance ride when he was a boy growing up. Modern technology had changed the cycling experience. Of course, this bike had cost a thousandfold more than what he had paid for his first Schwinn Manta Ray. Thinking about it always reminded him of his grandmother.

His fingers stung beneath his leather riding gloves when he thought about those days. He'd come a long way in his life. He could only hope his family would have been proud.

But for now, he had little time to spare for such sentiment with afternoon office appointments beginning at one o'clock. He hopped on his mount and steered toward River Road, one of his favorite places to ride. The picturesque hills and curves that snaked for miles along the Cumberland River bottom would help free his mind and calm his spirit. The adrenaline rush from the workout would anesthetize the pain of his emptiness.

Alex pulled her yellow Volkswagen Beetle to a stop in front of Dr. Abrams's office. "Are you sure you're okay going in by yourself?"

"I'm fine." Beth eased out of the car and steadied herself. Although shaky, she was determined to show some independence.

"I'll meet you in the waiting room after I find a parking place," Alex said before driving away.

Taking the elevator to the top floor of the building, Beth located the doctor's office and stepped inside. After signing in, she took a seat in the corner of the waiting room.

Magazines were stacked neatly on the mahogany table next to her chair. She shuffled through the medical and horticultural periodicals. Odd combination. Nothing interested her except the one question burning on her mind. Would her scan show healing this time?

She focused on deep breaths to calm her anxiety and looked around the room. It reminded her of photos she had seen of handsome English libraries or exquisitely decorated bachelor dens. Sienna-colored carpet had been paired with sage-colored grass cloth above and below the mahogany chair rail. The muted tones blended tastefully with the brown leather

KATHY HARRIS

192

chairs scattered throughout the room. The understated decor reeked of masculinity with the exception of the extravagant tassels at the end of the gold rope, which restrained brown, gold, and sage paisley-patterned draperies. Beth smiled to herself as she pictured Dr. Abrams giving in to a decorator on that final point. Doctor meets decorator design.

"Bethany." Dr. Abrams's assistant, Rena, snapped Beth back to reality.

Rena was staid, yet pleasant, just like the nondescript surroundings of the doctor's office. Judging from the casual ease with which she went about her duties, Beth guessed she had worked with Dr. Abrams for a number of years.

She wore burnt-orange trousers topped with a white lab coat. Her dark brown hair, which was swept back into a tight French twist, reminded Beth of a character from a vintage movie.

After doing a short physical exam, Rena led Beth to Dr. Abrams's private office, where more mahogany furniture awaited.

"Dr. Abrams will be with you shortly," the physician's assistant said and then disappeared down the hall.

Beth settled into a wing chair, which sat opposite of the doctor's massive desk. The room hadn't changed since the last time she had been here with Josh. She noticed that the paisley draperies, like those from the foyer windows, hung sans rope and tassels. Apparently the doctor had set his limits.

Medical books lay scattered on the desk and filled the bookshelves that lined the interior walls. Beth found the lack of personal artifacts in the room curious. There wasn't so much as a photo of an Irish setter to hint of the doctor's personal life.

A New York bike-a-thon poster, framed and hung on the window wall, was perhaps the most telling clue that he existed outside of his work. Framed diagrams of the human brain and medical diplomas from Vanderbilt and Columbia Universities were scattered among other certifications and awards. He appeared to be a well-educated and respected physician.

Beth trusted Dr. Abrams with her life. He had been the first doctor to reassure her after her initial trip to the emergency room in October. She had subsequently seen glimpses of a charming personality underneath the hardened shell of professional detachment.

"Good morning, Bethany," Dr. Abrams said, as he strolled into his office carrying a large manila envelope. "Let's hope for significant improvement."

He walked straight to the viewer on the wall behind his desk and placed the film into it.

Beth waited, hoping for good news.

After a minute or two, he finally turned to her. "These results show promise. Your dissection shows a slight reduction."

"That's wonderful," she exhaled audibly.

He switched off the light and took a seat at his desk. "How are you feeling?"

"My pain comes and goes."

"Any mood swings?"

Beth felt heat rise to her cheeks. "I'm all over the place, I'm afraid. I often wonder how my husband can stand me."

"Don't be too hard on yourself. You're not entirely responsible. Your medications are likely contributing to that."

"I tried to wean myself off the morphine a few weeks ago . . . and I couldn't," Beth admitted, hoping the doctor wouldn't scold her.

Dr. Abrams's blue eyes pierced her. "It's too soon. Please, don't do that again without consulting me."

"I'm just—"

"You need those medications right now," the doctor frowned. "We'll get you off them soon enough."

"I wish Josh could hear you say that. I'm afraid he thinks I'll never get off this stuff. He's worried that his wife will be a drug addict for the rest of her life."

Beth stared at a speck of lint on her black pants. Brushing it off, she continued. "I hope he's not right."

"It's not easy, but I have confidence you'll make it." The doctor leaned closer to her. "You seem to be a determined young woman with a strong faith." His expression softened. "I admire your tenacity in keeping the baby. Perhaps I shouldn't have been so quick to recommend against that in the beginning. You appear to be doing well."

Beth was certain she was blushing now. Having the confidence of Dr. Abrams uplifted her more than anything that had happened to her in a while. "Thank you. That means a lot, Dr. Abrams. The strength didn't come from me. It comes from my Christian beliefs."

"Whatever it takes." The doctor placed her film back into its envelope.

"Are you a Christian?" Beth asked.

Her physician raised an eyebrow. "An agnostic Jew."

"I guess I shouldn't have asked that. Sorry, I didn't mean to pry."

This time a slight blush colored the doctor's smooth, olive complexion.

"No worries. Religion isn't something I wear on my sleeve. I'll walk you to the foyer."

He scribbled a few notes on a sheet of paper, stood, and handed it to Beth. "Please give this to Debbie at the front desk. Let's do another scan in six weeks. Maybe we'll see enough improvement to completely discount surgery." He looked at her. "When are you due?"

"Ten more weeks."

"I'll stay in touch with Dr. Myers." He walked with her toward the door. "We don't want to risk you going into labor until your dissection is completely healed."

"I'll keep praying, Dr. Abrams."

When he opened the foyer door, Alex was sitting within view, and Beth noticed a change in his posture. "I'll see you in six weeks," he told Beth. Then he walked across the room to stand in front of Alex. "Nice to see you."

"You as well," she said.

They continued their conversation while Beth paid her account. Neither seemed to notice her as she approached. "I need to step out to the ladies' room," Beth mouthed to Alex, who responded with a slight nod.

Beth left through the front door and slipped down the hall. When she returned, Alex was sitting alone.

"Soooooooo?"

Alex walked over to her, and they hurried out to the hall-way, stifling their excitement like two giggling schoolgirls.

"He asked for my phone number."

# 31

Isaac. Isaac Ruben. Is that you?"

The familiarity of the voice, rather than the significance of the words, caught Ben's attention as he walked along the shade tree campus of Vanderbilt University. Fully assimilated, those two words brought back memories he had avoided for a long time.

Ben turned to the source of the voice. No one in Nashville knew him by that name. Who could it be?

"Isaac. It's Wade Martin." The stranger extended his hand and when Ben offered his own the sandy-haired man shook it vigorously.

"I don't—"

"Wade. From Columbia. Remember our statistics classes?"

Of course, how could he forget the most difficult course of his college career? Or the student who had helped him through it. "Wade! What are you doing in Nashville?"

"Been here about a year. Decided to try my hand in the music business." Martin laughed. "And, I emphasize the latter. *Business*. I'm not a singer. I'm an accountant."

Ben smiled at the thought of his old friend singing for a living. Martin's voice screeched and hawed through spoken words like a young child trying to learn the violin. "It's good to see you."

"What are you doing here, Isaac?"

"I'm finishing up my internship at Vanderbilt. Only three months to go. Can't you tell by the bags under my eyes?" He laughed.

Martin slapped him on the arm. "You look the same to me. I'm sure you're doing a great job. You were always ahead of the class in the medical sciences. I assume you specialized in neurology?"

Ben nodded. "Yes, still enjoying it."

"Hey, call me sometime. I'd love to have dinner when things quiet down for you. Are you in the book?"

"Yes. Yes. Let's get together. I'm living in an apartment in Belle Meade, and I'm listed under Abrams. Ben Abrams. I took my family name when I moved here."

"Will do. Good to see you."

# 32

## Present Day

Beth watched Alex maneuver her small car into a tight space beneath the cover of the Green Hills Mall parking garage. Water streamed down the windshield. Heavy rain had pelted them since they left home almost an hour ago, for what should have been a thirty-minute journey.

"I'm glad you're driving." Beth relaxed into her seat. "That was a trip."

"No problem. I deliver in rain, sleet, or snow." Alex grinned and switched off the ignition. "Besides, it's not every day I can help a friend pick out a Noah award gown."

"Especially a friend who is seven months pregnant." Beth rubbed her rounded tummy and smiled. "Isn't it fun?"

"You and Josh deserve this break. You've had a rough few months."

"I'm excited for him." Beth said. "His face brightens when he talks about the awards." She searched her bag for lip gloss. "It's about the only thing that makes him smile right now."

"You and the baby do too."

"Sure, when he's not letting himself be wound up in worry."

"Out of concern for your health?"

"Yes." Beth rolled the peach-flavored gel across her lips. "He's having problems on the road right now too. But he won't talk to me about it." She threw the tube of gloss back into her purse.

Alex studied her. "I'm no relationship expert. Hey, look at me, I'm a single woman." She blushed. "But it's better to get things out in the open."

"He's trying to deal with them on his own. You know, save me the stress." Beth focused on the massive concrete ballasts that supported the walls of the multilevel parking garage.

"Sharing cuts our worries in half," Alex said. "That includes you too. You need to be talking to someone, getting your fears out in the open. They have a way of growing when you keep them inside."

Beth turned to her friend. "You always make me feel better. I don't know what I would do without you."

"I hope so." Alex reached for the car door.

Beth touched her lightly on the shoulder. "I need to ask for your forgiveness."

"For what?"

"For my moods. My temper tantrums. I've been grumpy and unrealistic . . . and I'm sorry—"

"You're too hard on yourself, girlfriend," Alex said. "You've been through a lot. I'm not sure I could have handled everything as well as you have."

"Thanks, but you're being generous."

"Come on, let's go shopping." Alex said, before turning to exit the vehicle.

Beth hoisted her awkward body out of the passenger seat and straightened her rumpled blouse while she caught her breath. Carrying around twenty extra pounds wasn't easy.

"Where do we go first?" Alex asked.

"Let's start on the far side of the mall and work our way back." A mischievous smile spread across Beth's face.

"Like you can stay on your feet that long."

"I can do anything for shopping," Beth laughed.

"Okay. But, remember, you promised me lunch if I'm a good helper today." Alex placed a hand on her slender waist and sighed. "As if I need it."

"You're such a rail. I was never that thin, even before I was pregnant."

Her friend grinned. "I've always been able to eat anything I want, as long as I don't want too much." She grabbed Beth's arm. "Let's go shopping, Mama."

Two hours later, Beth had narrowed her search to two dresses. Her favorite was an emerald-green, one-shoulder, satin floor-length gown. But she also liked a salmon-colored, mid-calf-length cocktail dress, which would be more practical.

"What do you think?" she asked Alex while modeling the shorter dress.

"They both look great on you. You should buy the one that makes you feel comfortable."

"I love the green one, but I could probably get more use from the cocktail dress."

"How many times in your life will you wear a maternity cocktail gown?"

"A good point." Beth gathered the floor length gown into her arms. "I'll take this one."

After a stop in the Dillard's shoe department for matching flats, they returned to the car with Alex carrying Beth's bags. "So, what do you know about that doctor of yours?"

"Dr. Myers?"

"No, silly. Dr. Abrams." Alex opened the heavy mall door and held it for Beth.

"I don't know much at all. Rather mysterious. And he's kind of a serious person."

"Seriously good looking."

Beth grinned. "And seriously flirting with you the other day in his office."

"Do you think he'll call me?"

"Definitely." Beth had never seen her friend so insecure, almost childlike.

"Anytime you need me to take you to his office again, don't hesitate to ask." Alex's face flushed tinges of red as she clicked the door locks on the Beetle.

They stowed their shopping treasures in the trunk and settled into the car.

"Speaking of Dr. Abrams, I need your help with something."

"Sure." Alex glanced at Beth before putting the car into gear.

"I've been praying for God to help me get off these drugs before the baby is born." Beth took a deep breath. "I have a feeling he is telling me to try it."

"You've tried that once," Alex cautioned. "You weren't ready."

Beth stared into the distance. "Not right now. I want to wait until Josh leaves for the road, after the awards show next week. That will give my artery more time to heal. The results from my scan last time were encouraging. The tear is closing."

"You're not going to do anything without talking to Dr. Abrams, are you?"

"Not exactly. He told me I might be able to wean myself off the drugs soon." Beth fudged on the timeframe.

"I don't know."

"Please, help me. I feel so guilty taking the medicine while I'm carrying this baby."

Alex shook her head. "I just don't feel comfortable—"

"Please." Beth pleaded. "I need you to stay with me. Night and day, hour by hour, for at least two weeks until I can get through the worst of it. Dr. Abrams told me it would be hard. Probably the hardest thing I have ever done. But I know I can do it. God wants me to have a healthy baby." Tears trickled down her cheeks. "Or at least I hope he does."

Alex stopped at a red light and turned to her. "You know I'll help you. I have all the confidence in the world in your ability to get through it, and in God's plan to give you a healthy child. But let's pray about it."

"Thanks," Beth said. "I appreciate your help, and your prayers, more than you will ever know. God has brought me this far, and I'm confident he will get me through."

Alex pulled into the parking lot of a quaint little restaurant in the Vanderbilt area. "Is this okay?"

"Works for me. I'm starving." Beth opened the car door, and then turned back to her caregiver. "Remember, it's our little secret."

Alex nodded.

Once inside, they were immersed in conversation and enjoying large glasses of iced tea when Alex's cell phone rang. She checked the caller ID before answering. "*Restricted.* Probably a telemarketer." She punched the call button on the phone and answered.

Beth watched a smile spread across her friend's face.

"Hi, doctor, I mean Ben. Nice to hear from you. . . ."

Alex opened her mouth in a mock scream, while listening intently to the voice on the other end of the phone.

"I'd love to. What time? Yes, great place. I'll meet you there at one o'clock."

She clicked off the phone.

"That was your doctor asking me to lunch next Saturday!"

# 33

## Noah Awards Night

You look beautiful tonight," Josh glanced at his wife, who was sitting in the passenger seat of his Jeep as he drove toward downtown Nashville.

She smiled the little-girl smile he hadn't seen in a while. For months now, he had missed the happy-go-lucky woman he had married less than two years ago.

"Thanks, honey. I wanted you to be proud of me. I'm proud of you."

Josh extended his right arm across the console, and she placed her small hand inside his. Silence filled the empty space between them. Not the chilly void that had separated them for weeks, but unspoken contentment only lovers shared.

Incandescent blue streetlights near the Cumberland River softened the near-twilight sky above. Further ahead, amber lights that surrounded Courthouse Square provided an ambience, which warmed, almost caressed, the concrete cityscape.

Depending on nature's mood, April in Middle Tennessee could be fraught with winter or encouraged by spring. Splotches of color and earth tones now shared the landscape.

The optimism of this time of year, when dormant vegetation broke free from the bare earth, could be contagious.

"We're going to make it through this," Josh said, while changing lanes to turn left onto Fourth Street.

"I know," his wife whispered.

A few minutes later, the Bridgestone Arena came into view. The structure, which had been completed more than a decade before, fit comfortably within its surroundings on Lower Broadway. The building, with its saucer-shaped roof, sprung like a mushroom from the midst of the city, between the old Ryman Auditorium and the new Schermerhorn symphony hall. A tower of light jutted skyward from the front entrance of the steel and concrete façade.

He and Beth would be entering from the rear of the hall, so he took a right onto Sixth Avenue, then steered his green SUV onto the ramp that led into the arena's underbelly. Performers on the show enjoyed the perk of private parking under roof.

A somber security guard stopped them at the foot of the ramp. Once cleared, he told Josh where to park. They took a place on the back wall, near the entrance.

Stacy Powers, the publicist for Glory Records, greeted them as Josh was helping Beth from the vehicle. She spoke first to Beth. "Great to see you. How are you feeling?"

"Clumsy at times," Beth laughed. "But I'm making it."

"We've all been praying for you." Stacy hugged Beth and then turned to Josh. "Are you ready to do lots of press?"

"Sure. Lead the way." He grabbed his guitar.

They walked through the parking facility to a blue door, which led into the main backstage area. A long corridor in front of them snaked into the distance.

Stacy pointed to an alcove along the concrete block wall. "Josh, if you'll wait right here, I'll make sure everything is set."

—◆◆◆—

Panic threatened to ambush Beth. Her throat tightened, and she fought claustrophobia that had been set off by the hustle and bustle around her. She had attended few social occasions in the past seven months. None where circumstances had been so intimidating.

She leaned against the concrete wall behind her, taking comfort in its cool surface. A tall, middle-aged man wearing a business suit approached Josh.

"Phil! Nice to see you." Josh shook the stranger's hand and then introduced him to Beth.

"Beth, this is Phillip Crandall, my new label mate at Glory Records." Then turning to Crandall, "Phil, my wife, Beth."

"Your husband has been an inspiration to me." The man's boyish grin stretched from ear to ear when he shook her hand.

"Are you performing tonight?" Beth asked.

"No, just here to learn the ropes. I come from the ministry side of the business. This is all new to me." He stretched his arms wide and looked around.

Josh patted him on the back. "You'll do just fine. I've heard your music, man. Good stuff."

A few minutes into their conversation, Beth noticed Stacy Powers waving to Josh from a crowd of people. Beth nudged him, nodding toward the publicist. "I think you're needed," she said.

"Would you both excuse me for a minute?" Josh planted a kiss on Beth's cheek and suggested she wait for him in the artists' dressing room down the hall.

"Looks like I've been jilted at the altar." She laughed, already feeling somewhat comfortable with Crandall. "I have no idea where to find the dressing room."

"I can show you," Crandall said.

"Thank you. I'd love to sit down."

He glanced tentatively at her stomach. "When are you due? Is this your first?"

Beth felt the heat rise to her face.

"Sorry, I don't know when to shut up. That was personal, and I just met you."

"It's no problem," she laughed.

He offered his arm and escorted her toward the dressing room.

"You'll love being a parent. I have two," he said. "After we sit down, I'll bore you with photos."

Beth grinned. "That sounds great."

About thirty yards down the hallway, they stopped. Beth saw a handmade sign taped to the dressing room door. It read *Artists Only*.

"Is it okay for me to go inside?" She took a step backward.

"Absolutely. They're just warning the paparazzi to stay out." Crandall opened the door for her. "Isn't that what they're called?"

"I think so." Beth laughed, finding herself enjoying the man's company. "This is my first time at the Noah Awards. Thanks for taking me under your wing."

"It's a case of the blind leading the blind," he said, holding the door. "Like I said before, I'm just a minister. I'm still learning about the music business."

After stepping inside, Beth took a seat in one of the over-stuffed chairs that lined the wall of the room. "Minister, as in divinity school?" she asked.

"Yes. I majored in music in college and then attended seminary. I pastored a small church for a while, but it was my music that seemed to touch people. I sidestepped into a youth pastor role, and we started a coffee house. Everything began happening from there."

"How exciting."

"We built a recording studio to encourage young people in the church, and . . ." He blushed. "I'm sorry, too much information."

"No, it's fascinating." She clutched her stomach and took a deep breath. "Ouch!"

"Are you okay?"

"Just a swift kick. I'm expecting a soccer player."

They both laughed.

"When are you due?"

"In June."

"Is everything okay?"

"Why would you ask that?"

"I don't know. I'm getting the strongest impression that I need to pray for you."

Beth stared at him.

"Do you mind?" Crandall's cheeks colored slightly.

"No, of course not."

"Is it okay if I lay a hand on you while I pray?" He walked to her chair, and his hand hovered over her wrist.

"Sure." The compassion in his blue eyes almost brought tears to hers.

"Lord, I've just met Bethany. We don't know much about each other, but you know her, and you know her needs. I ask you to provide them and to bless her."

He took a long breath and continued. "Bless my friend Josh, and especially their new family member. One who, as you reveal in Psalm 139, you've already known, since before conception. You've seen his or her face, Lord, even before we will be blessed to do so. . . ."

Tears streamed down Beth's face. The words soothed her like none she had heard since October. The idea that God knew her child—had seen his or her face—filled her to overflowing with joy. *But how much did this Crandall guy know about her?*

In a flash, the face of a child appeared in her mind's eye. His face was perfectly formed. Beth's heart raced. Was this the child she carried?

Or could this be the child she had aborted?

A chill ran up and down her spine. She shifted her hand from beneath the gentle touch of Phillip Crandall, who was still praying, and pulled her shawl closer around her shoulders.

Crandall continued to pray, asking for God's protection over Beth and Josh. "Close the gap, Lord. Between heaven and earth. Between our failures and our forgiveness. Between our prayers and your mercy. And between what you want for us and what the adversary tries to destroy."

He lingered between each request.

"Thank you, Father. Amen."

Phillip opened his eyes and looked into hers. They both had tears.

"God is so good," he said. "I believe he has a special blessing for you and your child."

"Thank you." Beth wiped her eyes and smiled. "All children are a blessing. I wish I had understood that a few years ago."

---

Josh cupped his arm lightly around his wife's waist as Stacy Powers led them through a dark, backstage tunnel and onto the main floor of the arena. They were one of the last couples to be seated before the opening music.

Cameramen dressed in all black hugged the sidewalls of the hall, ready to be called into action. A giant jib arm, which was controlled by an operator seated on the main floor, hovered over the front row of the audience. It would soon swoop in for a close up of well-known Contemporary Christian diva, Drew Harlan, who stood idly on stage smiling and waving at people she knew in the audience.

Less than a minute after they were settled into their seats, Harlan stepped to the podium to welcome everyone and begin the show, which would be broadcast live from coast to coast. She wasted no time in introducing the first performers, a girl band known as the Angells.

Josh watched dry ice filter out into the first few rows of seats, not quite reaching row six, where he and Beth sat.

The girls rocked the house. Audience members clapped and swayed to the music. And the first award, for songwriter of the year, went to Peter Thomas, a cowriter with Josh on his single "He Has Come."

"Way to go, man," Josh shouted when Thomas walked past him en route to the stage to accept his award. His friend smiled and nodded. A cameraman caught the action.

"That's great." Beth leaned into him after the cameraman turned away. She placed her small hand in his. "A good sign for you."

He reached into his left jacket pocket and fumbled for the folded piece of paper that held his acceptance speech. He had hardly imagined winning, but of course, he had prepared in case.

The applause died down.

"First," Thomas said, "I want to thank the Lord. He is the author and finisher of my faith and my songs." Applause. "And thank you to my wife, Victoria, and my family." He blew a kiss into the audience and smiled.

Josh glanced to Victoria Thomas. She sat smiling, with a tissue in her hand, in the row behind and to the left of him.

Thomas continued. "Thank you to the artists who have recorded my songs this year, and to my cowriters on various projects, Martin Williams, Wally Conway, and Josh Harrison, who helped give wings to my words." He scanned the audience trying to pick out each man as he mentioned him, finally setting his glance on Josh. "Special thanks to Josh Harrison. Your incredible witness to me has been an inspiration."

With that, Thomas waved his award in the air, smiled, and exited stage right.

"He mentioned you! That was so nice!" Beth said, bouncing in her seat.

"Yes, it was." Josh whispered into her ear. "I'm speechless."

"I hope not," she teased. "Drew is announcing that it's time for the New Artist award."

Two members of the Angells returned to the stage. Taking turns, they read the name of each nominee. "Alison Anderson . . . Lane Bronson . . . Crossover . . . David's Sons . . . and Josh Harrison."

Josh knew they were all more deserving than he. Josh reminded himself that being nominated was enough. All he could expect.

"And the winner is . . ."

"Josh! Honey!" Beth screeched over the applause that had erupted. "You won!"

# 34

**Present Day**

Two days later Josh secured a parking slot on the street in front of the Victorian home that now housed the offices of renowned publisher Dixon Mason. The red brick, two-story building had once been a family residence, like most of the structures on Music Square East. For half a decade, beginning in the 1950s, the street had been known as Sixteenth Avenue South, a main artery of Music Row.

Several rocking chairs beckoned from the large front porch when Josh approached. If the weather had been warmer, he would have enjoyed waiting for Clint Garrett there. Dixon's porch offered a grand view of the music business, or what was left of it. Record labels had gone through a lot of changes in the past few years, with more in sight. No one knew how it would metamorphose or where the bleeding would stop. Several companies had moved off the famed "Row." Others had closed their doors completely. For sure, the music industry had taken a dive, along with the general economy.

Josh's Christian music record label occupied offices in Brentwood, about twenty minutes south, so Josh rarely spent time in this neighborhood. Yet there was something about

Music Row, the original hub of the Nashville music industry, that always reignited the fire of his desire for making it in the music business. Hundreds of thousands of dreams had been realized—or lost—on this street.

Josh opened the door and entered the reception area. A beautiful blonde girl sat at the large wooden desk. He guessed from her youthful appearance that she was an intern from either Belmont or Middle Tennessee State University.

"Hi! Can I help you?" The young girl's enthusiasm confirmed his intern hunch. Lifers were usually more guarded, and with good reason. Some unusual characters traipsed up and down Music Row.

"I'm here for Clint Garrett. I'm writing with him today."

"Josh Harrison?"

"Yes." He offered a smile.

"Clint called to say he's running a few minutes late. Please, have a seat." She pointed to a sitting area filled with antiques and wing-backed leather chairs. "May I bring you water, coffee, anything?"

"No thanks." Josh picked out a chair and a Billboard magazine to read.

Less than ten minutes later, Clint strolled into the room, having entered through the back hallway of the building. No doubt he had a reserved parking place in the back. He had made a lot of money for Dixon Mason during the past few years.

"Hey there." Clint grinned as he sauntered over to Josh.

"Man, you're looking good." Josh stood to shake his hand. Clint looked just as he remembered. A bit older, perhaps, and a little less cocky. But he was the same good-looking man who had captured the affection of country music fans everywhere. And he had retained that fascination, despite the decline of the music business and Clint's "bad boy" reputation. Most theories were that the latter had been a contributor to his success.

"It's great to see you." Clint slapped him on the back. "You've made quite a name for yourself lately. I saw the awards a couple of nights ago."

"Thanks." Josh's cheeks warmed. "You're not doing too bad yourself."

"I'm doing okay," Clint demurred. "I heard you got married."

"I did, a little over a year ago. We're having a baby in June."

"Congratulations, Bear."

Josh laughed. He hadn't been called by his nickname since he worked with Clint several years ago. It took him back to a less complicated time in life.

"Thanks. We're excited. So how have you been?"

"Let's go on into the writing room, and we can catch up there." Clint nodded down a long hallway. "That way."

Josh followed Clint through the corridor. A richly colored Oriental rug with hues of burgundy, navy, and dark green ran its length. As did dark, expensive-looking mahogany woodwork. Gold and platinum albums and BMI, ASCAP, and SESAC multimillion sales awards lined the deep green walls.

"Nice place." Josh ran his hand along the chair rail, as he followed his friend and former employer into a small but comfortable-looking room.

"Yeah, Mason has made some bucks in his days. I'm not sure he's enjoying it much now. He has cancer, you know." Clint's expression softened. "I hate it for him."

Just hearing the word *cancer* brought back unwanted memories for Josh. His mother had found it to be an unmerciful foe. "I'm sorry to hear it. I hope he regains his health."

Clint nodded. "Let's talk about good things. Make yourself at home while I unpack my guitar. There's a fridge in the corner. Help yourself to a drink."

Josh surveyed his surroundings. The room reminded him of concert hall dressing quarters, comfortable yet utilitarian. Paintings of sailboats and beach scenes hung on ocean blue walls for inspiration. An overstuffed leather sofa commandeered one corner. Two leather Captain's chairs flanked the fireplace. A substantial glass-and-wood coffee table anchored a plush rug to the pristine wood floor. Josh recognized the wood as pine, trees common to his home state of Alabama.

Most of his high school friends had grown up to work in the sawmills or paper mills. He had left a lot behind, but he had come a long way. Here he was cowriting with Clint Garrett. God had humbled him with the opportunity to live the life he had only once envisioned. Even better.

Josh watched Clint tune a vintage model Gibson guitar. Not long ago, Josh had been selling T-shirts for this man, the brightest star in the world of country music. Yet, Clint had called him for a writing appointment today.

"Got any good song ideas, Bear?" Clint looked up from the guitar, his blue eyes clear—clearer than Josh had remembered.

"I don't write many country songs." Josh hesitated. "I do have one idea. It's a play on the words dog and dawg. My working title is 'Old Country Dawg.'"

"Hmmm. Interesting." Clint grinned. "Let me throw out an idea. It's a song about forgiveness. Forgiveness that's bigger than the stars and smaller than a mustard seed." He strummed a G-chord.

"A Christian song?"

"Yes. That's why I called you. I thought we could write a few Christian tunes together. Are you willing?"

"Well . . . sure. That's what I do best. I just didn't—"

"Didn't think I cared much about Christian stuff?" Clint finished his sentence for him and smiled. "I didn't until about a year ago. I realized my life had gone down the wrong path. A long way down." He studied Josh's reaction. "I hope you can forgive me if I ever offended you when we were traveling together. I did some pretty crazy things—"

"No . . ." It was Josh's turn to interrupt. "Never, man. You were always good to me. I'm glad to hear you've made some changes, though." Josh hesitated. "You were doing some destructive things. I prayed for you. I prayed that you would get through it all."

"I knew you did. It used to make me angry when you told me that." Clint tweaked the tuning on his guitar. "But you always stood up for what you believed. I respected that, even if I didn't agree with you at the time."

As Clint continued to work with the strings, Josh noticed his wedding band was gone. "Are you and Kari still together?" he asked.

"Yes. Well, yes and no. We're trying to get back together. I did a lot of things to hurt her. I'm hoping she is willing to give me another chance."

"I'll pray for both of you," Josh told him.

Clint hit a discordant flourish. "Hey, we're here to make a living writing songs so we can feed our families. Let's get to work."

By the end of the afternoon they had completed Clint's song idea and begun a second based on one of Josh's ideas. They agreed to get back together in a few weeks and finish it up.

"It's great seeing you," Josh told him as they stepped outside onto the porch.

"A divine appointment," Clint said and then grinned.

A few minutes later Josh brushed moisture from his eyes as he drove away. Seeing the changes in Clint's life, and having the prayers he had prayed for his friend come full circle, gave him hope. Hope that he would get through what lay ahead in his own life. Whatever it might be.

# 35

## Present Day

Ben pulled the door slowly until a sharp click sounded summarily. Losing a patient was never easy. It was even more difficult when the person was so full of life. Frank Joseph had been a vibrant man about Ben's own age. He'd had a healthy heart, strong lungs, and an athletic build. But the tumor in his brain had been stronger.

Fate was a curious thing. It took many in the prime of life, while others sprinted across the finish line in triple digits.

Ben shook his head. The Joseph family appeared to be taking Frank Joseph's death in stride. Religious people intrigued Ben, especially Christians, the quiet, faith-filled ones, whose beliefs were eternalized not externalized. From the beginning, each member of the Joseph family had expressed peace about his or her husband, father, and grandfather's destiny—whatever it might be.

"God will work it out for the best," Mrs. Joseph had said one afternoon when Ben explained the seriousness of her husband's condition.

"We know God loves Dad even more than we do," his daughter had added before wiping her eyes with a tissue. "We trust the outcome, even if the unthinkable happens."

*How could people believe that God cared enough about them to trust their lives to him? Was that faith or ego?*

More likely hope beyond rationality. Or was it?

A beautiful, spring afternoon greeted Ben when he stepped into the hospital parking lot. The rain had passed for now. He would grab a bite to eat before heading to the countryside for a twenty-mile bike ride.

He set out for Elliston Place Soda Shop, only a few blocks away from the hospital. It was one of his favorite places for lunch. Comfort food for the difficult days.

Ben entered the diner through one of its double metal doors and took a seat in a vacant booth near the back of the tiny dining room. Within a few minutes, a young waitress appeared at his table, took his order, and returned with a thick, chocolate milkshake. Why not indulge and ride his bike a few extra miles?

Sipping his drink, he settled back into the creaky, green vinyl booth, allowing the ambiance to envelope him. The place hadn't changed in all his years coming here. It was something akin to a time warp. The restaurant still had its original—as in never remodeled—fifties décor, and that included miniature Wurlitzer jukeboxes mounted on the wall above each booth.

Ben flipped through the extensive selection of fifties, sixties, and seventies pop and country music. He had never paid much attention to popular music, and none of the titles meant much to him.

Turning his eyes to a table across the room, he watched two college-aged girls sitting and talking. Their books were piled high in front of them, and they laughed between sips of soft drinks. One of the young women, who was especially attractive, offered a provocative smile and then looked away.

At a table nearby, a drawn looking man dressed in a suit and tie scribbled on a yellow pad while his lunch companion talked. The second man, who wore a bright blue cowboy shirt embroidered with white and gold guitars, droned on and on. Within a few minutes, the first man pulled a camera from his briefcase and snapped a photo of the would-be, or could-already-be, famous country star.

A few businessmen and hospital staffers sat at the fountain bar, gulping down food. Some stared at cell phones. Others read newspapers. Each seemed to be as lost as he, blindly following a dream and not taking time to question what life was really about.

He had achieved his two main goals in life. To leave his grandfather's house and to become a doctor so he could help others. The first had been selfish, so he could only hope the second bought him *teshuvah*, or atonement.

Grandfather would gasp at his irreverence. Ben's rejection of the Jewish faith had dug an insurmountable chasm between them. But the past could not be mended. Grandfather had passed away at home, quietly in his sleep, with Mama Ruth by his side.

Now she was gone. The official diagnosis had been heart failure. However, Ben believed she had died from a broken heart. Despite their differences, his grandmother had been devoted to her husband, Levi Ruben.

Pangs of guilt overtook Ben when he thought about the number of times he could have flown to New York during the past year to see his grandmother but didn't. The two times he had gone she had welcomed him with open arms. And she had told him more about his parents during those trips than she ever dared to mention when Levi Ruben was alive.

The visits, and the information, had been both cathartic and confusing. Especially when she talked about the circumstances surrounding his parents' deaths.

He had always known that they had left Judaism for Christianity. But he hadn't known until this year that they had become evangelists for their new faith.

"I didn't want to confuse you more than you already were, Isaac," Mama Ruth had said to him when they sat together at her dining room table. "And I knew you had the spark of a rebel spirit in you, just like your mother. I saw how your grandfather's strict rules set you off, just like they did her. I didn't want to lose you too."

Mama Ruth had barely been able to walk at that point, but she had lifted herself from the chair and shuffled to the old mahogany breakfront. She pulled a leather-bound book from the drawer and laid it on the table in front of him. Two words were inscribed on the cover. *Holy Bible.*

"This was your mother's Christian Bible," she told him. "It's yours now. She would have wanted you to have it. It was one of the few personal effects returned to us after she died. I have kept it for this time in your life."

Mama Ruth opened the book and took an aged and yellow newspaper clipping from between its thin pages. The article, from a St. Louis paper, had told about the revival Ben's parents were to hold in Missouri. The story had been dated October 11, 1959.

They had been on their way to that revival when their plane went down.

"I hope this helps you, son." His fragile grandmother said, tears running down her cheek. "I know you are searching."

*It had only helped to confuse him.*

"Here ya go." The waitress set a burger down in front of him. The meal looked and smelled delicious. "Do you need anything else?"

"No, thank you," he said.

Ben looked across the room, where two women joined hands and prayed quietly before consuming their food. Perhaps that was something his parents and siblings would have done.

He picked up his napkin, placed it in his lap, and prayed silently. *If you can hear me, God, please make yourself known to me.*

# 36

**Present Day**

Standing in the doorway of the guest bathroom, Beth watched Alex paint a smile on her lips with crimson-colored liner. The fiery hue set off her friend's creamy complexion with paint-by-number freckles and her beautiful red hair, the color of the sassafras tea Beth's grandmother used to make.

"So you have a crush on my doctor, 'the Jewish version of Simon Cowell?'"

"I didn't say 'the Jewish version.'" Alex's cheeks bloomed as vibrant as the liner on her lips. "Simon Cowell *is* Jewish, isn't he?"

"I don't think so," Beth grinned.

"Google it and find out."

"You're trying to change the subject."

Alex smiled, for real this time. "Maybe."

Beth laughed and retreated to the guest bedroom, relaxing into a comfortable chair. "I can't wait to hear about your date," she said, loud enough for Alex to hear. "He's an attractive man. I love his blue eyes."

"Aren't they amazing?" Alex peeked around the doorjamb.

"Where are you going for lunch?"

"Saul's Mediterranean Pizzeria."

"All right! Regular food."

"Sorry to disappoint you, but Saul's is an organic restaurant," Alex shouted from the bathroom.

Beth sighed. "What else do you have in common?"

"For one thing, a childhood in New York. And most important, growing up Jewish and then leaving that path." Alex reappeared at the door. "I think he's a seeker."

"Maybe." Beth thought back to her conversation in Dr. Abrams's office. "I'm not so sure about that. Be careful, girlfriend, and don't lose your heart."

Alex sat on the side of the bed to pull on her boots. "I know. But I'm really drawn to this man."

---

Ben Abrams hadn't remembered being this excited about a date in years. He'd selected Saul's because it was casual. He wanted to keep the mood relaxed and get to know Alexandra Hayes better.

Saul's reminded him of a classic New York pizzeria from more than thirty years ago, a place he would have frequented during his college days. Alexandra appeared to be a decade younger than he, but he thought she would relate. They had talked enough in his office to realize how much they had in common.

Ben chose a table in the back corner of the room to wait for her arrival. Her entrance didn't disappoint. Ben glanced at his watch. She was right on time. She wore her fiery red hair pulled back in a braid and was dressed in a brown leather jacket, blue jeans, and a white cotton shirt. Every man in the room turned his head when she walked in. She smiled and waved at Ben when she saw him.

He stood and helped her with her chair. The floral scent of Alexandra's perfume mingled with the smell of green peppers, garlic, olive oil, and yeast. It was an oddly appealing combination.

Ben settled into the chair across the table from his date. "You look lovely today," he said.

"Thank you." She smiled and then glanced around the room. "This place reminds me of home."

"I thought you might enjoy it."

"Have you ordered?" She flipped through the menu.

"No. I've been considering my options. It depends on how much willpower I have today," he chuckled.

*Why did he feel so comfortable with this woman?*

"May I take your drink order?" A waitress asked as she stepped up to the table.

Ben nodded to Alexandra. "What would you like?"

"Do you have organic colas?"

"Yes, ma'am."

"I'd like that, please."

"Make that two," Ben said.

"Yes, sir. Are you ready to order?" The woman reached for their menus.

Ben stopped her. "We haven't had a chance to decide."

"Okay. Be right back with your drinks."

He turned his attention back to Alexandra. "So, what do you do when you're not caregiving?"

"I'm a starving artist." When she laughed, her freckles danced. "Actually, not starving, but not completely successful at this point." Her eyes connected with his. "The truth is, I love painting, and I'm happy just being able to do what I love."

The waitress set their drinks on the table. "Ready to order yet?" She pulled a pad from her apron.

"Not yet," Ben frowned. "Please give us a few more minutes."

The girl snapped around and walked away.

"Looks like we need to order," he suggested. "Before she has a breakdown."

Alexandra laughed. "Well, I want something extravagant with lots of cheese." She studied the menu in front of her. "I'm celebrating."

"Is it your birthday?" Ben couldn't imagine the coincidence.

"No . . . no. It's the first time I've been out for lunch on my own in a while. Caregiving has kept me tied down. It's nice to relax without having someone's life in my hands." She blushed. "Sorry, I suppose you never really get away from that feeling."

"It's an art," he teased.

She smiled.

"Do you know what you want to eat? Everything here is good."

"Can we share a pizza? Maybe a veggie one?"

"Absolutely." Ben waved the waitress to the table.

"Yes, sir."

"We'd like a large Veggie Margherita Pizza." He picked up the menus and gave them to her. "And make sure we have extra cheese."

The corners of Alexandra's mouth curled. "Thanks."

"What were we talking about?"

"You," she said. "I admire your career choice, helping people. What led you to it?"

"The flower shop."

"I don't understand."

"I worked in my grandfather's flower shop when I was a boy, actually until I left home for college." He exhaled a long breath of air, thinking about those days. "Are you sure you want to hear this?"

"Yes." She nodded and took a sip of her drink.

"I was fascinated early on with the human thought process. It was interesting how people went about choosing flowers for special occasions. It sounds like a stretch, but color and scent are neurological functions."

"Makes sense." She propped her chin on her hands, elbows resting on the table.

"There was a lot of motive in the process as well. Understandably, many people use flowers to express what they cannot. You'd be surprised, however, how some people use them to express what they don't mean yet feel obligated to say." He studied her beautiful face.

"I'd never thought about it like that."

"When I was a teenager, my grandfather suffered a stroke, and I watched him struggle with neurological issues." Ben drew in a deep breath. "That's when I began managing the shop. I had known long before then that I didn't want to make it my life's work, and I was miserable. But I had to do it, to take care of my grandmother. Later, my grandfather was able to build back up to a normal life."

"So your grandparents raised you?"

"Yes. My grandmother was my angel."

"Mine too," Alexandra nodded. "My mother left when I was a little girl. And I never knew my father. My grandparents meant everything to me."

"I lost both parents early in life."

"Do you remember them?" Alex asked.

"Not at all. Except through the photographs my grandmother kept for me."

"My grandmother shared my love of art. She encouraged me in it, and when the time came, she made sure I was able to attend one of the best schools available. I was a shy child, and art brought me out of myself." She sipped her drink. "Moore College is where I met people outside my faith tradition. It was a life-changing experience."

Alex's blue-green eyes drew Ben in as she spoke. They had much in common. Growing up in New York and leaving the Jewish faith. "Columbia was an escape for me. I couldn't wait to leave the confines of my grandfather's home."

The waitress delivered their pizza and provided plates and utensils.

"That looks and smells wonderful," Alexandra said. Then she bowed her head.

Ben felt vaguely voyeuristic watching her silent prayer, yet her self-assured grace somehow brought comfort to him. She appeared to be at peace with who she was. Something he envied.

She picked up her fork and slid a piece of pizza onto her plate. "Do you mind if I eat with my hands?" She grinned.

"Please do. I don't want to be the only one." He grabbed a slice of the fresh, hot pizza.

"Yum. Look at all that cheese," she said, before taking a delicate bite. "So what do you do for entertainment, to free your mind from your exhausting career?"

"I enjoy riding my bike. I usually ride about forty to sixty miles a week. And I garden," he laughed. "As much as I hated the flower shop, it seems to have stayed with me."

"I garden too. Mostly roses and flowering perennials."

"My yard is filled with daylilies," he said. "Much easier."

After discussing the merits of composting, they launched into a conversation about musical interests.

Ben took a second slice of pizza while Alexandra told him about the first time she had tried klezmer dancing. The custom dated back to the early centuries of Judaism and had religious origins. Klezmer dancing, which was similar to American-style square dancing, had recently reemerged within contemporary Jewish culture.

He listened intently while Alexandra exaggerated her attempts to master it. She had a self-deprecating and refreshing sense of humor. Something he didn't often find in such a beautiful woman.

"And then I fell to the floor. " She delivered the punch line to her story.

Ben laughed until tears filled his eyes and inhaled when he tried to swallow a bite of pizza. The crust attached itself to his throat, sticking halfway down. He made an effort to dislodge the food by coughing.

"Are you okay?" Alexandra asked.

He tried to speak but couldn't. He waved her off, certain he could get through it if he coughed enough. The expression on his face must have cued her that wasn't the case.

Within a few seconds, Alex stood up and rushed to the back of his chair. "Stand up," she said, helping him to his feet. She wrapped her arms around his waist and delivered a swift, upward thrust into his diaphragm.

Ben didn't have time to be embarrassed at the attention they had drawn because the room around him began to spin.

"Relax. I know the Heimlich," she whispered in his ear.

Just as he was about to lose consciousness, she thrust her wrists into his abdomen, and he heard himself cough. The food lodged inside his windpipe was expelled onto the floor. He remained bent and gasping for air.

Alexandra led him back to his chair and stood beside him with one hand on his shoulder.

He offered her a weak smile. A few seconds later, she returned to her seat.

"I was just going to tell you that I spent one summer working as a lifeguard," she said. A slow grin connected the freckles on her extraordinary face.

*Please, God, tell me you put this woman in my life.*

# 37

**Present Day**

Josh had a full day of errands before leaving for the road. After picking up his guitar from a repair shop near Music Row, he set out for a meeting at the bus leasing company across town.

He had made the decision after the Noah Awards to order a new lease bus. Although it was based more on practicality than pride, he was excited about the new coach. It would provide extra room and comfort for himself, his band, and his crew, and it would be one of the few Van Hool models out of Nashville. These days, most entertainers rode in Prevosts, but Josh had always loved the styling of the Van Hool. The extraordinarily tall windows, curving onto the roof, almost like skylights, filled the front lounge with light.

Rain poured from a murky gray sky as he approached a traffic signal near the intersection of Broadway and the frontage roads accessing the interstates that run through Nashville. A shaggy-looking, stoop-shouldered man caught Josh's attention. The man carried two grocery bags, one in each hand, and walked toward the center of Nashville's downtown area. He wore his coat collar up and held his head down, trying to shield himself from the downpour.

It was nasty weather for grocery shopping. Then Josh remembered there were no grocery stores within several miles of the center of downtown Nashville. This was a homeless guy, and rather than food, those sacks most likely contained all of his worldly possessions.

When Josh slowed his Jeep to navigate a large puddle of water, the traffic light at the corner of Broadway and Twelfth caught him. He made the stop and continued to watch the vagrant, who kept walking. Without looking either way, the man stepped off the sidewalk to cross the road, disregarding oncoming traffic.

Just as he did, a black Cadillac Escalade barreled through the waterlogged intersection, sending a giant geyser of muddy water in the pedestrian's direction. To avoid being soaked, the homeless man jumped backward onto the curb, almost losing his balance. He somehow remained upright, as much as his crooked carriage would allow. Once he had his feet flat on the ground, he offered a broad smile and a wave to the driver of the car that had almost upended him.

*Crazy old man.*

The light changed, and Josh eased through the water-covered intersection and onto the entrance ramp of the highway below. Low-hanging fog replaced the rain, and steamy puffs of mist tumbled around the wheels of the vehicles in front of him, like dust stirred up by the heels of horses.

After a few miles of driving north on I-65, Josh reached the Briley Parkway exit. He hummed a new song idea as he steered to the right, toward the river. A giant, white-barked tree in the low-lying right-of-way caught his attention. The old sycamore stood stark and bare beside the roadway.

Something about it reminded Josh of the homeless man. It had grown crooked and looked different from the other trees around it. Perhaps seventy feet tall, its trunk had bent about halfway up.

Josh speculated that the tree had encountered an obstacle many years before. Perhaps a fence. Or another tree. But, instead of stopping there, it had altered its path sharply to the left, and then began to grow straight toward the sun again.

Maybe the old vagrant wasn't crazy after all.

*Could it be he was just made of better stuff than the rest of us, with more faith and less discontent?* Perhaps the old man had chosen to look up through—or at least around—his problems while still smiling, knowing that a detour didn't have to alter the destination, it merely changed the path.

Josh stared into the misty, rain-soaked distance. Weather like this had always reminded him of what it must have been like in the Garden of Eden, before God took the nothingness and created green fields and four-legged creatures. Right after he changed the darkness into light and before he gave purpose to it all by creating man.

Shame stabbed him in the chest. If God could do that, he could bring purpose to the things that had happened during the last few months of his and Bethany's lives. If the old man could look up despite his problems, why couldn't he?

Josh had held himself up many times, standing onstage, asking people, even his friend Danny, to do what he hadn't been able to do: to keep the faith during the hard times. Perhaps he had encouraged others, but he still had to wrestle his own doubts to the ground.

Could he really give everything to God? Could he rely on him to get them through whatever lay ahead? Beth's addiction. A miscarriage? Eventually learning which one of his friends had been stealing from him?

Did he have that kind of faith?

It would have helped if his father had kept his. Or if his mother were still here to encourage him.

Josh knew in his heart that there was hope, even though he had a difficult time feeling it. Not all trees grow straight toward the sun. He must somehow grow beyond the obstacles in his path. The failures in his life. And the failures of those around him.

He must grow upward again.

Toward the light.

⸻

After a brief meeting at Rally Coaches, Josh turned his Jeep south toward Brentwood. The sky cleared about the time he approached the thriving residential and business community, which was a twenty-minute drive from downtown Nashville.

Glory Records occupied part of the first floor of a medium-rise office building in the prestigious Maryland Farms office park. Glory was a small but powerful label with product whole-saled by a major distributor in the industry. They had launched half a dozen contemporary acts into successful careers. Josh hoped he would become one of their high-priority artists now that he had won a Noah Award.

Although Glory had a small promotion and production budget, their twelve-member team included some of the music industry's finest professionals. Josh considered them almost family. They had stood by him, believed in him, and nurtured his career from the beginning.

He entered the yellow brick building through one of the giant glass doors and approached the reception desk. "Hey, Rhonda. How are you today?"

"Okay," the pretty brunette spoke without emotion.

"What's wrong?"

"Nothing. Just busy," she said, not looking up. "You can go on into the conference room. Mr. Benton is waiting for you."

"Okay." He offered a parting smile and turned toward the meeting room, which had an entrance off the lobby.

Greg Benton and Matt Holliman were already seated at the conference table.

"Josh." Greg stood and offered his hand. "Good to see you."

"You, too, man."

Matt stood as well. "Did Rhonda offer you a drink?"

"No. But I'm fine. Just ate lunch a couple of hours ago." Josh settled into a plump, leather chair on the opposite side of the conference table, his usual seat when he had meetings at the label.

Greg closed the hallway door before returning to his seat. "How's your wife doing?" he asked.

"She's okay. We're about two months from her due date and beginning to get excited." It was easier to give the short answer.

The smile on Greg's face faded, and he glanced at Matt before continuing. "This is lousy timing," he said. "But I've got some bad news."

"What?" Josh's first thought was concern for someone's health.

"We're having cash flow problems. And . . . we're going to have to release you from the label."

"What?" Josh repeated the question, this time in disbelief, as he scanned the faces in the room, hoping he had misunderstood.

"It's not you, Josh. Glory is going through some hard times right now. We're releasing five artists this week. I would appreciate your confidentiality before we talk to everyone, but we're cutting our roster to the core. We just can't—"

"We can't believe we're having to do this." Matt interrupted. "You're a breakout artist with lots of momentum. But we can't afford to develop anyone right now." Holliman's pale face blended into the ashen grey walls behind him. "It's killing us to have to do it."

"I'm shocked," Josh said, deflating his lungs with a single breath. "I knew the industry was down, but . . . "

"Let me put it this way." Greg Benton reached across the table, palms up, as if to allay any doubt of his honesty in the matter. "We're not sure how long we'll keep the doors open. This is better for you in the long run."

Josh couldn't imagine how this would be better. Nor did he want to extend this uncomfortable situation. He positioned his hands on the arms of his chair and pushed himself upward.

"Of course. Better for me. Right." He walked toward the door and, after several minutes of stilted conversation about keeping in touch and tying up loose ends, opened the door and left the room.

"Take care of yourself," Josh said to the receptionist as he walked quickly toward the outside doors.

"We're going to miss you," Rhonda said, her voice trailing off behind him.

⸻

Several times, Josh picked up the phone to call Beth and then put it back down. He needed to talk. To have her tell him that everything would be okay. But, right now, everything rested on his shoulders. Most of the reassurance would have to come from inside himself.

He prayed for strength where weakness now resided. If he didn't believe things would work out, his voice would give him away when he spoke to Beth. And he didn't want to alarm his wife.

Then a realization struck him. Perhaps Greg Benton had somehow found out that he had been witnessing from an empty heart. That he was a vacant body. A man without a soul dressed only in stage clothes.

*God, please help me find who I am again. Please help me find you.*

Josh knew he had to keep going on his own strength, if not God's. Somehow. He had no choice. He had to walk in faith and believe he was walking in the right direction by the Lord's leading.

One of his mother's old sayings came to mind. "Praise God," she would tell him, "and you will eventually understand how many ways he should be fully praised."

As Josh prepared to cross the Cumberland River into East Nashville, he picked up the phone and dialed Beth. He would suggest they go out to dinner. They would both feel better after discussing the record label situation over a good dinner. They would make alternate plans. Together.

He had time to work it out. For the next several months, he had a good position on a strong tour.

When Beth answered the phone, reality set in again.

"Hello," she said. Her voice sounded parched, almost unrecognizable. Another dry soul, this one consumed by drugs. He would be going home to a house where two empty people resided.

"Hi, hon. I'm on my way home. Would you like to go out to eat tonight? Maybe that Greek restaurant in Green Hills you like so much?"

"I'm not really hungry," she said, slurring her words. "I'm sorry. Can we just eat at home?"

"Sure. It's no problem. I'm not that hungry either," he said. "I'll pick up sandwiches on the way home."

Over supper Beth admitted to taking an extra Lortab because of excessive pain. They ate most of their meal in silence. Afterward, she followed Josh into the bedroom to watch him pack. He would be leaving at midnight for several days, beginning with a show in Atlanta tomorrow night.

Beth crawled between the blue flannel sheets, heaving a long sigh and propping her head on her elbow while he tossed things into his bag.

"I had a meeting with Greg and Matt at Glory Records this afternoon, and I don't have good news," he said, stopping his work to assess her reaction.

"What's wrong?" She frowned.

"They released me. They let me go."

"I don't understand . . ."

"I don't either." Josh stepped briefly into the bathroom to retrieve his shaving kit.

"But you just started working on your new CD," Beth said when he returned to the room.

"They're giving me the chance to buy the recordings back if I can find another label." He stuffed the kit into his bag.

"Do you think you can do that?" Beth settled into her pillow.

"I don't know." He zipped his canvas duffle.

She sighed, "That was so mean of them."

Then she dropped off to sleep.

# 38

**Present Day**

The sun rose through Alabama pine trees as Josh walked from the bunkroom into the front lounge of the bus. It was good to be back in his home state. After three sold-out shows in Georgia and South Carolina, the tour was now heading to Mississippi.

He wiped the sleep from his eyes. Everyone else was still in their bunk—and would be for several hours. Six-thirty in the morning was early for his crew. They had no reason to rise until closer to lunchtime.

"Good morning," Josh said, taking a seat to the right of his driver.

"Get enough sleep?" There was a grin in Danny's voice.

"Not really, but it's worth it to have this opportunity. Thanks for suggesting it."

"It's not that far out of our way, and I know how I would feel." This time Danny spoke with a hint of sadness. "How long has it been since you visited the cemetery?"

Josh reflected on the question. "My dad has been gone for close to a year and a half. It has been almost a year since I was there."

"Is this the exit coming up?"

"That's it. I could find this place in my sleep," Josh said. "And probably did several late nights coming home from college," he chuckled. "My dad was always waiting up for me, though."

An inexplicable emptiness of his parents being gone wrenched at his heart. Josh scanned the countryside, looking for solace in the familiar surroundings. A smattering of pines and a few wild, purple Wisterias in bloom decorated the immediate landscape.

This part of the world held many memories for him. Not the least of which involved football. Alabama was still a major contender in the SEC. The Crimson Tide had had a good run in the last few years.

Josh had chosen to attend the University of Alabama not only because of the school's proximity to his home but also because of his father's love for its former coach. Everyone in the state, and most football fans his father's age, had revered Paul "Bear" Bryant. Bryant had led the Crimson Tide to more major bowl games than any coach in the school's history. Most Alabamians shared a sense of pride in his accomplishments.

When Josh was a young boy, Samuel Harrison had often referred to Bear Bryant when he wanted to teach his son a life lesson. He had pointed out how the coach always taught his players self-discipline. "Through self-discipline you can win every game," his dad had said. "It will help you in every aspect of life, including the spiritual."

No doubt, that principle had stuck early. One day, when Josh was five years old, he refused to eat the green peas on his plate. Questioned by his father, he had looked up and said, "Call me Bear, Dad. I didn't let myself eat them."

From that point forward, the nickname stuck. Especially when Josh excelled or persevered.

Within fifteen minutes the bus pulled in front of Rock Creek Church. Danny eased the big Prevost to a stop beneath the shade of a few straggling pine trees, and Josh stepped into the cool, spring morning.

As he walked up the path toward the white clapboard church, he reflected on its steeple. Years ago, he and his father had carved the simple, wooden cross that sat on top of it.

The spire cast a long shadow upon the ancient plots to the west, the resting place of those who had planted the church more than a hundred years ago. When he was a child, Josh had enjoyed walking through the graveyard, reading the names of those who had gone before. Even then, many of the stones stood decayed and mute. The wind and the sediment had filed away the letters of long-forgotten names. Josh wondered now if the testimony of those who lay beneath had gone silent too. How long did our work remain after we no longer walked this earth?

Looking across the hillside, he marveled at the carpet of grass that already covered the ground. Several hundred feet away, a row of newly leaved trees stood guard, just before the land dropped to a creek below. It was a scene that had forever been painted in his mind the day they laid his daddy to rest beside his mother.

Josh walked toward the rise in the terrain, near the north end of the tree line. As he approached, he could hear the babbling of the water below. The sound took him back to days long ago, when he had fished in this creek with his dad. The stream always ran clear, cleansed by the rocks protruding from the brown, Central Alabama soil.

*From dust to dust.*

He had heard his daddy preach those words many times inside the old, white church behind him. The Genesis story of God creating man from the ashes of the earth had been one of his favorites as a child. That, and the beauty of this old cemetery, had almost led him to the study of archaeology.

He smiled. Perhaps his mother's love of music had been written stronger in his genes. He could see her now, sitting at the piano. Her face glowed when she played old hymns from a faded green songbook. She had known every page by heart, yet her expression displayed unexpected joy as she read each note.

Memories flooded back faster than Josh could comprehend. Daddy's sudden death from a heart attack. His mom's less merciful, extended relationship with cancer. Now Beth.

He choked back tears.

Was he destined to live his life alone? How long would it be before he knew if Beth would survive? If their child would live or die.

Tonight, he would sing for two thousand, but none could know the depths of his heart. He was thankful for that, because his faith had diminished to a shallow façade. Others saw only what he allowed them to see. Beth included. He couldn't let down his guard, for fear others would see that he was a fraud. An actor, who wondered if he could ever believe in complete joy again.

"Josh." Danny's voice pulled him back to the present. "I hate to bother you, but it's time to leave if we're going to make the show tonight."

Josh turned to see kindness and understanding on his friend's face. "Yes, we need to do that. Sorry—"

"No need to apologize," his driver said. "I spend a lot of time at my mother's grave." His voice faded into the rustle of the tree leaves.

Back in the bus, after a stop for fuel and a quick breakfast, Josh watched Danny merge into oncoming traffic, heading toward Jackson, Mississippi.

Several miles down the road, all of the colors appeared brighter. Perhaps it was the angle of the sun, or maybe Josh was refreshed by the time with his past.

"How do you do it?" he asked Danny.

"What?"

"How do you handle your mom's death so well? I know from experience, it's not easy."

"Look straight down the highway," Danny told him. He pointed with one hand, keeping the other on the wheel. "Do you see how it disappears into the horizon when there's a rise ahead?"

"Yes."

"That's like our journey in this life." Danny glanced at the bus's control panel. "We're traveling seventy miles an hour. That's too fast to stop if for some reason the road ends over that hill." He shook his head. "But we would never make our goal— the show tonight—if I didn't keep the pedal to the metal."

Josh studied Danny's face for a clue about what he was saying.

"However," his driver continued. "I have faith that the road doesn't end over that hill. My faith is based on past experience that I can trust the department of transportation to continue the road." He glanced to Josh. "Just as I know I can trust God for whatever is next. Even for those things I can't see."

Josh nodded.

"He has gotten me and my family through some tough times. The hardest, so far, being my mom's passing. But the Good Lord has promised that I'll see her again. I have faith the road doesn't end here, and when the Lord calls us to the other side of the hill, the view will be completely different. We will see things as he sees them."

Josh marveled at his driver's words. "You should have been a preacher. You missed your calling."

"Nah." Danny's face turned a dark shade of red. "I'm just grateful for the blessings of my faith. And a little emotional." He wiped his eyes with the back of his hand.

"Thanks for going out of your way today." Josh's response was interrupted by the ringing of his phone.

It was Clint Garrett.

"Hey, man."

"Where are you?" Clint asked.

"In Mississippi, on our way to Jackson." Josh scanned the road ahead.

"Are you ready for some good news?"

"More than ready," Josh said. "Did we get our song cut?"

"Better."

"YOU cut our song?"

Clint laughed. "No."

"What could be better than that?" Josh teased.

"Are you interested in recording for AMG Records?"

"Are you kidding?" *He had to be kidding.*

"I called Ken Buckingham to let him know you were available," Clint said. "And he wants to talk to you."

"No way!" AMG was Clint's label, the best in town.

"But there's one condition."

*Of course, he had known it was too good to be true.*

"You have to let me produce the project."

"All right!" Josh screamed loud enough to wake everyone in the back of the bus. Even if he did, they would be happy to hear the news. This could be the biggest break of his career.

"I'll take that as a yes," Clint laughed.

# 39

**Present Day**

A warm wind stirred the brown leaves from last year's fall against a backdrop of new life, chartreuse tufts of spring grass and flowering shrubs. Josh watched as Buster ran figure eights around the patio, making an attempt to catch them. The little dog had more energy than should be allowed at this time of afternoon. Or, perhaps, it was just that the convoluted merchandise reports had zapped Josh of energy.

His eyes stung from studying copies of the handwritten merchandise summaries Ryan had turned in for the month of February. The signs were there, just like his accountant had pointed out earlier in the day.

"Embezzlers try to make their numbers look ambiguous," Bob Bradford had said. "Look at the sevens on the report. They could easily be fours."

Josh had agreed when he studied the paperwork.

"His writing is extremely legible in other ways," Bradford had noted. "Alphabetical letters are written with perfect penmanship, but the digits are indistinct."

Once again, Josh agreed. But it was Bradford's last comment that intrigued him. "The brain will read the number it expects to see, although that may not be the number used in the computation."

To test his accountant's theory, Josh calculated the music CD sales total for the last week of February. Adding up the numbers resulted in a tally of one thousand eight hundred and fifty-four dollars. However, the total shown on the report was one thousand and fifty-seven dollars. A difference of seven hundred ninety-seven dollars.

Josh studied the numbers and confirmed the ambiguity of the handwritten digits. If he read the eight as a zero and the four as a seven, he could account for the missing money.

*Accident or intention?*

He ran totals for several more columns. Based on Bradford's premise, some amounts worked out, but some did not. The worst part, however, was that Ryan's numbers didn't jibe with the merchandise company reports. His road manager's numbers were short, leaving reason for concern.

Josh ran his fingers through his hair. He needed to know for sure. A false accusation would be not only embarrassing but also hurtful and counterproductive. In defense of Ryan, he held two positions, plus this recently added responsibility of merchandise accounting. Perhaps he had made an honest mistake and misread his handwriting.

Josh stretched his aching shoulders, and turned his attention back to Buster. The little terrier was now preoccupied with a cluster of bugs, some of the first of the year. Poised to attack, he eyed his prey. When none moved, the dog provoked them with a well-placed paw. A swarm of crawling creatures scurried across the patio in every direction. Buster ran after one, then the other, zigzagging across the cement.

Josh laughed, happy to take his mind off work for a few minutes.

It was an interesting game of getaway. Some of the insects stopped in their tracks when the dog approached. Others ran. Josh noticed that Buster always pursued the bugs that moved, and he ignored those who stood their ground.

Bingo! Why hadn't he thought about it before now? *Make the "bug" move.*

He would feed Ryan just enough information to make him uncomfortable if he were guilty.

He would make him move.

—————— ⌾ ——————

With so many things on his mind, Josh couldn't sleep. He would be leaving for the road again tomorrow, and he had checked his to-do list over and over. As always, his main concern was not what he had left to do, but what he could not control, the well-being of his wife, who lay asleep beside him. And their child, whose life was vulnerable to every decision they made.

Staying busy always helped assuage his fears, so during his days off he had jumped headlong into the physical preparation of the baby's room. The small, ten-by-ten-foot room lay directly across the hall from their master bedroom. According to Beth's request, he had painted the walls in rainbow colors, one pink, one green, one yellow, and one blue.

It had been Alex's idea to emboss a large letter into the center of each wall, spelling the word B-A-B-Y. She had volunteered to hand draw and paint the letters onto the pink, blue, and green walls. Beth's job was to embroider the final letter onto a pull-down shade for the window wall. The result had been spectacular. Standing in the center of the finished room gave the illusion of being surrounded by a huge pile of wooden baby blocks.

During the past two days Josh had built and painted a removable shelving unit for the nursery closet. The custom compartments, or cubbyholes, would soon hold stacks of diapers, baby clothes, and stuffed toys. The money to buy the materials for the project had come from his quarterly airplay royalty check from BMI. The amount had been enough to also buy bed linens and pay off the chunk of debt that Beth had run up for the nursery furniture. He would be leaving for the road exhausted but feeling fulfilled.

And ready to catch a thief.

———— ⬥ ————

"Josh, can I see you for a minute?" Ryan signaled from the bunkroom.

Josh followed his road manager into the back lounge and closed the door behind them.

"What's going on?"

"We have a problem." Ryan said, taking a seat on the right side sofa. "Some of the merch money is missing."

"What do you mean?" Josh sat on the sofa across the aisle.

"I put the cash in my bunk bag last night, like I always do. But for some reason, I couldn't get it off my mind. Even though it had already been counted and reconciled, I rechecked it this morning, and it's more than a thousand dollars short—$1,326 to be exact."

"Are you certain it was all there last night?" Josh asked, staring into his road manager's frosty blue eyes.

"Absolutely. I counted it four times. Twice last night and twice again this morning."

Josh repositioned himself in his seat. "What do you think happened?"

"I don't want to accuse people, but it's obvious," Ryan said. "Someone on the bus stole it."

Uncertain how he should respond, Josh hesitated, running his fingers through his hair as he thought about Ryan's accusations. Why should he trust the man he believed to be a thief? *Was this a preemptive strike?* A clever move on Ryan's part?

"Do you understand what you're saying?" Josh could feel his blood pressure rise. "You're accusing one of the men on this bus of stealing."

"I realize that, but there's no other explanation."

"Who do you think did it?"

"This is going to be hard for you, because I know how close you are to him. But I saw Danny messing around near my bunk last night."

"His bunk is next to yours."

"Yes, but he had a funny look on his face, when I walked in unexpectedly. I didn't think much about it until I found the money missing this morning."

"Is that the reason you recounted it?"

"It was. I know you don't want to believe that he—"

"No one is guilty until they are proven guilty. Do you understand?" Josh stood up. The brusqueness of his voice surprised even him.

Ryan sat back in his seat. "Yes, sir."

*Sir?* Ryan had never called him sir.

"Look," Josh said, poking an accusing finger at the man he believed was really stealing from him. "Keep this between you and me. Do you understand?"

"Okay, but—" Ryan shook his head.

"No one." Josh reached for the button that opened the pocket door. "There will be no false accusations on this bus. You bring me proof, or you bring me the missing money."

He walked into the bunkroom and punched the button on the wall beside Danny's bunk. The bunkroom door closed with a thud, not unlike the ache that now pounded inside his head.

⁓

Josh had been uneasy for two days, dreading the television interview he had committed to do to promote this evening's show. He smoothed his shirt, moistened his lips, and listened to the producer count down.

"And four, three, two . . ."

"Welcome back." The pretty, blonde anchor spoke directly into camera one. "We have a special guest this afternoon. Contemporary Christian entertainer Josh Harrison is with us."

She turned to him. "We're glad to have you, Josh."

"Thank you." He took in a deep breath, while pinching the loose skin between the thumb and forefinger of his left hand. Someone had told him once that it would help ease nerves. It didn't.

The reporter flashed a smile. "Is it correct to use the term *entertainers* for Christian musicians?"

He had never been asked that question. "Sure. Our goal is to entertain people, as well as to spread the message of the gospel."

"You're in town to perform at the civic center tonight, correct?"

"Yes. I'm opening for the Triumphant Two Tour, and I'm honored to be here."

She glanced at her notes. "You're opening for R. O. S. and Fast Train to Glory. Is that correct?"

"Yes, they're our headliners. There are five acts on the show all together. I've been blessed to be a part of this tour for about a year now, and I can tell you . . ." He took another breath. "These groups represent some of the best talent to ever walk onstage, no matter what musical format. I'm honored to be on the same show with them."

"Congratulations on your own successes," she cooed. "I understand you won a Noah Award recently."

"Thank you. I was humbled by that."

"And you got your start in country music? Is that right?"

"No. Well . . . yes. Not performing. I worked for country music star, Clint Garrett, for a couple of years. I was a member of his road crew."

"That must have been amazing. What was that like?"

"It was great. In fact, I recently did some songwriting with Clint."

"How nice. His career has certainly taken off, hasn't it?" She studied her notes.

"Yes. It has. And he's doing well personally."

"That's good to hear. I understand he fought a few demons in his life."

"Well, he did go through some rough spots. But Clint is the first to admit that. He's a Christian now—"

"Christian entertainers love to talk about the before and the after, it seems. Do you have a before-and-after story, Josh?"

"What do you mean?"

"Do you have a renewal story?"

How much did this woman know about him?

"Well . . . we all do." He offered a tentative smile. "None of us are proud of who we can be at times. But, through the strength of Christ, we—"

"I hope this isn't too personal, but I understand your wife is very ill and pregnant with your first child. How do you reconcile those things with your faith?"

Josh cleared his throat. "That's a good question." *One he preferred not to answer.* "I . . . my wife and I trust that the Lord will provide. In his grace."

"But an unborn child in danger? How do you deal with that?"

He squirmed in his seat. "You pray a lot. Sometimes, it's your troubles that lead you closer to God."

*Or to give up on God.*

"I understand your father left the ministry after your mother passed away." Her eyes darkened.

This woman was out to destroy him. Who had given her so much information?

"Josh?"

"Yes. Well, my dad did retire after my mom died. He was exhausted. And not well at the time." Josh dug deep into the mustard seed of faith that survived in his heart. "That's one reason Christian entertainers do what we do. To help people realize they—we—can make it through the difficult times with God's help. My faith is not perfect, but God's grace is perfect."

"Very well said." The reporter glanced to a production assistant, who was signaling that they were out of time. "Thank you, Josh."

The interviewer reached to shake his hand. "Would you perform a song for us after the break?"

"I would love to do that."

"Thank you."

She turned to camera two. "Josh Harrison. We'll be back after this."

—— ⚭ ——

*He had been set up.* Most likely by Ryan Majors. His road manager was trying to throw him off balance. To preoccupy him. Ryan had given away all of Josh's dirty little secrets.

Now, he—or someone—must face the repercussions.

# 40

**Present Day**

Blackberry winter," Beth said to herself as she opened the mudroom door to let Buster out before bedtime.

The little dog wouldn't budge. "What's wrong, Mr. B.?"

He looked at her with his big, brown eyes and gave a slight wag of the nub of his tail. "It's not raining right now, buddy. We can make a quick trip. I'll go with you."

He followed her outside and then scampered into the yard. Beth walked farther onto the patio to enjoy the night sky. The weather was right on target for the middle of April, unpredictable. They'd had no lightning or thunder today. Just rain, and lots of it.

Buster barked from the middle of the yard for her attention.

"I'm coming," Beth said. "You sure are needy tonight, aren't you, boy?" The dog smiled. At least his expression appeared to be a smile. She grinned in return. There was nothing like a dog to take your mind off your own worries.

She strolled through the backyard, while Buster moved on to his nightly routine of chasing bugs, sniffing clumps of grass, and checking the perimeter of his yard.

Night had fallen with no real fanfare. After the dog finished his business, she planned to go inside and relax in bed with a book. In the meantime, she would enjoy the peace and quiet of her surroundings. This was her favorite time of day and her favorite season of the year.

A feeling of gratitude descended upon her. Gratefulness for life came naturally in the spring, the earth's season of new beginnings. Honeysuckles bloomed on the nearby fence, wafting old memories. And a bed of spring flowers beside the patio reflected almost unworldly colors in the moonlight.

Without warning, she heard the rain hitting the leaves of the tall trees that grew in the far end of the yard. Another surprise downpour.

Pregnant women didn't jog, so she walked as quickly as she could toward the house. When she was halfway there, the rain found its way to the ground. The first few drops landed lightly on her face. The cool mist refreshed and tingled when it touched her skin, taking her back to her childhood. How many times had she walked in the rain when she was a young girl? She had always envisioned God opening up a giant sprinkler system, pouring out healing water for the benefit of all who dwell below.

The rain intensified, and the sharp pelts now stung. She detoured to the eave of the house, shimmying along the side before taking a seat on the back step, protected from the rain.

Invigorated, Buster rushed to her side and settled beneath her bended knees.

"Ooohh. Wet dog!"

He trembled from the chill.

Beth reached inside the door for a towel and then sat back down on the stoop. "Here, let me dry you off, Mr. B. Then we'll sit here for a while and watch the rain."

She enveloped the dog in the towel and rubbed him gently dry. After she finished, he snuggled beside her and closed his eyes.

Beth sat, mulling over the beauty of her surroundings, contented to watch the rain and take in the ambiance of the night. When the rain slacked again, Buster ran barking into the yard.

"Shhhh, Buster. You'll wake the neighbors."

"What are you up to, girlfriend?"

Beth jumped. "You frightened me!"

Alex had managed to walk through the back gate without Beth hearing her.

"The feeling is mutual," Alex scolded.

"What do you mean?"

Her neighbor took a seat beside her. "When I got up for a drink of water, I looked out the window and saw Buster playing in the yard. It scared me. What are you doing outside at this hour?"

"What time is it?"

"One o'clock."

"I must have lost track," Beth grinned.

"Why are you up so late?"

Beth pointed skyward. The clouds had moved on, and the half moon glowed in a sea of dark blue. "I've been sitting here watching the rain and thinking about things."

"It might be safer, and warmer, to do that inside."

"I suppose so." Beth drifted back to her reflections. "Have you ever thought you could see the dark side of the moon?"

"What do you mean?" Alex twisted her body so she could see the moon.

"Just look at it. You can almost make out the full circle, the perimeter, the edges, and even see the faint details of the dark part."

Alex studied the sky without speaking.

"Or is it an optical illusion?" Beth asked. "Kind of like seeing what you think is there, based on the part you can see."

"Good question. I have to admit I've never thought about it," Alex chuckled.

"I'm being philosophical tonight. But I think it compares to life," Beth said. "We always think we know how ours will turn out, you know, based on what we have lived so far. We have plans and dreams and expectations. But we don't know really, do we? Only God knows what's on our dark side."

"I agree," Alex nodded.

"And we all have dark things in our past. I know I do. But I want to do better tomorrow."

"One day at a time," Alex said.

"I'm starting tomorrow, and I need your help." Beth turned to her friend. "I'm starting to wean myself off the drugs tomorrow."

"Your painkillers? What will Ben say?"

"Ben? Have the two of you been talking about me behind my back?"

Alex covered a mischievous smile with her hand. "No. We haven't been talking about you. Not much anyway. I just don't want you to take any chances."

It was difficult to see the red on Alex's face in the moonlight, but Beth knew it was there. Her caregiver, neighbor, and now best friend had been seeing Ben Abrams for several weeks. Beth had never seen her so happy.

"What he doesn't know won't hurt him," Beth said. "And don't you tell him." She wagged a playful finger at her friend.

"I don't know, Bethany."

"It's okay. Really." Beth tried to assure her. "He told me how to do it a long time ago. I'll take it slowly."

"But—"

"Besides, I think my dissection is healed."

"I thought the last test still showed a problem?" Alex sat back in surprise.

"It did. But something happened at the Noah Awards." Beth repositioned her body, leaning into the corner of the mudroom wall. "One of the singers, a new friend of Josh's, prayed for me." She studied Alex's face again. "I know you will understand what I'm about to say, perhaps some people wouldn't, but I felt something. In my head."

Beth stroked her left temple with her fingers. "And in my spirit," she said. "I believe God healed me." A tear slid down her cheek.

"Wow . . . well, of course, that's possible. I just hope you're ready for the physical and emotional symptoms of withdrawal. It's not going to be easy. You know that from the last attempt."

"I'm ready," Beth said. "I want to do this while Josh is away. We have just over two weeks to get me through it before he comes home. Will you help me?"

Alex thought for a moment. "Yes, with one condition. That you talk to Dr. Myers and make sure you're doing what's right for the baby."

"I've already done that," Beth said. "And she has gone over everything with me."

"Then, I'm ready when you are."

Beth grabbed her friend's hands in hers. "It's going to take a lot from you. You'll have to stay with me night and day again. And . . . I'll probably be grumpy. I might as well tell you now." Beth offered Alex a wry smile.

"You've been grumpy before." Alex grinned and then leaned forward to give Beth a hug. "What do we need to do?"

"Come on inside, and I'll show you the schedule." Beth slowly got to her feet. "Tomorrow, I'll reduce my dosage by ten percent."

# 41

**December 13, 2002**

Despite concerns, Bethany knew she could do this.

She walked, almost confidently, through the door. She was in control of her destiny.

The interior waiting room wasn't as cheerfully decorated as the lobby. Several girls about her age, and one older woman, occupied the brown leather captain's chairs, which lined the dark green walls.

No one looked up when she entered. The clinic counselor instructed her to take a seat, and Bethany fumbled through the magazines on the corner table before settling into a chair.

The ambient sounds in the room, although low, contributed to her discomfort. In the far corner, a blonde girl, who appeared to be a few years younger than her, cried softly. She held a child's teddy bear tightly to her stomach. Her arms crossed around it while, with her head tilted down and her legs pulled up, she sat in an almost fetal position.

A few minutes later, a woman dressed as a nurse called for the young blonde. She wiped her eyes and brushed her long hair from her face. Then she stood, straightening her shoulders and throwing her head back.

Still holding the bear, the girl grabbed her backpack. She appeared to be no more than seventeen or eighteen years old.

As the young blonde approached, her faded blue eyes met Bethany's.

"Here," she said, thrusting the bear at Bethany. "Maybe this will help you. The wait is over for me."

Bethany took the stuffed toy and cradled it in her arms.

"Good luck," she said. But the young girl didn't reply. Instead, she stiffened her shoulders and followed the nurse down the hallway.

Several other women were called while Bethany waited. Her confidence in what she was about to do wavered as she watched the faces of those going before her. At one point, an older woman came into the room and sat beside her.

Most likely noticing Bethany's unease, the woman leaned close to her ear and whispered, "This is my third abortion, dear. No need to worry."

"Bethany McKinney," the nurse called from a nearby room.

Bethany stood, clasping the bear close to her side, and walked on shaky legs across the room and through the doorway.

"Have a seat." The middle-aged woman flipped through paperwork, then asked Bethany to confirm her identity and her age.

"You spoke to a counselor, is that correct?"

"Yes."

The nurse checked off a small, square box. "Any questions about the procedure?"

"No."

Another box checked.

Their conversation continued for fifteen minutes or so. More questions and checked boxes. "How many weeks since your last period?"

"About eight," Bethany said.

"Do you have any concerns?"

"How long will this take?"

"Most of our patients leave within two hours of the procedure. We follow federal guidelines."

"That's good," was all Bethany could think to say.

"Have you considered options?" The woman asked matter-of-factly.

"What do you mean?"

"Do you certify that you have been counseled about other options?"

"Yes, I understand." Bethany bit her lip.

"Sign here, please." The woman gave her the clipboard and the pen.

After Bethany signed the paper, the woman stamped it with a notary insignia, signed it, and placed it in a folder.

She opened the door to a small antechamber and motioned for Bethany to follow her. "There's a bathroom to your right. You'll need to put on a gown. They're on the shelf." She pointed to everything as she spoke. "There's a locker to store your clothes and personal belongings. If you have one with you, please turn your phone off and leave it in the locker. Once you are finished, take a seat here."

"Yes, ma'am."

Within a few minutes of Bethany completing her instructions, another older lady escorted her into a medical suite off the small room. The gray-haired woman looked like somebody's grandmother and smelled of gingerbread.

"Have a seat up here," she said. "And lie down."

Bethany's hands trembled as she did what she was told.

"Place your feet in these stirrups and try to get comfortable." She helped Bethany adjust her body. "Slide down a bit."

The grandmother-nurse exuded warmth when she explained about the procedure. "The doctor will use the suction aspiration method. It won't take more than fifteen minutes. We'll give you a list of dos and don'ts when you are ready to leave. Okay?"

"Okay." Bethany wiped a tear from her eye.

"Is this your first abortion?"

"Yes."

"You will do fine, dear. Don't be afraid. One day you will have children when the time is right."

Bethany nodded. "Will I feel anything?"

"You will likely have cramps or a slight tugging sensation. I'm about to give you a shot to calm you and a local anesthesia, which will numb your pain. You may have some nausea or sweating. That's completely normal."

Bethany's urge to run screaming out of the room was immediately met by a prick of her skin. The antidote to her fear had been applied. Yet nothing could take away the feeling of betrayal and dread that had begun to set in.

When the doctor entered the room, she knew she had made a mistake. But the sense of pain and regret emerging from deep inside her was somehow lost in the moment. Speaking few words, the doctor went about his work.

—◦◦◦—

**Present Day**

"Are you sure you want to do this?" Alex asked.

"I've never been more certain of anything," Beth said. "I'm ready."

If she could break free of the drugs, she could prove to God that she was doing her best—and then everything would be okay with her baby. At least, that's what she hoped. She was willing to pay the penance. But that didn't make it easier.

A few hours later, spiders of pain began to crawl up and down her legs. She rubbed her hand along her calf muscles in an attempt to bring relief. The leg pain was followed by sweat and clamminess. Soon, a snaking discomfort slithered through her insides.

Two days later, her craving for the narcotics raged within her system, and she wondered if she had made the wrong decision. Was it possible to deal with this without checking into a hospital?

Yet, she knew, if she did, Josh would have to know. She could not face him if she failed again.

The pain and restlessness interrupted her sleep. She would get up each night, walk around the room, and pray. Alex slept in the chair by the bed. She stayed by her side and walked with her. When Beth's body and mind were exhausted, they would catch an hour or two of sleep.

They were both tired. But Alex always endured, no matter what. Even during Beth's temper tantrums. Her moods were as unpredictable as her symptoms. But Alex never appeared to be offended. She refused to accept anything but the steadfast belief that Beth could do this.

Beth suspected that Alex spoke with Dr. Abrams each day to discuss their progress. That thought reassured her. It likely bolstered Alex too. The growing relationship between her care-giver and her doctor had been a positive side effect of Beth's illness.

Step-down days were the worst. There were times when she wanted to crawl outside her skin. The restlessness was a hunger that couldn't be satisfied. And she had uncanny bouts of sneezing. All signs that her body was being extricated from the bonds of its captor.

In two weeks, she had gone from seventy-five milligrams to twenty-five milligrams of morphine, and she couldn't wait to tell Josh. She knew he would be proud of her, but she was determined to surprise him—face to face, when he returned home from the road. He would be here soon, giving her a reason to stay strong.

She needed the boost because her worst symptoms could very well lie ahead. Today would be her first without any narcotics at all. She could already feel the tug between desire and determination. Insufferable anxiety would follow.

The child inside her stirred. *Dear Lord, please ease my baby.*

"Let's have a cup of tea and lunch," Alex suggested, peeking her head into the living room where Beth sat. "You have to keep your strength up. Besides, the baby needs nutrition."

Alex always knew what to say. Beth nodded and stood on shaky legs. She didn't care that much about eating, but she wanted her child to be well.

They walked together into the kitchen, where Alex had laid out an English tea, using Beth's best china.

"Oh, my!" Beth hiccupped. "How wonderful."

"Chicken salad sandwiches and grape cake with mascarpone whipped cream for dessert." Alex's eyes sparkled as she watched Beth's reaction. "We're celebrating your first day without the drugs."

After Alex said grace, Beth unfolded her napkin and picked up her fork for a bite of the dessert.

"So how does Dr. Abrams say I'm doing?" Beth asked.

A mischievous grin spread across Alex's face. "How did you know I had been consulting with him?"

"You don't think I expected you to let me do this on my own, do you?" Beth sighed. "Yum. That's great cake!"

"Eat your sandwich first." Alex gave her a stern look.

"You didn't answer my first question." Beth placed her fork on the table and picked up a quarter of her sandwich.

"Ben said he's proud of you," Alex blushed.

"You're becoming close, aren't you?" Beth asked while chewing.

"I hope so. I really like him." Alex scrunched her face, sending a posse of freckles upward toward her aqua-blue eyes.

"I'm praying for you both," Beth said. "He's a lucky man." She crunched on a carrot stick. "Does he have any idea how good you cook?"

Alex smiled, and then sobered. "Thank you for praying for him. He's seeking spiritual direction right now."

"No wonder God has you in his life," Beth said. "I'm so thankful for the good things that have come from the bad." She placed her hand on her tummy.

⚬≈≈⚬

Two days later, Beth sent up a silent prayer of thanksgiving. She could now dare to believe that she was free. Alex had been a strong and unwavering coach for the past two-and-a-half weeks. She had coaxed when Beth showed weakness and screamed when Beth had become belligerent. She had wiped tears—and even shared them—when Beth cried in desperation. Then she had prayed over her with a sweet and gentle spirit, which so eloquently revealed the heart of a friend.

The painkillers, now gone from Beth's system, had once been necessary to keep the devastating pain at bay, but they had also lured her with beautiful lies that she could forget her past, masking the truth of her situation.

She'd had to wean herself not only from the drugs but also from the denial that had lived inside her for years. She'd had to come to the realization that the only way to find true forgiveness was through repentance and confession.

God had forgiven her a long time ago. But she had never forgiven herself. She would never forget the past, but she could now put it behind her.

With a shovel in hand, she spaded the loose soil alongside her back garden fence. It was a great place to plant summer flowers—and to bury her past.

She took a breath of fresh spring air and looked around. New life exploded in every direction. The dogwood trees were in full bloom, and the purple clematis wound their way around the trellis beside the patio.

Gratitude filled Beth's spirit to overflowing. Many difficult days were now behind her, and she looked to the future with the eyes of faith.

She slipped the rusty red bear inside the gossamer bag she had made for him and gently placed the bag into the hole. Then, shovel-by-shovel, she covered it with dirt.

# 42

**Present Day**

Ryan, can I see you in the back lounge?"

Josh's lithe, sandy-haired road manager cracked open a bottle of spring water and took a long swig before answering. "Sure, man. What's up?"

Without comment, Josh led the way through the bunkroom, careful not to awaken those already sleeping. He closed the bunkroom door behind them. "Have a seat."

Ryan flashed a tentative smile and lowered himself onto the left-side sofa.

"I didn't want it to come to this, but I have no choice," Josh said, watching Ryan shift slightly in his seat. "Remember when we talked about the missing merchandise money a while back?"

Ryan nodded.

"I had hoped it would work itself out. That we would find out it was a mistake. You know, accidental."

Ryan looked directly at him, his eyes intense, but said nothing.

"It appears it's no accident." Josh ran his fingers through his hair and took a seat opposite his adversary. "Someone is stealing from me."

"Do you know who it is?" Ryan's mouth twitched, his expression wavering between surprise and affirmation. "Remember what I told you—"

Josh held up his right hand, signaling for Ryan to stop. "Are you stealing from me, man?"

"Josh . . . me? No. Why would you think that?"

"Because I've seen both sets of books and the wrong set is in your handwriting."

"What? Two? That's impossible." His road manager's lip quivered. "Are you kidding?"

"I wish I was," Josh cleared his throat and watched desperation, and then inspiration, cross Ryan's face.

"Now I get it . . . I've been set up." Ryan slapped his thigh. "Sometimes, when Mitch turns in his papers, I rewrite them. You know what a perfectionist I am." His eyes pleaded for a connection.

"That doesn't explain everything."

"C'mon, man. It's not what you think." Ryan's gaze moved from Josh to the floor and back again. He paused to take a breath. "Hear me out, please. Your problem is with Mitch and Danny."

"How can you say that?" Josh shook his head. Why couldn't Ryan just admit his offense? He drew in a deep breath and considered his words. "So how do you know that?"

"Because Danny offered to cut me in when I questioned him. Remember when we talked before?" Ryan sounded so believable. "I know I should have followed up with you about it before now. But I wanted to wait until this trip was over. You have so much on your—"

"So you just found out about it?"

"Yeah, man, I promise. Just this week."

Could Ryan be telling the truth? It was possible that Mitch could doctor the books on his own.

But Danny? *No way was he involved.*

"I know you think Danny is perfect. But he's not the loyal, meek little Christian you think he is. He's a lot different when he's with the rest of the guys," Ryan snorted. "I've always thought he was capable of something like this. He's a two-faced—"

"Stop it." Josh had had enough. "Where's your proof that Mitch and Danny are involved?"

"I realize this makes me look culpable. I should have said something sooner, but I've suspected for a while that Danny and Mitch were stealing from you." He lowered his voice as if he feared someone would hear him above the roar of the bus engine beneath them.

"But can you prove it?"

Ryan stared out the window of the bus for a moment, looking into the darkness. "I have proof at my house," he said. "I have the original merchandise paperwork in my files. The sales reports that are in Mitch's handwriting." Ryan's confidence seemed to grow with every word he spoke. "I wish I had brought this to you earlier. I had really hoped I was wrong, but now I know I wasn't."

"When can I see the evidence?"

"This week."

Josh rummaged through his bag for his songwriting journal and tore out a blank piece of paper. He scribbled Bob Bradford's office address on it. "Here," he said, holding the paper out to his road manager. "Meet me at my accountant's office at 9:30 a.m. on Tuesday."

Ryan rose to his feet. "I will be happy to."

"And bring everything," Josh said.

"Everything," Ryan repeated.

"You're going to have to prove this to me," Josh said before Ryan punched the button that opened the door. "You're their supervisor. The merchandise reports are in your handwriting, so the burden of proof rests with you."

"Understood," Ryan said, as he left, closing the door behind him.

Josh reflected for a few minutes on the conversation, thinking back to everything Bob Bradford had told him. Could Ryan be telling the truth?

He shook his head. There was no way he had misjudged Danny. At least in his mind, his friend was innocent until proven guilty, even if Ryan's words left reason to doubt.

A few minutes later Josh made his way through the semi-darkness of the bunkroom, heading toward the front of the bus. Ryan's curtain was closed, an indication that he had gone to bed. In fact, every curtain was now closed.

Josh decided to keep Danny company for a while before turning in for the night.

⚊⚊∞⚊⚊

Raindrops exploded on the windshield as the bus navigated the wet superhighway. It had been thirty minutes since they crossed the Ohio River into Kentucky, heading home on Interstate 24.

Josh threw a handful of M&M's into his mouth. "That's almost hail," he said.

Danny nodded, fighting the steering wheel only a few feet from where Josh sat. "It's the wind that worries me. Hail won't do more than raise the insurance premium. This wind is dangerous."

"I can feel it." Josh tightened his fingers around the arm of the jump seat.

"They said on the radio an eighteen-wheeler blew off the road in Clarksville. We'll be there in a couple of hours."

"Have you talked to anyone in Nashville?" Josh asked.

"I called my dad earlier. He said it was rough there too."

Josh considered calling Beth, but it was one o'clock in the morning. Besides, their last few conversations had been less than pleasant. She had been moody every time they had spoken recently. They had plenty to discuss when he got home. No need to stir things up now.

A gust of wind and Danny's voice snapped Josh back to the moment.

"Why don't you get some rest, boss? I can handle this." Danny gave him a sideways glance.

"I suppose I should. Beth has a doctor appointment in the morning."

A few minutes later, Josh climbed, fully clothed, into bed. No need to get too comfortable with just a few hours to sleep before they arrived in Nashville.

Only the sound of the diesel engine filled his ears, but he could feel the sway of the bus as it cut through the stormy night. Judging from the way the big coach rocked back and forth, the wind had increased. Yet, while it didn't take long before sleep overtook him, he awakened into a dark dream world.

The briny taste of salt wet his lips and stung his eyes. Somehow he knew he was inside the belly of a great whale. A shiver of terror passed through him, and he closed his eyes. When he opened them, he saw a man standing nearby. The man looked at him, smiled, and then began to pray.

Josh knew instantly it was Jonah.

Without warning, the fish wrenched from side to side, and Josh fell into the midst of the hot sordid rot of the fish's void. When he looked up, Jonah had disappeared. Still, Josh sensed he was not alone. Comfort began to spread throughout his body, like warm seawater running through his veins. In the utter blackness of this alien place, God spoke to him, making a promise.

*Everything will be all right.*

Almost immediately, Josh felt a rumbling that started deep within the great fish. A rush of water caught him up. He twirled and swirled within the putrid water, which now oddly reeked of brimstone. Josh flailed his arms, fearing he would drown within it. Then he felt himself being expelled from the murky prison.

It was then Josh realized that he had awakened from his dream into a nightmare. The black Prevost was out of control. He had ridden the highways for years, long enough to know what was happening. They were being tossed around unmercifully by the storm. He could hear the wind and the rain slamming into them. He could hear it above the whine of the engine. The smooth road had become rutted. The straight path crooked.

Life itself was on the line.

He did his best to sit up. He wanted to walk the hallway to the front of the bus and to see his fate. Before he could move, the world began to roll. He reached for the top of his bunk—or was it the bottom? And he held on.

They rolled and rolled and rolled.

*Oh, God, please . . .*

# 43

**Present Day**

The scream of the phone startled Beth from sleep. She looked at the bedside clock. A call at four in the morning never brought good news. Especially when Josh was on the road. She answered with breathy apprehension.

"Mrs. Harrison. This is Officer Wayne Pugh of the Kentucky Highway Patrol. Your husband has been injured in a bus accident."

Beth sat up in bed. "Is he . . . Is he okay?"

"He has been taken to Four Rivers Hospital in Paducah."

A few minutes later, Beth held her stomach, trying not to retch again, while Alex dialed the phone.

"This is Alexandra Hayes. I'm calling about Joshua Harrison. I'm calling for his wife. Yes. I can wait." She gave the phone to Beth.

Beth listened to music on hold for what seemed to be an eternity.

"Neurological ICU."

"Yes . . . this is Bethany Harrison. My husband is a patient. I'm calling to find out how he's doing."

"Harrison? Yes, he's stable, ma'am. He's unconscious, but stable."

"Can you tell me what happened?"

"I'm afraid that's all I can tell you at this time. However, I can have the doctor call you."

"Please . . . he can call my cell number. I'm leaving Nashville now and should be there in about three hours." Beth gave her number to the nurse and then repeated details aloud about the location of the hospital so Alex could take notes.

A few minutes later, Alex had their bags packed. "I've got my keys. We need to get going," she said.

"Let's take Josh's Jeep," Beth said, blinking back tears. "We can make better time in the rain."

***

Beth watched as Alex gripped the steering wheel, and the Jeep fought its way through a windblown downpour. Rain pelted the windshield. Alex eased her foot on and off the accelerator, navigating through pools of water and passing slower-moving vehicles.

Although Beth wanted to be there as soon as possible, she knew her friend was doing the best she could. Visibility was little more than ten feet ahead. Without warning, they would come upon eighteen-wheelers and other vehicles in ditches or pulled off the side of the road. Some temporarily escaped the hammering rain by parking beneath overpasses. But Alex never hinted that she wanted to stop.

Daylight broke about the time they crossed the double bridges, which spanned the Tennessee River in Kentucky. They drove most of the way in silence. Twice, Beth called the hospital, hoping to learn more about Josh. She was told only that his condition hadn't changed. A few times, she and Alex prayed out loud, for Josh, and for the others who had been riding the bus.

Shortly before they arrived in Paducah, the doctor called.

"Mrs. Harrison, this is Mark Franklin. I'm the neurologist on duty at Four Rivers."

"Please give me some good news," Beth said.

"We have the bleeding stopped, but he's still unconscious. We're about to take him down for scans. We should know more by the time you get here. Come on up to the third floor."

<hr />

A strange peace descended over Josh when he realized he was back in the water. This time, he was swimming in a river, sweet and amniotic. He could see the likes of heaven surrounding him, yet he knew it wasn't heaven. It was more like home. Home in Alabama.

The smells of childhood overtook him. A comforting mix of fragrant Wisteria, spicy pinewood, and the dusky perfume of his father's Bible.

He reached out to touch the soft, fleshy walls, which surrounded him as he floated in a sea of warm light. Somehow he knew he was back inside his mother's womb. There was no pain, only great anticipation.

A light in the distance called to him without words. It was a brilliant light, which both enticed and frightened him. Had death come? Or was it life that beckoned?

He heard a rumbling sound.

Josh knew instantly it was the voice of God. The tone and intensity brought both comfort and great dread at once.

*You entered this world because of my mercy, and you leave it by way of my mercy. Just as I have saved you from death, I have given you life. I have loved you, because you are my child.*

**275**

Josh heard himself questioning the voice. "What does all this mean?"

*Peace, be still*, the voice answered.

And then . . . silence.

—∞∞—

Beth walked into Josh's hospital room, not sure what to expect. But she wasn't prepared to see an empty space where his bed should have been. Her heart jumped into her throat. *Was everything okay?*

A nurse stepped into the room, just behind her. "Mr. Harrison is in scanning," she said. "Are you his wife?"

"Yes, how is he?" Beth's lip quivered.

"He's doing okay, honey." The nurse reassured her, and then noticed her baby bump. "When are you due?"

"Not quite two months."

"Well, you need to get off your feet. Make yourself comfortable." She nodded toward the chair in the corner. "Can I bring you something? Water? Orange juice?"

"Water would be great."

She turned to Alex. "How about you?"

"Yes, water, thank you."

Thirty minutes passed before they heard the faint whir of wheels. The noise grew louder, and then a knock. The door opened and a technician appeared.

"He's back." The young man flashed a smile as he guided Josh's bed through the doorway. Another technician followed, pushing with one hand, using the other to steady the bags that hung above Josh's head.

Beth focused on the pale, handsome man lying in the bed. He looked so vulnerable, yet at peace. He appeared to be sleeping.

It took several minutes for the technicians to rearrange the tubes and hook up the medicine dispensers. After they left the room, she hurried to her husband's bedside. He had a number of bruises and abrasions on his forehead and left cheek. And his head was bandaged. She stroked his arm and bent to kiss him on the forehead. When she did, he mumbled something she couldn't understand.

"Josh, it's Beth," she half-shouted in his ear.

His eyelashes fluttered, sending a chill down her spine. *Could he be waking?*

A few seconds later, he opened his eyes.

"Hi." She leaned over the bed and peered into his eyes.

"Hi, yourself," he whispered. The corners of his mouth turned upward.

"How do you feel?"

"I hurt all over. Where am I?"

"In the hospital. You were in a bus wreck."

"I know. Where?"

"You're in Paducah at—"

A tall man in a white coat entered the room and walked to Josh's bedside. "Mr. Harrison, it's Dr. Franklin. Are you nauseated?"

"A bit." Josh tried to nod. "Oh—"

"Try not to move your head more than you have to. You'll likely have a headache for a few hours—or even a few days. But you're a lucky man." He turned to Beth. "Are you his wife?"

"Yes," Beth said.

"He's fortunate. It appears he came through with only a concussion and several contusions."

Beth smiled, but her relief didn't last for long. The doctor nodded toward the hallway. "Would you mind stepping outside with me?"

"Of course." She looked to Josh.

"Mr. Harrison, I need to borrow your wife for a few minutes. We need to fill out some of your paperwork."

"I'll stay with you, Josh." Alex reached to touch Josh's arm and asked if he needed anything.

After Beth had stepped into the hallway, Dr. Franklin directed her to a chair. "Please, have a seat. We need your assistance. We've been unable to reach the next of kin of the driver of the bus."

Beth gasped.

"He's in critical condition. We need to talk to his family for surgical permissions. Can you help me?"

Beth's mind raced. "Yes . . . his name is Danny Stevens. He's single, so his father would be his next-of-kin." She fumbled for her phone. "I have his phone number, but I don't think I have his father's." She searched through every contact in her list. "Wait, here it is. It's Jim Stevens." She gave the doctor the number.

He scribbled it onto Josh's chart. "Thank you," he smiled. "I need to take care of this, but I will stop by to see your husband again before I leave. He's going to be fine." He offered a reassuring look. "Is this your first child?"

Beth glanced at her protruding tummy. "Yes."

"Boy or girl?" the doctor asked.

"We're not sure."

"Everything will be okay." He placed his hand on hers. "Try to relax as much as you can. I know this is traumatic for you. But we'll get your husband out of here and home soon." He turned to leave.

"Doctor, how is everyone else?" Beth had almost forgotten to ask.

He turned to address her question. "Surprisingly, nothing too serious. We're keeping everyone overnight to make sure there are no major underlying problems."

Beth took deep breaths as she walked back into Josh's room. The anxiety of the past few hours, and the loss of sleep, had caught up with her. Now that she was convinced that Josh would be all right, she remembered her appointment with Dr. Myers.

"Alex, would you do me a favor?"

"Sure." Alex turned to her.

"Would you mind calling Dr. Myers's office to let them know I can't make my appointment today?"

"I already did," Alex smiled. "And they reminded me that you need to watch your blood pressure. And," she pulled up a chair, "to stay off your feet."

"Thank you," Beth flung herself into the chair. Her throat was parched and her skin burned. Remnants of the morphine cravings.

Josh would be proud of her when she could finally tell him. But she wouldn't even consider it until she had him home and the reassurance that everything was going to be okay.

Alex interrupted her thoughts. "I'm going to the cafeteria to get us a cup of hot chocolate. Would you like something to eat?"

"Yes. That would be great." Beth cradled her stomach with both hands. "I think I'm finally relaxed enough to keep something down."

"I'll see what I can find. You and Josh enjoy each other's company for a few minutes."

Beth nodded toward the bed. "Looks like he'll be sleeping." She grinned.

"That's what you both need." Alex pulled another chair in front of Beth. "Prop your feet up and try to nap while I'm gone."

Beth felt the heat rising to her cheeks. "Just what you needed," she said. "Two of us to take care of. I'm so sorry."

# 44

**Present Day**

Beth and Alex made the decision to stay in Paducah overnight. The next morning, they released Josh, leaving behind
only Danny, who waited for a transfer by air ambulance to
Davidson County Medical Center in Nashville.

While Alex waited in the car, Beth accompanied Josh to
Danny's room for a quick visit before they left for Nashville.
She hadn't seen her husband cry since his father's funeral. But,
as she studied his drawn and battered face, she could tell that
he was fighting back tears for his friend.

Josh cleared his throat and placed his hand on Danny's hospital bedrail. "Hey, man, you hang in there. They're taking you
to Nashville to get you fixed up. We'll see you there. You can
trust those people. They will take good care of you."

Josh squeezed Danny's hand. Although he didn't open his
eyes, the big man squeezed back. Or, at least, that's what Josh
appeared to believe, because he smiled. However, Beth saw a
tear drop from her husband's cheek and fall onto the crisp,
white sheet which stretched across Danny's hospital bed.

"Let's pray before we leave for Nashville." Josh reached with
his free hand to clasp Beth's hand. She took Danny's other

hand, forming a circle of prayer, and Josh prayed. "Heavenly Father, we come to you with humbleness and great faith. We beseech you to forgive all our fears, our doubts, and our struggles. We give great thanks for your love and your healing. Please keep Danny safe on his flight to Nashville."

"Amen," Beth whispered.

Josh addressed his friend again. "Okay, man, we need to leave so they can prep you for the trip. Beth and I will see you in Nashville. We'll be praying for you. Don't doubt or worry a single minute. We're all praying."

This time there was no acknowledgment from Danny. Josh's face stiffened, and Beth prayed that Josh wouldn't have to lose his best friend.

⟪∞⟫

Several days later Josh grabbed an empty bag and a flashlight from the back of his Jeep Cherokee and slammed the hatch door closed.

"Wait for me here," he told Beth.

"Be careful, honey."

He smiled and gave her a quick hug. She had fussed at him all day. "I'm fine. Stop worrying."

He walked over to the big, black bus, which had been towed to a holding yard at the bus leasing company in Hermitage. The door had been shunted open by emergency workers, so Josh could easily step inside.

Although the coach had rolled several times, the majority of the damage had been done to the driver's compartment. According to the police report, it had struck a tree on the final rotation.

Silence hung in the air when Josh stood on the lower step in front of the jump seat, looking around. He had ridden in this seat many times, perhaps for thousands of miles, never dreaming something like this would actually happen.

The framework and exterior walls had held, just like they had been designed to do, but the interior was in shambles. Shards of glass littered the floor and covered the leather upholstery of the jump seat.

Never again would he look upon his travels the same. He was blessed to have come through the ordeal with his life. One of his employees was still fighting for his. He said a prayer for Danny and stepped up onto the landing beside the driver's seat.

It was covered with bloodstains and more broken glass. Josh averted his gaze and turned toward the rear of the bus. He shined his flashlight around the front lounge and galley, pushing Danny from his mind, as he started to make his way across the cluttered path, which had once been clear. And much easier to navigate.

No need to linger. The air was stale, and he walked through knee-deep piles of trash. Cereal boxes, kitchen utensils, and electronic equipment—the remains of their comfortable life on the road—were strewn across the carpet.

The bunkroom door, which had been ratcheted partially open, stood guard over the inner sanctum of the bus. Josh raised his light high above his head, providing a better view of the unlit hallway ahead. Bed linens and personal belongings were scattered across the floor. The late day sunlight filtering through the back lounge windows created an eerie glow at the end of the long, dark corridor.

He focused the flashlight beam on the ceiling and caught his breath when he saw a three-foot tear in the metal. Something must have ripped through the roof when the bus rolled down the hillside.

He tripped on a tangled mess of linens, and had to steady himself against the closet wall, before continuing toward the last row of bunks. Danny's bed was in the last row on the right, just below Ryan's.

Kneeling on the floor beside the bunk, Josh held the flashlight with his left hand and looked around for items of importance. Remarkably, some things still remained on the shelf above the bed. A disposable camera, a pack of gum, and a Bible. He fought back a tear as he reached for the Bible. It was the kind of thing he was hoping to find, to save for his friend. For when he recovered.

Josh placed the Bible into his bag and continued to peruse the area. Brightly colored postcards from cities they had visited on their tour lined the wall and ceiling of the small compartment. Nothing that couldn't be replaced. He shuffled through the disheveled bed linens and found a few CDs and Danny's toiletry bag. Except for his hanging clothes, that was probably everything. Josh stuffed it all into the bag.

He started to stand to leave and then remembered that some of the guys stored books, photos, and even cash underneath their mattresses. He'd better take the time to make sure nothing important remained. The bus would be heading to the salvage yard any day.

He switched the flashlight to his right hand, using his left to hoist the mattress, and began searching at the front, working his way to the foot of the bed. Nothing.

*Wait. There was something lying in the far corner.*

Josh stretched with his entire body, lowering his head and holding the mattress up with his shoulder. He grabbed the object with his thumb and forefinger and pulled. It appeared to be a canvas bag. He placed it into his large bag and let the mattress fall back onto its platform.

On his way back through the bus, Josh opened Danny's closet. He gathered loose items from the closet floor and tossed them into his bag. Then he grabbed the few hangers full of clothing, folded them over his arm, and made his way to the front of the bus and outside.

The cool evening air refreshed him.

Beth, who had been standing nearby, reached for the bag, freeing up his hands to carry the hanging clothes to the Jeep. He hung them on the clothing hook inside his rear passenger compartment.

"Is that everything?" Beth asked.

"All I could find for Danny," he said, grabbing an empty bag from the backseat of the SUV. "I'll be back after I gather my own things."

Beth still held the sack containing Danny's personal items.

"You need to rest," Josh said, opening the front passenger door for his wife. She climbed inside, placing the bag on the floorboard in front of her, and he slammed the door.

It didn't take him long to clean out his bunk and closet, and to go through the drawers in the back lounge. Soon they were on their way home.

"How bad was it?" Beth asked.

"Awful. But thank God it held together enough to keep us alive."

"Did you lose anything important?"

"Nothing we can't replace," he told her, stretching his arm across the console and resting his hand on hers. "I've got you. That's all that matters."

She smiled.

"Why don't you look through Danny's things and see if there's anything we need to take to the hospital for him. His dad might want to hold on to the Bible I found. It's at the bottom."

Beth leaned forward and rifled through the sack. "What's in the canvas bag?"

"I don't know. Open it," he said.

She unzipped the red bag and looked inside. "Josh . . ."

"What, honey?"

"It's filled with cash, small bills." Her voice was shaking. "There must be twenty thousand dollars in here."

Josh slowed the Jeep and pulled to the side of the road.

"Could that be the missing merchandise money?" He mumbled, almost to himself. *Was it possible he had been wrong about Danny? Could Ryan have been telling the truth?*

The halls of the hospital were silent, except for the low rumble of a surgical cart rolling along the corridor toward them. Josh paced back and forth while Beth hovered in the corner near the entrance to the neurological intensive care unit.

Danny would soon be taken into surgery, and Josh wanted to let his friend know he was pulling for him. Innocent or guilty of stealing merchandise money, his driver's life hung in the balance. Josh would not let him down now.

Jim Stevens had been sitting at his son's bedside since he had been transported to Davidson County Medical Center forty-eight hours ago. The older man appeared even older today, beaten down from grief and worry. He'd lost his wife, and he could now lose his son.

A few months ago this turn of events might have completely destroyed Josh's faith, but much had happened since that time. His own near-death experience. Beth's incredible break from drug addiction. And the lingering reminder from Danny that God directed our lives and stood by his promises.

With a loud pop, the twin metal doors of the ICU opened, and the two surgical attendants, dressed in green, wheeled the rolling cart inside.

"It won't be long," Josh said to Beth, who had finally taken a seat on the marble ledge of the nearby windows.

Six floors below them, cars and pedestrians went about their normal activities. Sunlight streamed into the hallway, a surreal contradiction to what was going on inside.

"Are you okay there?" he asked Beth.

"I'm fine. We'll be sitting in uncomfortable chairs in the waiting room soon enough."

"For quite a while, I'm afraid." The doctor had predicted an eight- to ten-hour surgery. "Maybe I should take you home after this. There's no need for you to stay."

"I want to be with you," Beth told him. "I almost lost you. I don't want to ever be without you again."

Moisture filled Josh's eyes for the second time today. God had given him much to appreciate.

A few minutes later, the ICU doors opened, and Danny's bed rolled into the hallway. Jim Stevens walked beside him. When he saw Josh and Beth, he motioned for them to step closer.

"I know you want to see him," he said. He backed away so Josh could approach the bed.

Josh nodded and grabbed Beth's hand, leading her with him to the head of the cart.

"I know you can hear me, man, even though you can't talk right now." He leaned closer to Danny's ear and spoke distinctly. "Beth and I want you to know we're here with your daddy. We'll take care of him while you're in surgery." Josh cleared his throat. "The doctors will take good care of you. We'll see you in the recovery room."

Josh fought back tears. He reached across the bedrail to lay his hand on top of Danny's, careful not to disturb the monitor wires and tubes, which ran every which way. He caught the attention of the technician standing nearby. "Do we have time to say a quick prayer?"

The man nodded.

Beth reached for Jim Stevens's hand and took it in her own. Then she offered her free hand to Josh. He took it and began to pray. "Dear Lord, we ask you to guide the doctor's hands, to give him strength and wisdom, so he can do his best for our friend Danny. We pray, Lord, that you would work through these doctors and nurses and heal his wounds, the trauma to his head. We love Danny, Lord, and we love you. In Jesus' name, we pray. Amen."

"Thank you," Jim Stevens said, backing away.

"We'll see you in the waiting room," Josh nodded.

The technicians motioned for Danny's father to stay with them as they prepared to roll the bed down the hallway. "You can stay with us to just outside the surgical suite, sir," one of them said.

Josh watched the old man, walking bent and tired, and following his son's gurney down the corridor. At the end, they disappeared into the elevator.

# 45

**Present Day**

Ben Abrams had prepared all of his life for this moment. He had long entreated God for an epiphany. For the certainty that he existed, and the assurance that he could have a relationship with him.

"Help me, God." He prayed silently over his patient, whose chances of surviving surgery—much less of a complete recovery—were in the low percentages.

"Give me the ability to save the unsavable," Ben pleaded. "I'll consider it a sign that you can also save me."

With that humble request, he picked up the scalpel and made his initial incision into Danny Stevens's shaved head.

# 46

Waiting wasn't easy. Josh occupied his time in the surgical waiting area by reading well-worn magazines, mindlessly staring at the soap operas playing out on a muted television, and praying.

Lots of praying.

Beth appeared to be resting comfortably. She had dozed off in a leather recliner next to him. That in itself helped him rest.

Jim Stevens occasionally walked the floor and made phone calls to his daughter in Florida, to keep her informed and to give himself the strength to deal with the possibility of losing his only son.

Four hours into the operation, a surgical nurse called to report that things were going as expected. Jim Stevens seemed to be buoyed by the news. However, Josh wasn't sure how much consolation could be read into that statement. She had also said the surgery would last another five hours, maybe more.

At one point, Josh walked to the cafeteria to bring back cold sandwiches and drinks for everyone. It had provided a nice break for him, and otherwise Mr. Stevens would have gone all day eating from the vending machine. He appeared to appreciate all of Josh's help, thanking him over and over again.

He knew Mr. Stevens had no idea about the money Josh had found in his son's bunk. If time proved Danny was the thief, it would break his father's heart. Josh vowed to himself never to mention it to Mr. Stevens if something happened to Danny. There was no need to bring more misery on this faithful, old man. He had been a pillar of strength and edification to his congregation, and to his family, for years.

But what would he do if Danny fully recovered and he learned his driver, his friend, had been stealing? Josh shifted in his seat. It was a problem he must confront when the time came. If that time came.

He glanced at the clock on the waiting room wall. They had three hours to go before they knew Danny's prognosis.

In the meantime, Josh would continue to ferret out the facts, as he knew them. There had to be a reasonable explanation for the twenty thousand dollars in Danny's bunk.

At two thirty, Ryan Majors walked through the waiting room door. He had a solemn expression on his face. His left arm was bandaged and hung in a sling from his shoulders. His usually robust road manager appeared gaunt and haggard, although he was still dressed to the nines.

Ryan nodded to Josh as he approached, but he reached first for Jim Stevens's hand. "I'm sorry to hear about Danny, sir," he said. "He is a fine man. I pray that God will be with you both through this."

"Thank you, son. And you are?"

"I'm Ryan Majors. I work with Danny . . . and Josh." He nodded toward Josh.

"I will tell Danny you came by. Were you in the wreck?" Mr. Stevens asked, noticing Ryan's arm.

"Yes, but this is nothing compared to your son's injuries. I'm sure he put up a good fight for all of us against the wind that night. According to the police report, we went head-to-head with a tornado."

Josh studied Ryan as he spoke and thought he noticed a tear in his eye.

After a few more words with Jim Stevens, Ryan turned to Josh. "May I see you outside for a minute?"

"Of course." Josh stood to follow him.

After they turned the corner and found a quiet place in the back hallway, Ryan made a request. "Please let me talk for a few minutes without interruption. I have some things I need to get out."

Josh nodded, running his hand through his hair and wondering what could be so important.

"Danny is an innocent man. If anything should happen, I never want you to doubt that." Ryan stared straight into Josh's eyes, not blinking.

Josh bit his lip while contemplating the statement. There was much he could say, but he held back.

Ryan averted his eyes to the floor and continued. "I know he's innocent because I am the one who took the money." Ryan shifted from one foot to the other. "I, alone, am to blame. Not Mitch, not Danny. No one but me."

"I appreciate—"

"No. Please, let me finish." Ryan held up his hand, looking directly at Josh.

Josh could see both fear and sadness in Ryan's eyes. His face was drawn and vulnerable.

"I have no excuse, except that I let my life get out of control. I know you don't care about the details, but I owe them to you." He averted his gaze again. "Or, maybe . . . I just need to get them out."

"Okay," Josh said.

"My wife left me. It had been coming for a while. In some ways I don't blame her. Perhaps I left her a long time ago. Got too big for my britches, as my dad would say." He paused to reflect, and then continued. "In some ways, she did too. Our success happened quickly. We moved into the big house, bought the expensive furniture, and became addicted to the high life. We were both grasping at things that didn't matter and ignoring the things that did."

Josh's heart softened to Ryan. It was a story that could very well have been his own.

"Lacy was lonely with my being gone all the time. To compensate for that, she wanted more things. More club memberships. More clothes. Things to occupy her time. I was afraid of losing her, because I do love her." Ryan looked into Josh's eyes again. "And I did the only thing I knew to do. I know it was wrong. I knew it was wrong at the time. But I thought I would pay you back."

"May I speak now?"

"Yes. I just want to say I'm sorry. I'm sorry . . ." Ryan looked away.

"You accused an innocent man," Josh said. "That's the worst thing you could have done."

"I know," Ryan nodded.

"The money can be paid back, but a man's reputation can never be repaired."

"I will apologize to Danny after he gets through this." Tears ran down Ryan's face.

"What if he doesn't?"

"I don't know how I will live with myself." Ryan wiped his face with his sleeve.

"As for the stealing, you know I have to—should—turn you in to the authorities."

"I fully expect that." Ryan stiffened. His lithe frame looked like he could break in two at any minute.

"But I won't."

A look of surprise crossed Ryan's face.

"Not if you repay the money."

"Thank you—"

"Let me finish. I heard you out," Josh said. "God has taught me a lot in the past few months. And I had a lot to learn." He cleared his throat, fighting back emotions. "If he's taught me anything, it's that mercy and forgiveness trump everything."

Ryan nodded.

"My faith has sometimes been weak. But God has given me mercy so that I might have faith." He looked into Ryan's eyes. "And that I might show mercy."

"I'll pay you back soon."

"Do you still have my accountant's number?"

"Yes."

"Please work it out with him."

"Thank you," Ryan nodded. "I'll set up the payments—with interest—after I find another job."

Josh studied him, trying to determine if Ryan was, indeed, sincere. "You have a job. With me."

"What?"

"You're still my guitar player. You're the best in the business."

"I didn't expect—"

"But I'm going to have to discharge you as my road manager," Josh said. "That's a pay cut, you understand."

"Yes . . . I do. Certainly. I can't expect you to trust me."

"It's too much for one man to handle," Josh said.

"I'll pay you back, Josh. One way or the other. I have my house up for sale. I promise, you'll get the money."

"I believe you will." Josh offered Ryan his hand. "We'll work it out. But I have to ask you one thing."

"Yes?" Fear crossed Ryan's face.

"Did you set Danny up before the wreck?"

Ryan looked away momentarily, and then back to Josh. "You found the money? The twenty thousand?"

"Yes."

"I guess that's a good thing, huh? I mean, that's a start on what I owe you."

"Yes, it is." Josh laid a hand on Ryan's shoulder.

"Thank you."

"Okay. Get that arm healed up, man. I need to get back to Beth and Mr. Stevens." Josh motioned toward the waiting room. "I hope you can work things out with your wife."

"Me too," Ryan said, smoothing his shirt. "Can I ask you one more thing?"

"Sure."

"Will you pray for me?"

"Of course."

Back in the waiting room Josh stood watching Beth sleep. Jim Stevens had also dozed off. Ryan's confession was almost too much to take in. An unexpected end to a bad situation. A nightmare that had been resolved.

Now . . . if only Danny would make it through surgery.

"Would a member of the Danny Stevens family, please come to the phone?" The attendant announced over the loudspeaker.

Jim Stevens awoke, startled. "Was that for me?"

"Yes." Josh took a deep gulp of air.

Jim Stevens rose quickly from his seat and rushed to the reception desk. Josh awakened Beth and whispered that the call had come.

From his chair, he watched Jim Stevens pick up the phone and identify himself. He could only see Mr. Steven's face from a distance of several yards. At first, his expression was stiff. He listened and didn't speak. A few minutes later, his shoulders shook, as if he were having a seizure. Then the old man began to sob.

Josh's heart climbed to his throat. *Oh, no. The worst has happened.*

He stood up and met Jim Stevens halfway back to their seats. A big smile crossed his face as he approached.

"He made it," the old man said. "He made it."

Josh grabbed Danny's father by the shoulders and hugged him. Then Beth hugged both of them.

"What did they say?" She asked, brushing back tears.

"Dr. Abrams said it was the most difficult surgery he had ever performed. He said Danny's situation was worse than he had expected once he got inside, but that everything went perfectly." Jim Stevens shook his head. "He said he felt like he had divine assistance with this one. That he couldn't take the credit."

"That's what he said?" Beth's eyes filled with tears.

Jim Stevens took a long breath. "Yes. And he said he thinks Danny will recover completely."

# 47

**Present Day**

When Josh visited Danny in his hospital room six days later, he couldn't believe how much progress his friend had made in such a short time.

"You look great, man."

"The good news is I feel better than I look," Danny laughed. "Ouch!" A pained grin spread across his face. "It still hurts to move my head."

"It'll take a while, but you're almost over the hill."

Danny gave him a confused look. "What do you mean? I don't think thirty-five is so old."

Josh chuckled. "That's not what I meant. Don't you remember what you told me on the road awhile back? That we sometimes have to see with faith and not worry about what's over the next hill?"

"I remember," Danny nodded, slowly this time. "I can tell you for sure, I'm ready to coast for a while." A grin spread across his face.

"So when can you go home?"

"Not until next week," Danny's smile faded. "I can't wait to get back on the road and drive that new Van Hool you've got on order."

Josh stared at him, not sure how to break the news. "You mean you were planning to drive again?" He took a deep breath to deliver the bad news. "I've already hired a new driver."

"You have?"

Josh watched Danny's eyebrows knit together. "It's because of the wreck, isn't it? It wasn't my fault . . . " Danny looked sullen.

"It wasn't your fault. In fact, from what I've heard, you probably saved our lives." Josh shook his head. "I just think you'll be too busy to drive."

"What do you mean?"

"I'm hoping you'll agree to be my new road manager."

"Really? You want me?" He poked at his chest. "To be your road manager?"

Josh could see the excitement in his friend's eyes.

After thinking about it, he frowned. "Are you asking me because you don't trust me to drive?"

"No, I'm asking you because I trust you completely."

Danny had no idea about the things that had happened between Josh and Ryan, including the stolen money Josh had found under Danny's mattress.

"So what's Ryan going to do?"

"Play guitar."

"You mean . . . I'll be his boss?" A sly grin emerged with Danny's full understanding.

"Yes. Payback is—"

"Oh, son, I'm sorry. I didn't know you had company. I'll come back later." Jim Stevens turned to leave just as he entered the hospital room.

"Please don't, Mr. Stevens. I was on my way out the door." Josh nodded to the chair beside the bed. "Please have a seat."

"How is everything with you, young man?" The elder Stevens offered his hand to Josh. "Has your wife had her baby yet?"

"No, sir. She's not due for a few weeks."

"Please give her my regards. She's a sweet young woman. Pretty, too." He winked.

"Thank you. I'm on my way home right now. She's cleaning the house. Nesting I think it's called." Josh chuckled.

"Josh and his wife have been through a lot," Danny told his dad.

"We all have," Josh said. An old thundercloud of fear hovered around him when he thought about the last obstacle in the road they were traveling. "Now, if Beth can just deliver a healthy baby."

"We'll be praying for you," Jim Stevens said. "Don't you doubt that. In fact, my entire church is praying."

"One more hill," Danny added.

Josh smiled and nodded.

*He had one more hill. But God hadn't brought him this far for him to give up now.*

<hr />

Beth had been contemplating her decision for weeks. Today she would finally do something about it. After Josh left for the hospital, she settled into the rocking chair in the nursery and dialed the phone.

Pamela Morris answered on the second ring.

Beth took a deep breath before introducing herself. "Mrs. Morris, it's Bethany Harrison. I met you at Nell Stevens's funeral."

"Yes, of course, I remember you, young lady. Have you had your baby yet?"

"No, ma'am. I'm due next month. I'm a bit nervous, I must say."

"Don't worry, my dear. I had four of them. You'll forget the pain quickly, but you'll always remember the first time you hold them. They're a blessing."

"That's why I'm calling you." Beth bit her upper lip, uncertain of how much she wanted to relate. "I've thought a lot about our conversation last fall and, after I have the baby, I would like to volunteer with your group. Do you have a need for office help? I'm a bookkeeper's assistant."

"Why, yes. That would be lovely. May I ask why you feel so strongly about our group?"

Beth gathered her thoughts. "I want to do it in Nell Stevens's memory. Not that I could ever replace her, but as a tribute to what she tried to do in my life."

"I seem to remember you said you hadn't met her," the older lady said.

"I didn't think I had at the time you and I spoke. But I realized later, after thinking about it, that I may have."

"Really? How did you know her, honey?"

"I believe she was the woman in front of the abortion clinic who tried to counsel me before I had my abortion many years ago."

———— ∞ ————

Beth set out to clean and organize the baby's room with renewed vigor. For the first time in years, she felt truly free. Things had come full circle, and she was moving beyond the guilt and denial that had haunted the last decade of her life. She would now be able to help others make an informed decision when they had an impossible choice.

Of course, they would have to choose for themselves, just as she had done. But, if she had been more aware of the facts—including the lingering emotional and physical side effects of an abortion—she would have chosen differently. No doubt about that.

She wanted other women to have those facts before they decided. To understand the implications of what they were about to do and to know they had options. She wanted to assure them they were not alone.

Volunteering wouldn't change her past. But it would help her stay focused on the present, where God wanted her to be.

In that present, she was now busy preparing the house for her baby's arrival. There was so much to do in the three remaining weeks of her pregnancy she could keep herself occupied night and day. Thankfully, Josh was home to remind her not to wear herself out.

She sang a favorite childhood lullaby while she folded and stored linens, dusted furniture, and made notes in her pregnancy journal. When she glanced at the clock, it was twelve thirty. Past time for lunch by the baby's schedule.

On her way to the kitchen, Beth detoured to open the living room draperies. A brilliant rush of color greeted her when she pushed the fabric aside. What had been muted yellow and brown bushes only yesterday were now vibrant sheaves of gold Forsythia blooms. The massive, nine-foot stems that represented little more than overgrown hedges fifty weeks of the year, had come into their own. The warm, spring weather had transformed them into beads of liquid sunshine.

As Bethany stared in awe, the child inside punched her back into the moment. "Settle down," she said, rubbing her tummy. "Ouch! Hey, stop it," Beth playfully chastised.

Without warning, she had the feeling of losing her stomach, like that of dropping inside a speeding elevator. That sensation was followed by a stream of water trickling down her legs.

Her water had broken, and it wasn't time.

———— ⧟ ————

After calling Josh, Beth phoned Dr. Myers's office.

Alisha put her on hold while she spoke briefly to the doctor. "According to our records your pregnancy is a week short of term. Dr. Myers wants you to check into the hospital immediately."

"Okay." Beth took a seat on the kitchen bench to digest the news. "Is my baby in trouble?"

"We don't know that." The nurse reassured her. "But the best place for you is under a doctor's care. I will call Davidson County Medical Center and have everything ready for you to check in. Can you be there within the hour?"

"Yes," Beth said. "I'm waiting for my husband to come home. He will drive me."

"That's great. You don't need to be driving right now." Alisha cautioned. "Lie down and wait for him. Take it easy until Dr. Myers can see you."

Beth's final call was to Alex, who dropped what she was doing to help Beth pack. Within a few minutes she had Beth's bag ready to go. Ten minutes later, Josh raced through the front door. He picked up the bag and almost swept Beth off the sofa.

"Let's go," he said. His face looked drawn and tight. Only ten days ago, he had been in the hospital.

"Honey, relax. I'm okay."

Although she said the words, Beth couldn't completely convince herself all was well. Something pricked at her spirit. Was

God telling her she had more of a faith trial ahead? She prayed for the strength to put her baby's life into his hands. To believe everything would work out.

*Please, God, take care of my child.*

Her contractions had started by the time they arrived at the Davidson County Medical Center. Within the hour, Dr. Myers completed her exam. The doctor removed her stethoscope and sat on the edge of Beth's hospital bed. "Are you uncomfortable?"

"A little," Beth said, biting her lip. "But I can tolerate it."

"You're having premature labor pains," the doctor told her. "I'm hoping your body will slow down and give us more time. There's a chance it will, and if that's the case we'll have to watch you for infection. You're where you need to be, kiddo," Dr. Myers patted Beth on the arm. "We're going to keep a close watch on you. I'll be monitoring your blood pressure, the baby's vital signs, and your dilations."

"Is everything okay?" Beth asked.

"It is right now. Of course, premature is never optimum."

Beth nodded.

"How are you holding up?"

"Okay." Beth wiped a tear from her eye.

"Isn't that your husband standing in the hall?"

"Yes, ma'am."

"Let's invite him in. I'd like to share everything with him too."

A few minutes later, Josh stood beside the bed, rubbing Beth's shoulders, while Dr. Myers discussed Beth's and the baby's risks.

"We'll take it an hour at a time," she said.

Twenty-four hours later, Josh walked into the midst of chaos. Beth's room was filled with medical staff. Her blood pressure had skyrocketed. Nurses were prepping her for surgery.

"We can't wait any longer or we'll be putting Bethany and the baby at risk," Dr. Myers told him on her way out of the room. "I'm scheduling a C-section immediately."

Josh tried to stay out of the way, while staying close enough to reassure his wife. In the end, it was Beth who reassured him.

"Everything will be okay," she insisted, smiling up at him from her bed. "God has been with us from the beginning. That first morning when I came to the hospital, he knew we had a child on the way. He knew her then, and he knows her now. Soon, we will know her."

"Her?" The word caught in Josh's throat. "Why do you say that?"

"I have a feeling. Just like I believe everything will be okay."

He caressed her forehead with his lips. "You're warm."

"She has a slight fever," the nurse working next to him said. "It's another sign of toxemia."

"So there's a name for what's happening?"

She nodded, preoccupied with her work.

"Oh!" Beth screamed.

"Excuse me." The nurse pushed Josh aside. "What is it, dear?"

"My contractions. They're worse."

"Get Dr. Myers on the line, stat," she barked to her assistant.

"Yes, ma'am."

The younger woman snatched the phone from the bedside table and dialed a series of numbers while her supervisor checked Beth's vitals. Then she timed her contractions.

"Mr. Harrison, if you don't mind, would you please step across the room. I need to check your wife's dilation."

Within minutes, the assistant passed the phone to the nurse in charge. "It's Dr. Myers."

"Bethany Harrison's contractions are increasing rapidly," the supervisor told the doctor. "She's already at six centimeters."

Josh heard Dr. Myers on the other end of the phone shouting orders.

"Yes, doctor. We'll prepare her."

Slamming down the phone, the older woman announced to her subordinate, "We're preparing for vaginal delivery."

"What happened?" Josh asked.

"Things are moving faster than we expected. We think the baby is too far into the canal for a C-section."

Soon, the birthing room technicians arrived. They worked quickly, double-checking paperwork with Beth's wristband, unplugging monitors, and re-hanging medical dispensers. Within a few minutes they had Beth ready to move, beckoning Josh to follow as they wheeled his wife's bed out of the room, down the hallway, and into the elevator.

He had many questions. But the look of urgency on the attendants' faces told him everything he didn't want to know.

# 48

**Present Day**

Josh shivered as he looked around the surgical suite. The large, monochrome cube—white floors, white walls, and white ceiling tiles—was devoid of human warmth. Cold, sterile-looking equipment clung to the edges of the well-lit space. Two powerful examination lights hung from the ceiling, focusing on the surgical cot in the center of the room where Beth lay.

What must be millions of dollars worth of medical technology—and almost a dozen, highly trained doctors, nurses, and surgical assistants—attended to his wife. But he knew his reliance had to be on God.

Josh stuck his hands into the pockets of his jeans and shuffled to the side of the room.

"Sir, please take a seat," a technician in green scrubs instructed as he rushed by.

Josh obeyed without thinking, still concentrating on his allegiance to a higher power. The Lord had brought them to this moment. Not only physically, but spiritually. Despite Josh's many concerns over the past eight months, God had moved them safely to this point in their journey.

The crooked had become straight. The rutted road smooth.

He remembered the words God had given him in the midst of the bus wreck. *Peace, be still.*

Beth's screams of pain interrupted his thoughts.

He saw Dr. Myers's staff gather around her and heard muffled fragments of their conversation.

"I don't know how much she can help us."

"I agree."

"Dilation is ten centimeters, doctor."

"The baby isn't moving," someone else said.

"Get Dr. Abrams on the phone," Dr. Myers ordered. "I'm concerned about that dissected artery. I know it's healed, but too much pressure and she could still be in trouble."

"BP is up another two points systolic."

"I can see the top of the head—"

"I don't have a choice at this point," Dr. Myers shouted. "Prepare the vacuum extraction pump. She has to have help. I don't want to lose them both."

<hr/>

Pain and sedation obscured Beth's senses. If pressed, she could, perhaps, remember being wheeled into the delivery room. She had memories of having complete confidence that Dr. Myers and the hospital staff would take good care of her baby. And of Josh hovering around the room, watching and waiting.

But now exhaustion consumed her. She needed help. She was ready to get this done.

Snippets of the conversation penetrated her reality, even though she had no concept of time. Or fear.

Until she heard the whine of the surgical vacuum.

She fought the straps that held her to the cot, but she couldn't move.

Why had Dr. Myers deceived her? Had she decided it was Beth's life or the baby's?

Old memories rushed back, convincing Beth of impending betrayal.

"No—save my baby—not me. Please . . . save my baby."

*God, please. Take me, not my child.*

⸝⸝⸝⸝

The words of Micah 6:8 came to mind. *To do what is right, to love mercy, and to walk humbly with your God.* Josh knew that mercy had been given freely, although hard earned, to both him and Beth. They had revisited the altar of God, laying their faith and fears upon it, and God had been faithful and generous.

At seven twenty-three in the evening, Beth gave birth to a baby girl. Elizabeth Rose Harrison came into the world praising God at the top of her lungs. Her mother, while still groggy, was doing fine.

The baby's great-grandmother, Elizabeth Randall, received a phone call from Beth's mother, Liz McKinney, about an hour after the birth, announcing the arrival of her namesake. And Josh had no doubt that little Rose's paternal grandmother, Rose Harrison, had special knowledge of the baby girl who had been born today by God's grace, for her name had been called by him even before she was conceived.

⸝⸝⸝⸝

Bedlam surrounded Beth. People scrambled around her hospital room, laughing and bumping into each other while they prepared for her and baby Rose—as she was to be called—to go home.

Her mother had volunteered to transport all of the flowers, plants, and teddy bears in her SUV. Friends, family, and even fans of Josh's music had sent more flowers, cards, and e-mails than Beth could fully comprehend. One special arrangement had come from his new record label, AMG Records. Josh had finalized the deal earlier this week during Beth's hospital stay.

Beth saw the relief on her husband's face the day he received that call. He had told her their financial future, and Rose's, would be secure for a long time if things went well. *On the other side of the hill, the view will be much different*, her husband had said. It had become his favorite saying.

With Bob Bradford's help, Josh had devised a financial plan that would allow Beth to stay at home with little Rose for as long as she chose. He had presented it to her the day after her daughter was born. That same day, she had told Josh about her call to Pamela Morris.

"Everything's ready. All we need are the release papers," Josh said, settling into the chair beside her bed. Her mom had just left with the last cartload of flowers.

"Dr. Myers's nurse will be here soon," Beth reminded him. "Would you hold the baby for a few minutes while I get dressed?"

Josh smiled and reached out to receive his daughter.

"She looks a lot like you. A lot like your mom." Beth marveled at the resemblance. "I'm so—"

"Great! I didn't miss you." Dr. Abrams strolled into the room. He had a broad smile on his face. "How are you feeling?"

"We couldn't be better." Beth spoke for all three of them.

"I'm glad everything worked out so well for you."

"We're blessed," Josh stood up to shake the doctor's hand, juggling Baby Rose as he did.

"That's why I'm here." The doctor took a seat on the edge of Beth's bed. "I want you to know I've been blessed, as you would say, too." He paused to reflect. "Without the two of you, I wouldn't have met Alexandra."

Josh and Beth shared a knowing smile.

"You make a great couple," Beth grinned. "We already feel like you're part of our family, Dr. Abrams."

"It's Ben."

"I don't think I can call you by your first name," Josh said. "It doesn't seem respectful enough for the man who saved my wife's—and my best friend's—life."

Ben Abrams shook his head. "I didn't save Bethany or Danny Stevens. God did." He cleared his throat. "I've been humbled in the past few months to watch him working in so many lives, including my own."

Beth had heard samplings of this from Alex, but she had no idea to the extent Ben Abrams had come to believe.

"I've come a long way since I lost my parents and siblings more than fifty years ago. I think they would be proud of me."

Beth noticed tears in the corner of his beautiful blue eyes.

"I can't imagine how awful it would be not knowing your parents." Josh glanced down at the baby in his arms. "Who raised you?"

"My grandparents," Dr. Abrams said. "Both devout Jews by an odd twist of fate. I knew, even during my childhood, that my parents had become Christians. But I only learned recently they were also evangelists. They devoted their lives to the ministry."

Bethany and Josh exchanged glances again.

"That had to be mind blowing," Josh said. "How did you find out?"

"Shortly before my grandmother died she told me several things I had never known. That my parents' airplane crashed in a hayfield outside the small town of Mercy in Southern Illinois—"

"Mercy? That's close to where my grandparents live." Beth sat up in bed.

"Really?" Dr. Abrams looked surprised. "I would love to hear about it. I have to admit, I've always been curious to learn more about the accident, and the place where it happened."

"I can understand that," Beth said. "But it may be more of a coincidence than you realize." She dug back into her memory for the story her grandfather had always told. "My grandfather—"

"Oh, sorry . . . I didn't realize you had company. I'll be right out here." Liz McKinney spun around to exit the room.

"Mom, please join us. I need your help with something."

She gave her daughter a puzzled look and stepped closer to the bed.

"Remember the story Grandpa used to tell? You know, the one about him saving a baby from a plane crash. Do you remember the details?"

Ben Abrams looked from Beth to her mother.

"Yes . . . let me see," Liz McKinney said. "It would have been in 1959. I was four at the time and don't remember it very well. But Daddy has told the story over and over."

Color drained from Ben Abrams's face. "That would have been my parents' plane," he said almost matter-of-factly. "I was the baby your father saved."

# EPILOGUE

The Neimann farm had been bought and sold twice since Mrs. Neimann passed away in 1963. Even though few in the community still remembered the plane crash, a call to the new owner and a quick explanation gained access to the upper pasture.

Jack Randall moved slower now. Arthritis had settled into his hips more than a decade ago. But his memory was unaffected by the years since he had last walked this farm.

The old, wooden barn had decayed and fallen into itself. It had been replaced by a large, steel building. Pipe and cable fencing encircled the lot, instead of the sagging wire and wood fence that had once been there.

The new tenants were taking good care of the place. Jack believed that Albert Neimann would be proud.

And so would Ben Abrams's parents. Their son had grown into a fine man.

Jack studied his guest. He appeared to be keenly interested in everything around them. His intense blue eyes sparkled in the sunlight. They were moist with tears that had probably been a long time coming.

Jack wiped a few of his own from his cheek.

"The plane was over there." Jack pointed to the center of the grassy field. "By the time I came upon it, your family had been respectfully taken away."

The doctor nodded.

"Over there, in that fencerow, was a large bale of hay." Jack spread his arms as far as he could reach. "A big, loose stack that had been around for a year or two. Soft, yet supportive."

Ben Abrams shook his head. "I don't know how I survived it."

"I'll tell you something, young man," Jack said. "You landed on the prayers of your mom and dad. And God's will." He looked into the blue eyes that had haunted him for fifty years. "You were supposed to be here."

"It's humbling," Ben said. "I'm not sure I've kept up my side of the bargain."

"God's ways are not always understood in this life. I think you're exactly where you're supposed to be."

Ben smiled at him. "I hope so. I want to think I've become the man my parents would have wanted."

Jack laid a hand on the doctor's shoulder. "You've got plenty of time to accomplish more, Lord willing," he told him. "And a fine start at it with that young woman you brought with you."

Ben's eyes sparkled again, and he turned to look behind him where Alexandra, Josh, Beth, and Baby Rose were waiting at the car.

"Let's ask them to join us."

"I'll go get them," Ben said.

"I'll walk with you," Jack winked. "There's still a lot of mileage left in these legs, but it's just in lower gear."

Ben laughed as they turned to walk back toward the road to Mercy.

# Discussion Questions

1. In the prologue, Jack Randall is compelled to go to the site of the plane crash. How might his life have been different if he hadn't gone? Have you ever been prompted by God to do something unusual or unexpected? If you responded to that urging, how did your life change because of it?

2. In chapter 1, Josh Harrison feels confident that he has made the right choices in life. But doubts set in quickly. Why? How could Josh have been better prepared to face his trials?

3. Bethany Harrison had a near-death experience in the ambulance on the way to the hospital. Why did this experience leave her torn between the possibility of going to be with the Lord and returning to her earthly existence? How did this affect her actions later?

4. Early in the book, Dr. Ben Abrams holds little regard for people of faith. Why did he feel that way? What happened to change his beliefs? Did this happen through one event or a series of events?

5. Who besides Bethany Harrison planted a seed of faith in Dr. Abrams's life? Who influenced him positively as a child?

6. Bethany's unexpected pregnancy brought back memories of her "secret sin" from the past. How did this make her feel? Did she believe that God had forgiven her? Why did she have a difficult time forgiving herself?

7. What did the rust-colored teddy bear represent to Bethany? How did burying the bear play a significant role in her healing? Do you think she should have asked Josh, or even Alex, to be with her when she buried the bear, or was it something she needed to do alone? Why?

8. Alexandra Hayes provided assistance to Bethany in many ways. Can you list three? Was one of those roles more important than another?

9. How did Nell Stevens's death affect her son Danny's faith? How did Danny's faith subsequently have an effect on Josh?

10. Isaac couldn't understand why his grandfather would disown his daughter, Isaac's mother. Isaac felt that his grandfather had "thrown her away like a faded flower," an analogy from Isaac's work in the flower shop. How is this ironic in light of Dr. Abrams's recommendation that Bethany abort her pregnancy? How is it different?

11. In chapter 37, Josh realizes that a detour doesn't have to alter our destination—it may merely change our path. Can you think of an example of this in his life? In Bethany's life? In Ben Abrams's life? In your own life?

12. During and after the bus wreck (chapters 42 and 43) Josh's nightmare/dream coincides with the physical trauma of the storm going on around him. What other symbolism is represented in the dream? How did the dream reassure Josh in the midst of the storm?

13. *Mercy* is often defined as "loving-kindness," especially when it is not deserved. In chapter 46, Josh tells Ryan that he is offering mercy because he has been shown mercy. In what ways did Josh believe God had given him mercy? Did others receive mercy as well? In what way?

14. Bethany was confronted with an extraordinary number of problems within a short period of time: a life-threatening illness, medically related drug addiction, an at-risk pregnancy, marriage difficulties, and even guilt from her past. Yet, despite her doubts and fears, her life became a witness to her doctor. Who else did Bethany's faith affect? Who might it affect in the future?

15. In chapter 38, while walking through the cemetery, Josh contemplated if it was possible for our testimony to continue even when we are no longer alive. Can you think of an example of this happening in the book? What examples can you give from the Bible? How about in contemporary society?

16. In the epilogue, Jack Randall tells Ben Abrams that he landed on "the prayers of his mom and dad." Do you believe that prayers can transcend time? Can you think of examples from your own experience?

17. Throughout most of the book, Bethany sought forgiveness from God. Had it been there for her all along? If so, why did it take so long for her to accept it? Read Romans 3:23 and 1 John 1:9. How do these verses apply in your life?

Abingdon Press fiction
a novel approach to faith

Plan your escape.

BKM122220002 PACP01110786-01

# What They're Saying About...

**The Glory of Green,** by Judy Christie
"Once again, Christie draws her readers into the town, the life, the humor and the drama in Green. *The Glory of Green* is a wonderful narrative of small-town America, pulling together in tragedy. A great read!"
—Ane Mulligan, editor of *Novel Journey*

**Always the Baker, Never the Bride,** by Sandra Bricker
"[It] had just the right touch of humor, and I loved the characters. Emma Rae is a character who will stay with me. Highly recommended!"
—Colleen Coble, author of *The Lightkeeper's Daughter* and the *Rock Harbor* series

**Diagnosis Death,** by Richard Mabry
"Realistic medical flavor graces a story rich with characters I loved and with enough twists and turns to keep the sleuth in me off-center. Keep 'em coming!"—Dr. Harry Krauss, author of *Salty Like Blood* and *The Six-Liter Club*

**Sweet Baklava,** by Debby Mayne
"A sweet romance, a feel-good ending, and a surprise cache of yummy Greek recipes at the book's end? I'm sold!"—Trish Perry, author of *Unforgettable* and *Tea for Two*

**The Dead Saint,** by Marilyn Brown Oden
"An intriguing story of international espionage with just the right amount of inspirational seasoning."—*Fresh Fiction*

**Shrouded in Silence,** by Robert L. Wise
"It's a story fraught with death, danger, and deception—of never knowing whom to trust, and with a twist of an ending I didn't see coming. Great read!"—Sharon Sala, author of *The Searcher's Trilogy: Blood Stains, Blood Ties,* and *Blood Trails.*

**Delivered with Love,** by Sherry Kyle
"Sherry Kyle has created an engaging story of forgiveness, sweet romance, and faith reawakened—and I looked forward to every page. A fun and charming debut!"—Julie Carobini, author of *A Shore Thing* and *Fade to Blue.*

Abingdon Press fiction
a novel approach to faith

AbingdonPress.com | 800.251.3320